Crystal Avarice

Books by Troy D. Wymer

Lightyears Trilogy
Lightyears
Lightyears II: Intragalactic Terrorism
Lightyears III: Ominous Intervention

Treasures From Afar

Xeno Tryst Duology
Xeno Tryst
Feathers of Shardaa

Crystal Avarice

Crystal Avarice

TROY D. WYMER

WymerNovels, the "Atheneum of the Mind" tag line, and books logo are trademarks ™ by Troy D. Wymer

Published by WymerNovels

www.WymerNovels.com

ISBN: 979-8-9916986-4-1

First Edition: 2024, Version 1.2

Published in the United States

DEDICATION

This novel is a dedication to my late mother, Nancy Lou Wymer. My mom was a loving, caring, giving, supportive, and selfless person who enjoyed helping others. She was relentless at praying for people and she poured everything into her children. I am blessed to have had her as my mother. She is greatly missed. Until I see her on the other side, I will always cherish our precious memories. In honor of my mom, I have named one of the main characters in Crystal Avarice *after her with Nancy Louray. Many of my mom's traits and idioms have been incorporated into the character.*

—Troy D. Wymer
September 18, 2023

Preface

When I was eleven, I created a comic story that I called *Wilcox Brown, Private Investigator.* There were mysteries to be solved and Wilcox Brown was the man to do it. Other than myself, the only other person that probably saw my comic was my mother. I had some influence with a variety of mystery shows on television in the late 1970s and early 1980s. A few years later, I began reading a lot of mystery novels. At the time, it was my favorite genre. One of my favorite novels was *The Green Turtle Mystery* by Ellery Queen, Jr. Since I write science fiction space opera, but wanted to write a mystery, I combined the two genres. Wilcox Brown has been resurrected from my comic in my new space opera mystery novel, *Crystal Avarice.*

An appendix is at the end of this book with a terminology glossary.

—Troy D. Wymer
May 7, 2023

CHAPTER ONE

"Nancy! How have you been?" Avalaur asked.

"Good. I'm a little tired, but good. How are you doing?" Nancy Louray asked.

"Well, now that we'll be eating lunch, I'm going to be doing a lot better. I'm starving!" Avalaur said.

"I'm hungry as well. It's nice of you to fly here to Kesron and have lunch with me. We have so much catching up to do," Nancy said.

"Yes. And the Country Barn is one of my favorite restaurants," Avalaur said.

"So, how's the family?" Nancy asked.

"Good. My two children are a handful, but it's all good," Avalaur said.

They strolled along the wooden walkway toward the entrance. Red siding covered the building. It had been an old barn that was renovated and turned into a restaurant. Located on the outskirts of Kethan, one of Kesron's largest cities, the Country Barn offered the perfect mix of countryside and city atmosphere. The restaurant was located on the edge of many essential farmlands that extended beyond the city. Their importance for adequate food supply was celebrated with several festivals during the harvest season.

A gust of wind drifted across the nearby fields and suddenly blew Avalaur's blond hair around. She straightened it up the best she could. Avalaur opened the door and they entered the restaurant. They were immediately greeted with mouth-watering scents emitting from the kitchen. They found a booth next to the window and made themselves comfortable. The menus were already laid out before them. Nancy slid her menu to the edge of the table.

"I already know what I want," she said.

"Well, since you live here on Kesron and come to the Country Barn all the time, I'm sure you know the menu well. I, however, need to look. Mashed potatoes sound good," Avalaur said as she browsed.

"Their potatoes here are not as good as mine," Nancy said.

"Of course not. Your mashed potatoes are the best. Next time you make them, you better invite us over," Avalaur said.

"You can count on it. I love the company. I'm sure we can find something for the kids to do. We'll have to make a day of it and go shopping," Nancy said.

"Yes."

A waitress stopped at their booth. "Hello, ladies. Can I start you both off with drinks?" she asked.

"I'll have a cola," Nancy said, "but light on the ice."

"Same for me, but I want all of my ice," Avalaur said.

"Okay. I'll have those out in a moment," the waitress said.

The waitress left to get the drinks.

"So, what are you getting?" Avalaur asked.

"Grilled chicken, mashed potatoes, and green beans," Nancy said.

"Mmm. That sounds good. I think I'll try that too," Avalaur said. She closed her menu and placed it on top of the other menu at the edge of the table.

"I don't miss waitressing. I waitressed for years at a few different restaurants when I was younger," Nancy said.

"I don't think I would like that either. I'm just not a people person. I would end up flipping someone off or something," Avalaur said.

"You mean, you would give them your best finger?" Nancy asked.

They both laughed. "Exactly!" Avalaur said.

Nancy looked over at the kitchen as the cook threw a couple of large meat slabs onto the grill. Flames rose up from the surface for several seconds before settling down. Avalaur followed Nancy's gaze.

"Flames always trigger me," Nancy said. "When I was a little girl, I was in an apartment fire. The entire building was on fire. I looked outside from my upstairs bedroom window and saw my siblings and mother in the street with other people who had escaped. I was so scared, I didn't know what to do. I hid underneath my blankets and prayed. Apparently, one of the neighbors saw me when I had looked out the window and she called my father at his work. He immediately left work and sped home as quickly as possible. He ran into our burning apartment and up the stairs as flames began to enveloped the room. I remember him grabbing me from the bed, throwing me over his shoulder, and running down the burning steps. I held onto him for dear life as smoke surrounded us. As we reached the first floor, the staircase collapsed. He ran out the front door and across the street to safety just as the fire trucks arrived. We were both coughing for some time. I learned that two boys from one of the other apartments died in that fire. It's very sad. I'm so thankful that my father rescued me that day. It was an answer to my prayers. God definitely heard them. Since I have survived that horrific childhood ordeal, I have the ability to carry on my lineage one day by having a family of my own. I will tell my children how blessed I was that day."

"Wow! It's no wonder that you are triggered by flames. I'm sorry you had to go through that awful experience. Thank you for sharing that with me, Nancy. The story is definitely something that is worth passing down to your children someday," Avalaur said.

"Yes," Nancy said.

"Speaking of having children someday…you are approaching that menopausal age. If you're going to start a family, you had better do it soon. When are you going to find a man to marry?" Avalaur asked.

"I don't know. I've dated some real winners, I'll tell you. But I do have some very strong feelings for my boss," Nancy said.

"Wilcox? You're kidding me! That's awesome, Nancy. But he is ten years older than you…not that it matters. Did you tell him yet?"

"No. He's always so busy with his work. There's always a mystery to be solved. He has not shown any interest in me, or anyone else that I know of, for that matter," Nancy said.

"Well, at least you know there isn't anyone else. Now, you just need to give him the right signals," Avalaur said.

"Yeah, sure…the right signals. We're a good team solving

mysteries. I wouldn't want anything like that to get in the way of our work," Nancy said.

"Look, Nancy, you have feelings for Wilcox and they aren't going to go away. If a relationship develops, then you're just going to have to figure out a way to incorporate it into your everyday mystery solving work."

"I doubt something will spark. Wilcox doesn't see me like that. He's so focused on his work, any signals I give off are completely ignored. But I'll keep trying," Nancy said.

"You need to tell him about your feelings. After all, it sounds like you've felt this way for some time now," Avalaur said.

"Yes, I have. Perhaps, I'll find the right moment. And how is *your* relationship doing? I've been praying for you and your family."

"The kids are great. My husband and I are doing great. The three Cs are key to every successful relationship," Avalaur said.

"Three Cs?" Nancy gave Avalaur a questioning look.

"Yes. Communication, compromise, and cunnilingus," Avalaur said.

They both started laughing.

"I'm sure you're right," Nancy said.

The waitress stopped at their table with drinks. "Two colas, one with light ice... Have you two had a chance to look at the menu?" the waitress asked.

"Yes. I'll have the grilled chicken, mashed potatoes, and green beans," Avalaur said.

"Same for me," Nancy said.

After taking their orders, the waitress left.

"I appreciate you meeting me for lunch, Avalaur," Nancy said. "It's nice to get away from the office for a little while."

"Yes. My space flight home took me right by Kesron, so the timing for your invite to lunch was perfect," Avalaur said.

"It's not very often that I get to see my best friend from school," Nancy said.

"You'll have to drop by our place on Symphainia some time," Avalaur said.

"Definitely."

Soon, the waitress stopped at their table, holding a large tray. She placed their meals onto the table in front of them. "Would you both like refills on your drinks?" she asked.

"I would," Avalaur said.

"Yes, please," Nancy said.

The waitress disappeared into the kitchen. They enjoyed the food and catching up on things. Eventually, they finished their meals, paid, and stood from the booth.

"Safe travels on your way back to Symphainia… Contact me when you arrive so that I know you made it home safely," Nancy said.

"I will. You never know with space travel or even the weather on Symphainia," Avalaur said.

They hugged and parted ways.

"Thank you," Coradelle Hershall said.

"You're welcome. Enjoy," the man behind the counter said.

She adjusted her small purse, grabbed her coffee from the counter, and left the cafe. The streets of Kethan were moderately busy with both pedestrians and vehicles. It was the largest city on Kesron. Coradelle traveled to Kesron in order to hire the private investigator that she had researched. Perhaps he could help her. Gazing at the small shops along the street, she sipped her coffee.

"Mmm." Coradelle savored the taste.

Among the many small, niche shops, there was a bakery, a clothing store, an art gallery, a chocolate shop, and an ice cream shop. It was the perfect shopping district with most stores within walking distance. She noticed her destination ahead. Coradelle stopped in front of a small, narrow building and looked up at the old sign above the door.

"Wilcox Brown Agency, Private Investigators," she read.

Coradelle tried the door, but it was locked. She looked at the slogan on the window that read: Solving mysteries for over 30 years. Coradelle peered into the window at the dark office. It looked very cluttered.

"*Great!* I traveled all the way from Ryamesh and he's not even open."

She noticed a small note attached to the inside of the door that indicated they were out to lunch. Coradelle immediately felt relief that her trip to Kesron was not wasted. There was a bench in front of a bakery and donut shop a couple of doors down. She walked over and rested on the bench, draping her long, blond hair over her shoulder. She would just have to wait for their return. Coradelle pulled a comm from her purse and dialed her friend.

"Hey, Alivia. This is Coradelle. How are you?"

"Good. What's up?" Alivia Bexley asked.

"Oh, I'm just about to hire an investigator to help with my father's deed to that planet. I'm just waiting for the investigator to return from lunch. So, I figured I would call my best friend and talk," Coradelle said.

"You're still dealing with that? I thought you were going to give up. I know you didn't get anywhere with the Settlement Agency," Alivia said.

"Well, this is going to be my last ditch effort to get the deed. Like you said before, it may be a lost cause. I just wanted to give you an update," Coradelle said.

"Okay. Well, Coradelle, good luck with everything. Try to stay positive," Alivia said.

"Thanks. I'll keep you posted," Coradelle said.

"You better. Okay, I'll talk to you soon."

"All right. Bye," Coradelle said.

She ended the transmission and put the comm back into her purse. Coradelle took another drink of her coffee and smiled at a bird chirping in the tree next to her. She looked up and squinted at the sun.

What a beautiful song, she thought.

Wilcox Brown finished the last few bites of his lunch and leaned back in his chair. He was a man in his fifties and his black hair was starting to show signs of gray. Across from Wilcox, sat his friend, Adamorr, who was an Axynnian. In population, the Axynnian species were second common to humans. Adamorr had short, light brown fur and amber eyes. Wilcox and Adamorr were both casually dressed for the informal lunch. The Lush Vine was one of Wilcox's favorite restaurants. It was located on Xeralosa, not far from Kesron. Their table was in a quiet corner toward the back of the dining area. White flowers with a dash of cerise decorated the top of a half wall next to their table.

"That was quite delicious, Adamorr. I appreciate you buying this time," Wilcox said.

"No problem. And, yes, it was very good food. So earlier, before the food arrived, you mentioned that your work load is light. What do you attribute that to?" Adamorr asked.

"I'm not sure. It's not like crime has gone down. The market is not saturated with private investigators…at least not on Kesron. I haven't had a big case in some time."

"What's the largest case you've ever worked on?" Adamorr asked.

"Well, I don't know if it was the largest case, but it certainly was the strangest and still remains an unsolved mystery. I was hired by the old Space Agency to investigate what appeared to be an ancient, derelict ship that was discovered on the edge of uncharted space. Our team went aboard and found the skeletal remains of an unknown alien species. We didn't know their origin. There were several of these skeletons lying on the ship floor at various locations. I'll never forget how tall these beings must have been. Their ship malfunctioned and they became lost, drifting helplessly in space…apparently for several years before the Space Agency discovered the ship in that territory. It is presumed that they starved to death. There were also strange blue crystals that we saw at various locations on the ship," Wilcox said.

"So, there *are* more than just our two species…" Adamorr said.

"Yes. The odd thing about that case was that the military arrived on scene. They came in and took over the entire investigation. We were no longer permitted to search the ship and we were told to leave immediately. We never had a chance to check the ship's computer and retrieve the information about their galactic origin that was most certainly there. That was years ago. The ship is no longer there and the military never answered any of our questions. I tried to go through the proper channels in the Marrithious Government to no avail. Even our government leader at the time was quiet about it," Wilcox said.

"You know, I've been all over this side of the Marrithious Galaxy, including some of the uncharted regions, and I've seen a lot of strange things, but I've never come across another intelligent species besides our two species. There is so much we don't know about our own galaxy," Adamorr said.

"True. And their spaceship was very large, rounded, and odd looking," Wilcox said.

"My son is into spaceships right now. He has a poster of all kinds of different spaceship models on his bedroom wall," Adamorr said.

"How is your family?" Wilcox asked.

"They're good. The children are getting older every day. So, do you ever regret not starting a family? When are you going to find someone?" Adamorr asked.

"There is one good thing that came from the military taking over that investigation. At the time, I met this sexy commander named Victoria Ediira. Over the years, we've hooked up on occasion. It certainly wasn't love. It was more of a mutual understanding that our urges needed to be met. I believe she is now a general in charge of a large portion of the military. Yeah, I'm probably too old to start a family now, but my lack of a relationship is for good reason. I need to focus on my work and solve cases," Wilcox said.

"Well, some men start families in their fifties," Adamorr said.

"Speaking of work…I should get back to the office. At least you live here on Xeralosa. I have to fly back to Kesron. It's the good thing for lightspeed-plus capabilities that enable us to travel much faster than the speed of light. And you know how much I like space travel. Not!" Wilcox said.

Adamorr knew Wilcox was avoiding the subject of a loving relationship with someone. He always avoided it.

"Okay. It was nice having lunch with you. Have a safe trip back to Kesron and I'll see you soon," Adamorr said.

They both stood up from the table and pushed their chairs in. Wilcox shook Adamorr's furry hand and they parted ways.

I wonder if Nancy is back at the office yet. I'm running late, Wilcox thought.

Outside, the sun brightened Xeralosa's landscape. Large rocks could be seen among the tall grass across from the restaurant. Xeralosa was a sparsely populated planet and was decorated with beautiful scenery. In the far distance, Wilcox saw a blue sea, the sunlight glistening on its surface. Seabirds could be heard singing as they soared high above the beige sands of the beach. The faint sound of waves splashing against the shore was calming. Adamorr had lived on Xeralosa his entire life. Wilcox found Xeralosa peaceful and enjoyed lunch with his friend on occasion. At least Wilcox wasn't far from Kesron. He headed for his ship, *Enigma*, that was resting on a landing pad in the distance.

When Wilcox entered the *Enigma*, he caught his arm on a sharp piece of metal at the entrance.

"Ouch! What the hell?"

He looked down at the tear in his shirt sleeve and immediately saw blood emitting from the wound.

Chapter Two

Coradelle looked up from the bench she sat on and noticed a woman with dark brown hair stop in front of the investigator agency and unlock the door. She quickly stood up from the bench and threw her empty coffee cup into a nearby trash can. Coradelle made her way back to the office and entered. The old door creaked when she closed it behind her, bells jingling from the top of the door's glass window.

Nancy quickly turned around from the back of the office. "Oh, hello."

As Coradelle entered, she was immediately greeted with the scent of old papers and books.

"Hi. My name is Coradelle Hershall and I'm here to see Wilcox Brown regarding a missing deed."

"Okay. I'm Nancy Louray. It's nice to meet you, Coradelle. Wilcox is not back from lunch yet, but I can get started by taking down some information. You can have a seat right here in front of his desk. Let me grab a pad of paper and I'll be right back."

As Nancy left the desk, Coradelle looked around the cluttered office. Walking across the square-tiled floor, she took a seat in one of the two chairs in front of Wilcox's desk. A few of the square floor tiles were broken. There were stacks of binders on Wilcox's desk and an array of papers littered across its surface. Next to his desk was a coatrack with an old jacket resting on one of the hooks. Nancy's desk was somewhat better, only with a stack of crooked forms at one corner. The shelves along the turquoise-colored walls were not much better organized than the desks. Several gray and green filing cabinets had a similar mess on top of them. The top drawer of one green filing cabinet had a mismatched gray color. A large bookshelf could be seen along the back wall, containing many law books. Cobwebs hung from the ceiling. Coradelle began to think that hiring Wilcox Brown would be a mistake.

"Okay… You said your name is Coradelle Hershall?" Nancy stood next to the desk with a pad of paper and an ink pen.

"Yes."

Nancy collected all of Coradelle's contact information.

"Tell me about this missing deed that you mentioned."

The familiar sound of jingling bells startled both of them. They looked toward the door as Wilcox Brown entered the office.

"Good afternoon, ladies," he said.

Wilcox removed his fedora hat and placed it on the coatrack next to his desk.

"This is Coradelle Hershall. She was just about to tell me about a missing deed she needs help with," Nancy said.

Wilcox sat down at his desk, across from Coradelle. Nancy noticed a tear in the sleeve of his shirt and blood stains.

"What happened to your arm?" Nancy asked.

Wilcox looked down at his sleeve. "I cut it on the entrance of the *Enigma*. There is a sharp piece of metal on the hinge of the ship's airlock door. The wound is fairly deep. I bandaged it, but I think I'll need a new shirt at some point. I hate space travel. Anyway, I need to have the hinge to the airlock door fixed."

"How deep is it? Do you need to see a doctor? Does it hurt or is it sore?" Nancy asked.

"What do you mean? What's the difference? I appreciate your concern, Nancy. I'm sure it will be fine. I didn't have another shirt on the *Enigma,* but, now that I think of it, I do have an extra shirt in the office closet," he said.

Wilcox stood from his desk and walked over to the office closet. He grabbed a different shirt and stepped into the back bathroom to change. A moment later, he returned to his desk.

"Okay. So, Coradelle…about this missing deed?" Nancy asked.

"Yes. I would like to hire you to solve a mystery regarding part of an inheritance from my late father, Robert Hershall. The part of the inheritance that I never received was for a deed to a planet. I never received the deed from the Settlement Agency. I received his life insurance credits and his belongings, but not the deed," Coradelle said.

Nancy finally sat down in the chair next to Coradelle and wrote down the information. Suddenly, Nancy saw a faint vision in the distance of the office. In the vision, Coradelle ran for her life along the side of a white building. There was a circular, blue logo on the side of the white building. In the vision, Coradelle looked behind her at her pursuers and then screamed. Nancy shook her head.

"Are you all right?" Coradelle asked.

"Sorry. Ah, yes," Nancy said.

Nancy had experienced different visions in the past, but she did not always understand them.

"How do you know your father had a deed to a planet as part of his inheritance? Are there other siblings involved?" Wilcox asked.

Coradelle stared at him for a long moment, her blue eyes difficult to read. Nancy noticed Coradelle become slightly emotional.

"Are *you* okay?" Nancy asked.

"Sorry, it's just that I miss my father very much. He died unexpectedly last year. I am his only child, so there is no part of the inheritance that would go to any siblings. And he was not married to my mother," Coradelle said.

Coradelle reached into her small purse. "I have this document from my father that I found among his belongings. It states that he purchased the planet from a real estate agent named Bryson Wieler. It shows the amount of credits he paid and shows the name of the planet as Staraliss. But the Settlement Agency told me there is no deed nor such planet. I *know* there is! He brought me there when I was a little girl, just after he purchased it. I was about eight years old. He was so excited to show me. It was a very long flight. When we arrived, I remember seeing all the wilderness and white pine trees. We could hear wolves in the distance too. There was such a beautiful waterfall and a river with large rocks, cutting through the forest. We walked around and he showed me where he planned to build a house. He wanted to build a large house on the planet one day for us to live in, but he never got around to it. He only brought me there the one time. When I was a teenager, I asked him about it and he said he still planned on building the house one day. Apparently, he never did because he didn't have the deed. I know the planet should have been part of the inheritance."

"Do you know if he brought anyone else there?" Wilcox asked.

"Maybe his old friend Maxboro Lawson… I'm not sure, but I think my father may have proposed marriage to my mother on Staraliss," Coradelle said.

Wilcox looked over the purchase agreement and handed it back to Coradelle. As Nancy wrote down all the details, Wilcox stood up and walked to the back of the office.

"Would either of you like a cup of coffee?" he asked.

"Yes. That would be great," Coradelle said.

"Yes, please," Nancy said.

"Nancy, can you make two copies of that purchase agreement?" Wilcox asked.

"Yes," Nancy said.

Coradelle handed her the paper. As Nancy made copies on a machine next to the wall on the right, Wilcox brought back a tray with three cups of coffee and a container of creamer, sugar, and stir sticks.

"Thank you," Coradelle said.

Steam came up from the cups. Nancy returned to the desk with the copies. She put some creamer and sugar into her coffee, as did Coradelle. Wilcox liked his coffee black.

"If you don't mind me asking, how old are you?" Wilcox asked.

"I'm thirty."

"Tell me about your childhood," he said.

"I was raised by my father. My mother and father split when I was a child, just before he purchased this planet. They were never married. My father and I lived on Ryamesh…actually, I still live there. After I moved out on my own, I would visit my father quite often. We would have lunch and we had game nights. Once in a while, he would tell me that he still planned on building that house. Now, it's a dream that is never going to be fulfilled."

"And what about your mother?" Nancy asked.

"My mother is Mercedes Brantt. She's always distant to me and never home for me to visit her. It seems like she's always gone on some galactic adventure. I often wonder what my life would have been like if they had not split up," Coradelle said.

"Do you blame yourself for that?" Nancy asked.

"Not at all. My mom was an ass to my dad. He raised me by himself and I had a wonderful childhood."

"Are you sure he didn't sell the planet and that is why the deed is not part of the inheritance?" Wilcox asked.

"I'm sure. He was still talking about building a house on the planet just before he died," Coradelle said.

"How *did* your father die?" Wilcox asked.

Coradelle looked past Wilcox at some unseen image in the distance as tears welled up in her eyes. "I don't know. There was nothing wrong with him. The doctors couldn't find anything wrong with him. On the death certificate, it says the cause of death is unknown. His friend Maxboro was pretty shaken with the news as well."

"I'm sorry. I don't mean to bring up the sensitive subject. It just helps if we know everything surrounding the case," Wilcox said.

Nancy reached over to her own desk and grabbed a box of tissues, handing one to Coradelle.

"Thank you, Nancy," Coradelle said.

"So, there was no known cause of death? That's very odd," Wilcox said.

"Correct. That's also what all the doctors were saying. He was in great health. There was no sign of an injury, no blood, no nothing," Coradelle said.

"Okay. Well, we have multiple cases that we are working on, but we are waiting for more information on most of those cases, so we can focus on your missing deed. Here is a list of our pricing," Wilcox said. He handed Coradelle a laminated price sheet.

Nancy looked at Wilcox. "We have *two* open cases," she said.

"Okay, *two*," he said, rolling his eyes.

Coradelle looked at the price sheet and then looked back up at Wilcox. She took a long drink of her coffee.

"That looks reasonable. I appreciate you taking on the case. So, what do we need to do first?" Coradelle asked.

"First, Nancy will take your payment. You mentioned you did not receive the deed from the Settlement Agency. I think we need to go to the Settlement Agency and ask a few questions. Is this the Settlement Agency on Anneriss?" Wilcox asked.

"Yes, it is on Anneriss. The representative that was assigned to settle my father's inheritance is Chaslin Anders. When I asked him about the deed, he said there wasn't one. I know better."

"Okay. We will start there at the Settlement Agency. Are you two ready for a trip to Anneriss?" Wilcox asked.

They all stood up and Wilcox grabbed his hat from the coatrack. Nancy ran Coradelle's payment. Afterward, they all maneuvered around some boxes toward the door.

"We can take the *Enigma*. Just be careful when you enter that you don't cut yourself on the door hinge," Wilcox said.

After stepping onto the sidewalk, Nancy locked the office door.

"So...I'm not judging, but why do you keep your office so cluttered? How do you find anything?" Coradelle asked.

Wilcox laughed. "No offense taken. We keep it that way for good reason...so that we throw off any intruders that may break in and try to get information. I've been doing this for thirty years and I've seen just about everything. It's kind of a security feature in disguise. Nancy and I know where the cases are filed and it's not where any intruder would think," Wilcox said.

They made their way past the many shops that lined the street. Turning a corner, Wilcox led them to a nearby landing pad located behind his office and the other shops.

"Here we are. Coradelle, I'm sorry it's not the latest ship model, but it still flies and gets me to my destinations," Wilcox said.

"That's quite all right. My ship isn't new either," Coradelle said.

"Nor is mine," Nancy said.

"Watch yourselves on the corner of the door there," Wilcox said.

They each entered the *Enigma* and Wilcox closed the airlock door. Nancy and Coradelle strapped themselves into the passenger seats as Wilcox made his way to the ship's controls. He sat down, strapped himself in, and engaged the ship's engines and anti-gravitational units.

"Oh, I forgot to mention that the last time I was at the Settlement Agency, I told them to fuck themselves," Coradelle said.

Chapter Three

High Commander Novish Shirom looked out the window from his office, high above Deslorr Canyon. The cloudy sky was dark and torrential rain pounded against the glass. He could barely see the river that flowed along the large boulders at the bottom of the canyon. Novish did see his reflection in the window. His eyes were a greenish-gray color, separated by a sleek nose. Little to no hair could be found on his head. Instead, it was crowned with a bumpy, uneven surface. He had several skin shades of light orange, beige, green, and black with varying patterns, mixed and spotted. A slightly wet residue adorned his face, glistening in the room's overhead lighting. It was the result of leaking glands in his face, common to his species. His height was approximately three meters tall. Novish Shirom was a typical looking Sharrixian. The high commander wore a solid gray military uniform with a burgundy cape.

As the pouring rain lightened a bit, Novish was able to see a portion of the building that protruded outward from the rest. It was the building's docking bay entrance. The rain pounded on the black surface of its overhanging section. He noticed a single ship slowly lower itself into the canyon and toward the overhang. Several red lights could be seen along the bottom of the ship. The docking bay entrance was surrounded by flashing white lights. Two large, metal doors separated as they opened to either side of the docking bay entrance. The sleek scout ship slowly moved forward out of the rain, the large doors closing behind it. As the military high commander, Novish Shirom knew the pilot would immediately head to the briefing room. He turned away from the window, walked past his large desk, and went out the tall, electronic door.

"Right on time for the council meeting..." he whispered.

Returning from a Sharrixian Government mission, a sleek scout ship entered the thick, gray clouds in the atmosphere of Lairdain Tannis, the seat of the Sharrixian Government. Visibility was near zero as the ship's instruments automatically guided it toward a large, tall building that was constructed into a canyon wall. The pilot was instructed to immediately report to the military high commander, Novish Shirom.

As the tall alien pilot exited her ship, she stepped over the dripping water that ran down the ship's hull. She made her way across the large docking bay floor. Some rain water had entered the docking bay at the entrance while the doors were open. A janitorial team made their way toward the ship to clean up the water. Metal beams could be seen far above the landing area. Several other ships were parked along one side of the bay. Across from the ships, containers rested against one wall with various identification numbers on them. The pilot proceeded up a yellow, metal stairway toward the second level.

Two very tall Sharrixians stood in a briefing room filled with electronic equipment and displays of various galactic maps and charts. Several different beeping sounds could be heard emitting from some of the devices. Workers sat at the controls in front of the two individuals who stood there.

"We've been in contact with the human military leader, Victoria Ediira. She is supposed to be investigating the situation on our behalf," Commander Gedlo Othan said.

"When is the last time you received a communique from her?" Commander Covlan Prilston asked.

There was some hesitation. "It's been some time now. We're just waiting for a response," Gedlo said.

A tall electronic door on their left swiftly slid aside as another Sharrixian entered the room. He wore a flowing, burgundy cape over a high ranking military outfit. He walked over to where Gedlo Othan and Covlan Prilston stood and stopped next to them. He was Novish Shirom, the highest commanding officer in the Sharrixian military.

"We are still waiting for a reply, sir," Gedlo said.

At that moment, the entrance door opened once again. They turned to see a pilot walking toward them, still in her black flight suit. Similar to the males, she also had a bumpy, uneven surface on her head. She held a tablet in one of her gloved hands.

"High Commander Novish Shirom, I have a report for you," the pilot said. She handed Novish the tablet.

Novish looked at the report on the tablet and sighed. He handed it back to the pilot.

"Thank you, Versill," Novish said.

"Yes, sir," Versill said. She took the tablet and left the briefing room.

"It appears that our human military friend, Victoria Ediira, has met with our special operations officer Versill and everything is on track. We have not received a communique due to galactic interference with the signal. That is why I sent Versill as a messenger to meet Victoria at a planet half way across the galaxy. Now, we must have patience and wait for Victoria to complete her investigation," Novish Shirom said.

"The galactic interference explains why we have not received Victoria's communique," Covlan said.

"Where is the justice for our Gatherers who have died at the hands of the humans?" Gedlo asked.

"I understand your concern, Gedlo. Patience… Now, I must go and explain this to the Sharrixian Council. We all want answers, but we must have patience. It's already been years, a little longer isn't going to change anything," Novish said.

Novish walked toward the exit, his cape flowing behind him. As the electronic door closed after him, Gedlo and Covlan looked at each other and sighed.

As Novish made his way along the brightly lit corridors of the Sharrixian Government Building, another tall figure turned a corner from an adjacent corridor and walked in-step with him. She wore an elegant red dress which accentuated her cleavage with its low-cut design.

"Queen Empress Aminarra! I presume you just arrived from the Lythinarr Palace and you are en route to the Sharrixian Council meeting as well?" Novish asked.

"That, I am," Queen Empress Aminarra Vistona said. "I hope your pilot was able to meet with the human."

"That, she did," he said. "I have some promising information to share."

She looked at him and smiled, the wet residue sheen on her face visible in the corridor lighting. Her greenish-gray eyes were surrounded with black eye liner. Long, silver earrings swayed when she turned her head. They continued walking in silence through a maze of corridors until they reached a large foyer with intricate details in every piece of architecture. The floor at the center of the room was decorated with a pattern, shaped like their planet of Lairdain Tannis, with various shades of blue and purple crystals. Above the center of the room, a large chandelier hung, its blue shades of crystal matching that of the stone floor below. White couches decorated the room on either side. Before them was an old-style double door on hinges that led to the Sharrixian Council room. The doors were decorated with black crystals around their parameter.

Important meetings for the Sharrixian people took place in the room. This meeting was no exception. The only difference was that the meeting would involve the human species from across the Marrithious Galaxy. As the two of them entered the council room, they noticed that most of the other members were just making themselves comfortable in the chairs that surrounded a large, oval table in the center of the room. In the center of the table was a tall, sparkling, white vase. Queen Empress Aminarra Vistona closed the doors behind her and sat at the head of the oval table on a throne-like seat, which was specifically designated for her. There was a low murmur of conversation that died down until the room became silent. Other than the queen empress and the high commander, there were six members of the council. Queen Empress Aminarra stood up at the end of the table.

"Good evening, Sharrixian Council. As a founding member of this council, I have called this special meeting to address our progress with the human investigation.

"It has been almost twenty years since the tragic incident of our people being murdered by the hands of the humans. We all want justice. Since we launched our outbound flight years ago to investigate the incident ourselves, we have been in contact with the human military. The entire human race is not responsible for the killing of our people. There is a specific group that the human military is investigating. However, the entire human race may pay the price, if we do not see justice soon," Queen Empress Aminarra said.

"We have literally been waiting for years for their investigation," one of the members said.

"I understand it has been many years since their military had first contacted us, but we are getting close to a resolution. High Commander Novish Shirom has some breaking information to share with us regarding the situation," Queen Empress Aminarra said.

As Queen Empress Aminarra made herself comfortable in her throne-like chair, High Commander Shirom stood from the guest chair.

"Thank you, Queen Empress Aminarra," Novish said.

"We've heard this all before," another council member said.

"I understand," Novish said. "The communications across the Marrithious Galaxy—as we've come to call it as the humans do—have been spotty. There has been much galactic interference with the signals. Our briefing room communications technicians have worked diligently to receive signals. We have sent and received partial signals, but it has been getting worse in the last several years, due to the supernova in the Pixellis Star System. So, it was decided to send out a special scout ship half way across the galaxy to better communicate with our human military contact. Versill, one of our special operations military officers, was able to meet with our human military contact, General Victoria Ediira, on the planet Rafith Astonn. It is located midpoint across the galaxy. We have learned the ongoing investigation that has been in the works for years with the human military is close to being resolved. It is an investigation that began when our very own outbound flight of the *Credence* was discovered by the humans. We had sent it out to investigate the portal attack, but the ship had malfunctioned and the crew had become lost. We are told that we will be contacted once the human military investigation has concluded. Victoria did apologize for the lengthy time that it has taken. We must have patience."

As Novish sat back down, the council member to his left shifted in her chair.

"Have we no voice in decisions anymore?" she asked.

"Of course, you do," Queen Empress Aminarra said. "I founded this council so that I could get input from representatives across Lairdain Tannis. Your voices matter."

"I don't understand why we can't just go through the portal instead of all the way across the galaxy," one of the other council members said.

Queen Empress Aminarra quickly stood from her throne with a fire in her eyes. "I forbid it!" she shouted.

High Commander Novish Shirom and the six members of the council recoiled in their chairs.

"I'm sorry, Queen Empress Aminarra," the man said. "I know it is forbidden because of the murders that have taken place."

"We will have justice for our people…one way or another. If we cannot get justice through the human military, we will take it upon ourselves to launch a full military assault against the humans, the Axynnians, or anything else that gets in our way. For now, we wait. This meeting is finished," Queen Empress Aminarra said.

She turned around, opened the double doors, and walked out of the council room. Novish Shirom had to quicken his stride to catch up to her in the corridor. The other council members were left chatting among themselves.

Queen Empress Aminarra looked at Novish as they both walked along the corridor. "In the morning, I will travel from the Lythinarr Palace to a meeting I have in the city of Grand Meadows. When I'm finished, I will come here to the Sharrixian Government Building so that you and I can go visit the portal. I have questions to ask you. The weather will be sunny tomorrow. I'll contact you in the morning."

"I will see you then," Novish said.

Queen Empress Aminarra turned at a corridor intersection, her red dress trailing behind her. Alone, Novish continued through the Sharrixian Government Building toward his office.

The morning sunlight brightened the landscape before them as they looked out the ship's observation window. Following Deslorr Canyon, they made their way between two sheer cliffs. The river water below was very high, due to all the rain. The large, gray boulders peaked out as the water rushed over them, twisting and turning along is rocky path. The high cliffs eventually shortened as the ship flew along, revealing an oasis of greenery stretching far into the distance.

"Lairdain Tannis is such a beautiful planet," Queen Empress Aminarra said.

"Yes. I've been on some desolate planets for military training. Nothing beats home," Novish said.

As the oasis thinned, they began to see salt plains with small pockets of trees scattered about. Soon, the trees and salt plains disappeared and were replaced with dry, rippled streams in the desert sand, created from the pouring rain the day before. Many shrubs decorated the sand.

"We're almost to the Crystal Field," Novish said.

As they flew farther along in the desert, reddish-colored outcrops and rock formations became visible. One particular rock outcrop was massive with an extensive rock wall face. The aerial view of the large rock outcrop showed the desert continuing around its parameter. They began to see shiny crystal objects along the desert floor, the sun's light glistening from their surfaces. Ahead of them, a shimmering field was fixed against the large, reddish rock wall.

"There's the portal," Queen Empress Aminarra said.

Novish Shirom slowed the ship and lowered it to the ground. It landed with a hiss that blew some particles of sand into the air. He disabled the engines and they both unstrapped themselves from their seats. The morning sky above the rock wall was very bright. Heading for the exit, Novish grabbed a pair of sunglasses.

There was a slight breeze in the desert heat. Novish walked around toward the front of the ship and stood with his arms folded. His burgundy cape ruffled in the wind. Queen Empress Aminarra stopped next to him. She wore comfortable attire for the excursion. Her beige shirt complemented her taupe pants. Before them was a shimmering, bluish field of energy that stretched across the face of a large rock wall. The shape of the field was slightly oval, but with a rough, nonuniform border. A low humming frequency emitted from the shimmering field.

"The portal..." Novish said. "This is where it all happened. Our Gatherers were killed here almost twenty years ago. They were collecting the crystals for our current Sharrixian Government Building's design and architecture. The humans were spotted coming through the portal to our side and harvesting our crystals. Our Gatherers chased them back through to the other side, but only one of the five Gatherers that chased after them came back through alive. The other four were never heard from again. The Sharrixian that returned was badly injured, but he gave details of what happened and described what the other side looked like. He said it was very similar to this side, but had a forest in the distance. We can see a little bit of that through the portal. The Gatherer who returned saw the humans shooting at them. He said there were several ships the humans had landed in and they had crates full of crystals they were loading. The Gatherer revealed that the other four Sharrixians had been killed on the other side of the portal by the humans. The Gatherer who had witnessed this later died of his injuries. One of the four Gatherers who did not return was my uncle Riilan," Novish said.

"I'm sorry. I was not aware that one of the missing Gatherers was your uncle. And that is why I forbid our people from entering the portal. But, if we have to fight…" She trailed off.

"If we have to fight, we will pursue every avenue at our disposal. We would need to fly across the galaxy to engage the humans on a grand scale. However, this portal is wide enough for our Stormrider fighter ships to fit through," Novish said.

"Do you know how long this portal has been here?" Queen Empress Aminarra asked.

"It's been here as long as any of our people remember. Most likely, it's a natural phenomenon," Novish said.

"Yes, it has. Where are your guards?" Queen Empress Aminarra asked.

"They're here…among the rocky outcrops and out of sight," Novish said.

Moments later, two military officers appeared from around a monolith of sandstone and proceeded toward them. Heavy laser rifles were slung over their shoulders.

"Queen Empress Aminarra… High Commander Shirom… It is nice to see you both," one of the guards said.

"How are things out here?" the high commander asked.

"Uneventful," the other guard answered.

Novish gazed across that section of the desert at all the shiny crystals that decorated the sand. He knelt down and removed his glove. Picking up a large, black crystal with his bare hand, he looked at the many edges on its translucent surface. Novish tossed the black crystal back down to the sand where it landed next to a blue one. Standing up, he put his glove back on.

"I don't understand their obsession with these," Novish said.

Chapter Four

Coradelle Hershall entered one of the many glass doors at the entrance of the Settlement Agency as it quietly slid aside. She was followed by Wilcox Brown and Nancy Louray.

"It may be a little awkward to speak with Chaslin Anders again, since I was very pissed off the last time I spoke with him," Coradelle said.

"I'm sure it will be fine," Nancy said.

"I would hope that they are understanding. I mean, you recently lost your father. They deal with settling wills all the time," Wilcox said.

They walked down a large corridor. The marble floor and bright lights above gave off a cold vibe. Their steps echoed against the walls. Abstract artwork decorated each side of the long corridor. A set of black doors could be seen on the right in the distance. Two women passed them, followed by an older couple as the three of them continued onward.

"This is the first time I've been on Anneriss," Nancy said.

"Really? Well, it's only my second trip here. I didn't think I'd be back when I left upset," Coradelle said.

"I've been here several times, but never to enjoy my stay. It's always been on business. I mean, Anneriss is literally filled with office buildings. There are financial institutions, insurance companies, the Settlement Agency, investment firms, attorneys, and all sorts of business offices here. There are a few industrial areas as well," Wilcox said.

They reached the set of black doors, which automatically opened to the sides as they approached. Coradelle found herself in the same large, cold hall that she had been in before. The three of them stepped through to the other side of the doors and looked around at the very large hall. The ceiling was at least two stories tall. The same marble floor that was in the corridor decorated the large hall. A fountain was fixed in the center of the hall, its continuous flow of water echoing against the distant walls. For the most part, the room was empty, except for some furniture in a waiting area to their right. Two white couches faced each other, separated by a white table with a single decoration centered on it. On the left side of the room, a man was speaking to a secretary through a long rectangular opening along the wall. A countertop was fixed at the base of the opening.

"We can wait over here on the couches," Coradelle said.

The three of them walked over toward the couches and made themselves comfortable. Nancy looked at the fountain in the center of the room. With intricate detail, it portrayed an animal jumping over the flowing stream of water. They overheard part of the conversation between the man and the secretary.

"Yeah, this was a great sale for me. I made some good credits on it. I mean, as a real estate agent, I haven't made this many credits since back when I used to sell entire planets," he said.

"Wow! I've never heard of anyone buying an entire planet," she said. Her voice did not echo as much as his.

"Purchasing an entire planet back in the day was not entirely unheard of. But now, it is very rare. The deal I just closed was for a large piece of land on Xeralosa. It was still a pretty awesome sale," he said.

"Well, Bryson Wieler, I'll let your representative know that you stopped by. Do you have the paperwork he gave you?"

"Oh, yes. Thank you for the reminder," the man said.

The man set a briefcase on the counter before the secretary and shuffled through some papers. In the waiting area, Wilcox turned his attention to the decoration sitting on the center of the table in front of him. Nancy followed his gaze as he observed it.

"That's a beautiful blue crystal," Nancy said.

"Yes, it's quite interesting and unique. It also looks familiar," Wilcox said. He leaned forward on the couch and picked up the crystal. As he rotated it, the lights high above reflected from the many angles on its surface. Several different shades of light blue emitted from the crystal. The color was a mixture between aquamarine and sapphire. Wilcox set it back down onto the table. The real estate agent left the hall and Coradelle Hershall stood up from the couch.

"If you two want to wait here for a moment, I'll go ask the secretary if Chaslin Anders is available. He's the settlement agent that was assigned to my father's case."

"Okay," Wilcox said.

Coradelle walked past the fountain and toward the secretary, her steps echoing high into the ceiling. Wilcox felt the wound on his arm tingle under his shirt and he rubbed it. He immediately thought back to when he cut it on the ship entrance.

"Hi. I would like to meet with Chaslin Anders. Is he available?" Coradelle asked.

"May I tell him who's here?" the secretary asked.

"Let him know that Coradelle Hershall is here with a few more questions."

"Okay. I'll let him know. You can have a seat in the waiting area and he should be right with you," the secretary said.

As the secretary picked up a comm, Coradelle walked back toward the couch. Wilcox watched her return and noticed a single door along the wall next to the secretary. Coradelle sat back down on the couch across from Wilcox and Nancy.

"She's contacting him. It should only be a few minutes," Coradelle said.

Wilcox leaned across the table toward Coradelle and whispered in a low voice. "Did you hear that real estate agent say that he used to sell entire planets?"

"Yes. Back when my father was alive and about twenty years younger, it was not that unusual…if you had the credits to do it. He saved up a lot for that planet. And it was such a beautiful place. Honestly, I wish he would have been able to build his dream home there," Coradelle said.

The single door next to the secretary opened and a man exited. He started across the hall toward the waiting area.

"Here he comes," Nancy said.

As the man maneuvered around the fountain, he noticed Coradelle and stopped in his tracks.

"You again? I thought the name the secretary mentioned sounded familiar. She said you had more questions. You know, you didn't have to be so rude when you left here last time," he said.

"Chaslin, this is Wilcox Brown and his assistant, Nancy Louray. I hired him to investigate this issue with my father's will," Coradelle said.

Wilcox and Nancy both stood from the couch.

"Hi, Chaslin. I'm Wilcox Brown, Private Investigator."

Nancy nodded her head in greeting.

"Last time Coradelle was here, she had some choice words for me. I tried to explain to her that there is no such planet as Staraliss," Chaslin said.

"Coradelle has a purchase agreement that says otherwise," Wilcox said.

"You didn't mention that last time you were here," Chaslin said, looking at Coradelle.

"The purchase agreement was a recent discovery, after going through some of his things," Coradelle said.

"This copy is for you," Wilcox said, handing him the purchase agreement. "You can file it in the official settlement record."

Chaslin Anders looked over the agreement. He immediately noticed a couple of things that made him swallow hard and turn a bit pale. It was very evident that he was suddenly overcome with anxiety.

"I...I see it does say Staraliss. But that planet is not on the space charts. If you search for yourselves, you'll see...it...it's not there," he said with a shaky voice.

"I know better. As I said before, I was there when I was a child. This document proves that it exists," Coradelle said.

"Look, I see that it has the planet that you had mentioned listed here. But...but there was no deed to a planet in his inheritance. I've stated that last time you were here. We've given you everything from his estate," Chaslin said.

Coradelle looked furious and turned toward Wilcox.

"Settle down, Coradelle. We'll get to the bottom of this," Wilcox said.

Wilcox reached into his wallet and removed a business card, handing it to Chaslin.

"Look at this from my perspective," Coradelle said. "I know Staraliss exists. I was there when I was a kid!"

"Contact me, if you find out anything else," Wilcox said.

"Okay. If…if anything else comes up, I will let you know," Chaslin said.

"Thank you," Wilcox said.

"Once again, I'm leaving here empty-handed," Coradelle said.

The three of them headed toward the entrance doors. Chaslin stood in place and watched as they exited the hall. As soon as the black doors closed behind them, he headed back toward the door next to the secretary at a quick pace, reaching for his comm.

"Hey, Quinlan. This is Chaslin. I think we have a problem…"

As the *Enigma* lifted from the surface of Anneriss, Wilcox, Nancy, and Coradelle sat in silence, as if they had been defeated. Wilcox made an adjustment at the ship's controls. Coradelle removed the original purchase agreement from her purse and focused on the word Staraliss for a long time. She wondered if she was wasting everyone's time with this investigation. Something else on the purchase agreement caught her attention. She had read the document before and had seen the real estate agent's name, but this time her eyes got big.

"Ah…guys, the real estate agent listed on this purchase agreement is Bryson Wieler. Isn't he the real estate agent with the briefcase who we just overheard talking to the secretary back there?"

Wilcox and Nancy quickly looked at each other.

Chapter Five

Upon arriving back at the office, Wilcox walked directly over to the coffee pot.

"If you're pouring, I'll have a cup as well," Coradelle said.

"You might as well pour me one too," Nancy said.

Coradelle sat down in the chair in front of Wilcox's desk. Nancy turned on her computer and sat down at her desk across the aisle.

"It sounds like they're trying to pull some funny business. I'm going to do some research on this real estate agent. His name being on that document seems very suspicious," Nancy said.

Wilcox brought the coffee back to the desks. He sat down and took a drink from his cup.

"Coradelle, when we left the Settlement Agency on Anneriss, you said you were leaving there empty-handed again. With the discovery of that same real estate agent's name on the purchase agreement, I think we left there with a vital piece of information. Before you get too involved with your research there, Nancy, let's talk to Coradelle a little more about her father," Wilcox said.

Nancy focused her attention from her computer to Wilcox and

Coradelle.

"Coradelle, if your father was never given the deed to the planet that he purchased, I would think he would have reached out to the real estate agent. Do you know if he did?" Wilcox asked.

"I think so. Each planet in the Marrithious Galaxy has slightly different protocols, but where he lived on Ryamesh—where I live—you are supposed to contact the real estate agent with any issues. He paid for the planet outright, so he should have been very pissed that he did not receive the deed. I really wish I knew where the planet Staraliss is and I would go there just to prove it exists. The name does not appear in the space navigation system. Do you think he got ripped off? I mean, has this ever happened to anyone else?" Coradelle asked.

"We certainly have a bunch of research to do with this real estate agent, but I will have Nancy also look to see if there are any similar cases in the database," Wilcox said.

Coradelle drank her coffee and again looked at the purchase agreement that she had retrieved from her purse.

"Thank you," Coradelle said.

"Don't worry, Coradelle. We'll get to the bottom of this. One of the copies I made earlier of that purchase agreement was for our records. It's going to take time to do our research, so as soon as we have some leads on the case, we will reach out to you with updates. Nancy has all of your information. There is nothing more that you can do at the moment. When you get back home, just try to relax and understand that you made a great decision in hiring me to help you with this case," Wilcox said.

Coradelle finished her coffee and set the small cup back onto the desk. With a heavy sigh, she looked up at the two of them.

"I just want to honor my father. I mean, I could just let this whole thing go, but I have a right to know what is going on. If something is fraudulent or deceptive here, I owe it to him to see that justice is done," Coradelle said.

"You are absolutely right. We'll do our best to figure this out," Wilcox said.

"Thank you guys. I appreciate it," Coradelle said.

"It's hard enough losing a parent, let alone trying to find out what happened to the deed. You will be in my prayers," Nancy said.

"Thank you," Coradelle said.

She stood up from the chair and headed for the door.

"Have a good day," Nancy said.

The bells attached to the top of the door jingled as Coradelle shut it behind her.

In a small, remote office within the Settlement Agency on Anneriss, the air was a bit chilly. The white walls made it seem even colder. Three men sat at a round table in the office. They had varying shades of brown hair. The business suits they wore looked fairly similar to each other. Chaslin Anders sat in one of the chairs and shivered slightly, rubbing his arms.

"Sorry for the cold. The environmental temperature control units in this area of the building are being serviced at the moment. Chaslin, as the settlement agent for the Robert Hershall inheritance, you gave me assurance that there would be no issues with our operation," Quinlan Zale said.

"I thought we had everything under control and all loose ends tied up. I didn't realize Robert's daughter had a copy of the purchase agreement," Chaslin said.

The three of them looked at the copy of the purchase agreement that sat on the table. Wilcox Brown had given Chaslin a copy of the document earlier during his visit. One of them slid the paper across the table toward himself to have a closer look.

"Not only is the planet Staraliss listed on here, but my name is on here as well. I put my confidence in you to have all of the copies of the purchase agreement destroyed. As the Settlement Agency director, *you* should have had this under control," Bryson Wieler said, glaring at Quinlan Zale.

"I thought we took care of this as well, Bryson. Apparently, Robert Hershall had another copy that his daughter discovered. And this investigator that she has hired also made a copy. So, there is no hiding the document at this point. Wilcox Brown may become a problem for us," Quinlan said.

"Well, we may need to take care of the problem, like we did before," Bryson said.

"At some point, we need to consider if all this is worth the compensation we're getting for this side gig," Chaslin said.

"News of this problem must not reach the boss of our operation, if you know what's best for you both," Quinlan said.

Silence filled the small, cold room.

"All these years and we've had no issues…until now. So, what do you propose we do?" Chaslin asked.

"I think we need to mop this up. We can start with Coradelle Hershall. She really is a loose cannon," Quinlan Zale said.

"I agree. I'll have some of our team in the network take care of Coradelle," Chaslin said.

"Be careful. We don't need people in this Settlement Agency learning about our internal operation," Quinlan said.

"I understand," Chaslin said.

"Well, if we're done here, I have properties to sell," Bryson Wieler said.

Nancy continued searching through the database for similar cases to see if there was a pattern. The information she had found about the real estate agent Bryson Wieler was not helpful. There didn't seem to be anything nefarious about him that she could find. Across the galactic network, there were many private databases that investigators and government authorities had access to, which were not normally accessible to the public. One of the lesser known and lesser used databases was currently pulled up on Nancy's computer. She slowly sifted through information regarding similar-case criteria.

Wilcox Brown was out running errands and finishing up another case that they had recently solved. As Nancy sipped her coffee, she looked out the front window of the office. The sunlight came through and brightened the bookshelves along the wall, highlighting volumes of legal books. Suddenly, the comm rang and she answered it.

"Wilcox Brown Agency. This is Nancy. How can I help you?"

"Hi, Nancy. This is Avalaur. Do you have time for lunch today?"

"Hi, Avalaur. Unfortunately, I already grabbed a bite to eat. But don't worry, I'll have you and the family over for mashed potatoes and other good eats soon enough. We are currently on a case that is getting time consuming, so I'm not sure when I'll have time for that dinner. But it will happen," Nancy said.

"No worries. Good luck on your case," Avalaur said.

"Thanks. How are you doing, otherwise?" Nancy asked.

"Oh…the kids are getting out of hand lately," Avalaur said.

"You need to put your foot down and get after them. Don't let them take advantage of you, Avalaur."

"You're right. You're right. Well, I'll let you get back to work," Avalaur said.

"Okay. Well, you have a good lunch, wherever you go. I appreciate the offer. Perhaps next time," Nancy said.

"Yes. Take care, Nancy."

"You too."

Nancy ended the communication and set the comm down. She sat for a moment and smiled. It was nice to have good friends. She focused back onto the computer screen. As Nancy scrolled down the page, she suddenly stopped and looked closely at the information that was displayed before her. Her jaw dropped slightly as she breathed in quickly.

Shit!

She quickly picked up the comm and contacted Wilcox.

"Hi, Wilcox. I wish you were here. You'll never believe what just pulled up on this old, obscure database I'm searching in," she said.

"Okay. What did you find?" Wilcox asked.

"I was searching for similar patterns for the Coradelle Hershall case in the obscure PI Index Database. Coradelle's father, Robert Hershall, is listed in a previous unsolved case by another agency."

"Seriously?"

"Yes! I'm just now looking at the details. I didn't see this before because no one uses this old database anymore," Nancy said.

"I'll be back in the office shortly and then we can go over the details of your discovery. Nice work, Nancy. See you soon," Wilcox said.

Wilcox settled the *Enigma* on the landing pad behind his office and disabled the engines. After opening the airlock door, he was careful by the entrance where he had previously cut his arm on the sharp hinge.

I need to get that fixed, he thought.

He took a moment to remove his shirt and check on the deep wound. He noticed it had stopped hurting earlier. Removing the bandage he had applied the other day, he was shocked to find that it had completely healed. Astonished, he gasped.

What the hell? How did that heal so quickly? he thought.

He rubbed his arm and felt the same tingling sensation that he had felt back at the Settlement Agency after he held the blue crystal decoration from the table. Wilcox put his shirt back on and stepped out of the ship. Closing the entrance, he headed toward his office.

The familiar sound of the jingling bells rang as Wilcox opened the office door. Nancy looked up and suddenly got the flutters when she saw his handsome face.

"Hi, Wilcox. Your shirt is not tucked in very well," Nancy said.

"Hello. Hey, you should see my arm. It's completely healed," he said.

He unbuttoned and removed his shirt again to show her, but kept his hat on. Upon seeing his bare chest, Nancy immediately breathed in deeply and smiled. He showed her where the deep cut had been on his arm.

"Not even a scar... Isn't that the strangest thing you've ever seen? It's like I never got cut in the first place," Wilcox said.

Nancy swallowed hard as she tried to control her emotions. Her attraction to Wilcox was evident to her, but he did not seem to notice.

"Ah...yeah, that's pretty odd," she finally said, breathing heavily.

Wilcox put his shirt back on and tucked it in completely this time. As Nancy cooled down a bit, she focused on the computer in front of her. Wilcox leaned over her and rested his hand on her desk. She looked up into his green eyes and took a deep breath.

"So, tell me what you've found about Coradelle's father."

"Um...I was searching for similar cases, but I stumbled across a case that actually involves Robert Hershall himself. It looks like he hired another agency to locate the missing deed to the planet Staraliss that he purchased. This was about six years ago...so five years before Robert died," Nancy said.

"Now, we're onto something. Great work, Nancy! Scroll down farther," Wilcox said.

They gazed at the computer as the information populated on the screen.

"Look!" Nancy exclaimed.

"So, he hired an investigator named Everett Quarton to find this deed. Let's contact Everett's office and compare notes," Wilcox said.

Nancy clicked on a link to Everett Quarton's contact information.

"Well, his agency office was located on the planet Marauve, but..." Nancy said.

"But?"

Wilcox saw what Nancy was referring to.

"The agency closed two years ago, after the investigator mysteriously died," Nancy said as she read the screen.

"This keeps getting more interesting. So, he mysteriously died?" Wilcox asked.

"Apparently. It looks like he was still working on the case for Robert Hershall at the time," Nancy said.

"So, it is really the same unsolved case that we have now taken on. If his agency on Marauve is no longer there, I wonder where Everett's case files are. See what you can find out about Everett's death. There must be more information," Wilcox said.

Wilcox removed his hat and placed it on the coatrack next to his desk. He sat down and turned on his own computer.

"I'll see what I can find," Nancy said.

"I'll see if I can find something as well," Wilcox said.

They both sat for hours researching information on Everett Quarton. It became late and office hours were over. Nancy stood up and walked over to lock the door and close the blinds. The late hours were taxing on her, but sometimes the extra time was needed for certain cases. When she sat back down, Wilcox looked at her.

"I didn't realize what time it was. You don't have to stay late. We can pick this up in the morning," he said.

"That's okay. I don't mind staying a little longer," she said.

"Wait a minute. I think I have something," Wilcox said.

Nancy walked over to his desk and looked at his screen.

"It says here that a family member of Everett Quarton took care of his funeral arrangements and his estate after he died. It was his nephew, Remywl Yortix. I'll see if I can find a location for this nephew of his," Wilcox said.

"Perhaps he knows what happened to Everett's case files," Nancy said.

"According to this, Remywl Yortix lives on the remote planet of Velassine. Everett died at his agency on Marauve. I wonder if his files were moved or destroyed," Wilcox said.

"Velassine…" Nancy repeated.

"I think, in the morning, we should pay his nephew a visit," Wilcox said.

"I believe Velassine is quite a distance from here," Nancy said.

"Yes, it is. So, I will see you in the morning, Nancy."

Nancy walked over to her computer and shut it down.

"Okay. I'll see you in the morning. I'm glad your arm is feeling better," she said.

"Me too. Have a good night, Nancy," he said.

"Do you want me to leave this door unlocked for you?" she asked.

"Yes. I'll be right behind you in a few minutes."

"Okay. Don't forget to turn off the coffee pot," Nancy said as she unlocked the door and exited the office.

The night air was chilly. Nancy's apartment was not far from the office. She walked by the dark windows of the closed shops along the sidewalk. Nancy was exhausted and was looking forward to lying on her couch where she slept. She thought about Coradelle and said a prayer for her. As Nancy walked along, she also thought about her friend Avalaur. Nancy continued with a little prayer for Avalaur's family. She knew, from what Avalaur was going through, raising children had its difficulties. Perhaps, someday, she would get to experience a family of her own. A girl and a boy would be the perfect family to her. She wondered if Wilcox would ever notice her interest.

Why don't I just tell him how I feel? she thought.

As Nancy arrived at her apartment, she paused at the entrance and looked at her reflection in the glass door. Her dark brown hair shifted slightly from the wind as she noticed her green eyes in the reflection.

Why doesn't Wilcox notice me?

She dismissed the thought and went up the steps to her apartment.

Wilcox arrived at the office in the early morning. Nancy was already there with a fresh pot of coffee.

"Good morning, Wilcox," she said.

"Hi, Nancy. You looked very tired yesterday. I hope you got some good sleep."

"I did. Thank you. So, are you ready for today's adventure?" she asked.

"You know how much I like space travel. Not! But, yes, I am ready. We'll see what information this Remywl Yortix is able to provide. First, I need a cup of coffee. Thanks for making a fresh pot. It smells delicious," Wilcox said.

"You're welcome."

Wilcox walked to the back of the office and poured himself a cup of coffee and then turned off the coffee pot.

"Would you like a cup?" he asked.

"No thanks. I've already had one."

"Okay. Bring your note pad. I think we're going to need it," Wilcox said.

"I already have that packed in my bag," Nancy said.

"Nice. Let's go," he said.

Nancy put a note on the door stating they were out solving mysteries. She grabbed her white sweater and bag. After locking the door, they headed for the *Enigma*.

Velassine's scenery was absolutely gorgeous. As the *Enigma* flew along the treetops of a colorful forest, Wilcox and Nancy gazed out the observation window at the inspiring landscape. In the distance, on the port side of the ship, a dark blue lake could be seen. There were only a few towns on the planet. Most of it was undisturbed wilderness. The coordinates to the home of Remywl Yortix brought them to the town of Kawthas. Wilcox settled the ship onto a landing pad outside of Remywl's home. As Wilcox and Nancy exited the ship, they were greeted with the warmth of sunshine. The light brightened the green grass along the front of the luxurious home. They made their way along the walkway that led up a few stone steps to the front door. The house was made of elegant stone with various colored patterns, including shades of beige and gray. It was two stories tall with white trim along the windows and doors. Two matching white pillars adorned the front entrance. They came to a stop at the taupe colored door and Wilcox rang the bell. They could hear heavy music playing inside the house. After a long pause, Wilcox rang the bell again.

"Perhaps, he did't hear the door bell," Nancy said.

Wilcox sighed. A moment later, the door opened to reveal a middle-aged man with long, brown hair and a beard. He wore a black shirt and blue pants. The man adjusted his glasses as he looked at the two of them. Loud, heavy music was blasting out the door to greet them. Thudding drum beats and crunching guitars dominated their ears. The man pressed a button on the remote in his hand and the metal music was paused.

"Hello. Can I help you?" the man asked.

"Hi. My name is Wilcox Brown and this is my assistant, Nancy Louray. I'm a private investigator and we are working on a case that involves Everett Quarton. From what I understand, he is a relative of yours. Are you Remywl Yortix?" Wilcox asked.

"Yes, I am."

"I got your address from the information we found on Everett Quarton. If you don't mind helping us, we have some questions about our investigation," Wilcox said.

"Everett Quarton… Ah, yeah, I can help you. Come on in," he said.

Remywl led them to a beautifully decorated living room and gestured for them to have a seat on the gray velvet couch. A fireplace was located in front of them, trimmed with beige stone. Pictures of what appeared to be family members decorated the cream colored walls. A few tall, green plants were positioned at various locations around the spacious room.

"Would either of you like a refreshment?" Remywl asked. "I have coffee, tea, water, cola, ale, and mixed drinks."

"Sure. I'll have a black coffee," Wilcox said.

"I'll have a cola with light ice," Nancy said.

"Okay. I'll be right back," Remywl said.

He left the living room and disappeared down a hall.

"This is a nice house," Nancy said.

"Yes. It is very stylish," Wilcox said.

From the couch, they both peered around the room. A black piano sat behind one of the gray velvet chairs. On top of the piano, a bouquet of red roses rested in a vase. The petals were vibrant. The stereo equipment was lit up with bright LEDs. Against one wall was a shelf, filled with a large metal music collection. Soon, Remywl returned with a tray of beverages. After handing Wilcox and Nancy their drinks, Remywl took a cola for himself and set the tray down onto the intricately designed, wooden coffee table. He sat down in the gray chair.

"Everett Quarton was my uncle. He was also a private investigator. A couple of years ago, he unexpectedly died at his agency office on Marauve. He did not have anything wrong with him, yet he died. To this day, our family does not know how he died. Even the doctors could not explain it. He had nothing wrong with him. He seemed to be healthy. It was a strange and mysterious death. I'm very delighted to know that you are working on this. Perhaps you can find out what happened to him in this investigation of yours," Remywl said.

As Remywl took a drink of his cola, Wilcox and Nancy looked at each other.

"That is very interesting. The case we are working on had a similar death. And our case led us to Everett. Apparently, he was in the middle of working on a case that involved our client's father. Do you know if Everett's case files were moved from his agency office on Marauve and archived or if they were destroyed?" Wilcox asked.

Wilcox took a drink of his coffee.

"After he died, there was a break-in at his agency. Someone ransacked the place. They were looking for something. But I doubt they found it. You see, my uncle took most of his important case files home to the North Harbor Mansion every night…for that very reason," Remywl said.

"Well, that's good. And where did your uncle live?" Wilcox asked.

"He lived here on Velassine, sort of… I'm sure you saw Lake Methora in the distance when you arrived here in Kawthas," Remywl said.

"Yes, we did. It is a beautiful, dark blue body of water," Nancy said.

Nancy took a long drink of her cola.

"I am the heir to his entire estate. After going through the Settlement Agency, I became the owner of his North Harbor Mansion on Lake Methora. It was his home, but he traveled so much, he was rarely there. If you're flying over, you can't miss his mansion. Unfortunately, I haven't cared for his mansion like I should. It has been neglected and some areas are in a state of disrepair. There is just so much to do. And I just cannot bear to go there. I get very emotional over his death. Oh, he was a lover of music, like me. After he died, I…I had a dream that he was alive. I was sitting by myself at a round table in a room for some event. There were other people in the distance of the room. I turned to my right and there was my uncle Everett. I looked at him in disbelief, knowing that he was dead. He smiled. I told him I had lots of questions for him and asked him if he could sit with me at the table. He agreed and walked behind me to come around and sit on my left. But as soon as he was behind me and out of my vision, he disappeared. I turned around and he was gone. That's when I woke up and realized it was just a dream. Even now, a couple of years after his death, it still seems so surreal. One of these times, I'll get over there and clean up his mansion," Remywl said.

Wilcox and Nancy could see the tears welling up in Remywl's eyes.

"I'm sorry for your loss and that you had to go through that. He must have been a wonderful uncle to you. You will be in my prayers," Nancy said.

"Thank you. He was awesome. I miss him terribly. Anyway…I know he would bring home his important case files and keep them in his home office when he did not need them at his agency. He was quite the sleuth. Feel free to head over there to his mansion and take a look around. I really don't want to go there. It is very emotional for me. I hope you understand. It will be night soon and the power is no longer on at his mansion, so you may want to bring a flashlight. If you need one, I have an extra," Remywl said.

Wilcox finished his coffee.

"I have a couple of them on the ship. Has anyone else ever came here asking questions about him?" Wilcox asked.

"No. You two are the first ones. There was a rumor going around here in Kawthas that someone landed at his mansion a couple of years ago, after he died. I don't have any proof of that, however. I hope you two find the answers you're looking for in your investigation. If you happen to find out why my uncle died, please let me know. He was a good man and I miss him dearly," Remywl said.

"If we find the answer to that mystery, we will certainly let you know. We appreciate your time. I'll do my best to locate North Harbor Mansion and try to leave it as undisturbed as possible," Wilcox said.

"Oh, you'll see it from the air. You can't miss it. There is a door on the back side of the mansion that should be unlocked. His office is on the second floor. Good luck," Remywl said.

"Thank you," Nancy said.

They all stood up and Remywl led them to the door. Wilcox and Nancy stepped out onto the porch.

"Good luck," Remywl said.

"Thank you. We appreciate your help in this matter," Wilcox said.

Chapter Six

The late afternoon sunlight brightened the trees as the *Enigma* flew above the forest at a slow velocity. In the distance, Wilcox and Nancy saw the dark blue waters of Lake Methora. The lake was vast, expanding for kilometers into the distance. A handful of very small islands could be seen in the lake, each decorated with several evergreen trees. A break in the forest revealed the North Harbor Mansion grounds. A road for ground vehicles led from the forest across the grounds to a parking garage. Wilcox landed the *Enigma* on a ship landing pad in the center of an overgrown lawn and disengaged the engines. From the observation window, they noticed a stone walkway leading from the landing pad toward a very impressive, but eerie, four-story mansion. It was decorated with stone walls in its entirety.

"Wow! That mansion is awesome," Wilcox said.

"I have a feeling it's going to be creepy," Nancy said.

"Well, since we don't have much light left in the day and the power has been turned off, it may very well be creepy. I'll grab those flashlights," Wilcox said.

After Wilcox took the flashlights from the *Enigma's* storage area, they stepped out of the ship and onto the mansion grounds. The once immaculate lawn was overgrown with tall, yellow grass. Ahead of them, the stone walkway that led from the landing pad split and went around a circular fountain that sat in the middle. Water was no longer flowing from it and it had become tarnished with a green corrosion. As they walked past on the right of the fountain, they peered inside and noticed the water level was very low with algae growing in it. Leaves floated in the standing water. They continued along the stone path that made its way through the overgrown grass. Soon, they went up two steps onto the front porch. The door of the large mansion stood before them. Four stone pillars supported a covered entry, mostly wrapped with green ivy. On the right of the mansion, there was a round turret section that extended to the third floor.

As they stopped at the front door, Nancy noticed weeds that had grown through the washed stone landscaping that surrounded the mansion. Wilcox tried the door, but it was locked.

"Remember, Remywl said the back entry door was unlocked," Nancy said.

"Oh, that's right. Let's head around back," Wilcox said.

Stepping down from the porch, they turned to their right. Moving beyond the stone walkway, they made their way through the tall grass and weeds. Walking along the left side of the mansion, they passed a large chimney that was made of the same type of stone as the rest of the mansion. Soon, they found themselves on a patio. A slider door led from the patio to what looked like a dining room. Wilcox tried the slider door, but it was also locked. He turned back toward Nancy and noticed that she was looking out beyond the patio. Wilcox followed her gaze. Through a cleared patch of woods, Lake Methora was very visible, its choppy waves splashing against the rocks of North Harbor.

"Isn't that something?" Nancy gazed at the distant water.

"Yes. It's very beautiful, yet treacherous at the same time," Wilcox said.

They both stood on the patio for a long moment, soaking in the beauty of the lake. As a seabird flew overhead, Wilcox turned to continue around toward the back of the mansion.

"Shall we?" he asked.

Nancy turned and followed him back into the tall grass. Ahead of them, the back corner of the mansion was visible. They turned the corner and noticed a small walkway that led to the back entry door. The daylight seemed to dim slightly as they reached the door.

"Here we are," Wilcox said.

Wilcox turned the door knob and the door opened. He looked at Nancy and stepped inside. Nancy followed him into a back entryway. She shut the door behind them. Beyond the small entryway was a long hall that had several doors leading from it. Despite the fact that the mansion was wired for power, evenly spaced candles were located along the walls of the hallway. The unlit candles were left at various used stages, some of which had formed drips along their lengths. Unique patterns were designed into the flooring of the hall. Opening a door to their left revealed a laundry room. The door on the right led to a kitchen. They both stepped into the kitchen. Nancy walked by a large island with a stove in the center. Wilcox opened a door at the back of the kitchen and peeked inside. There was a pantry with various expired items on the shelves. He followed Nancy as she passed the sink and he looked out the window toward the nearby forest. Nancy opened a refrigerator in the corner of the kitchen and stared into the dark interior at items covered in mold that had dissolved into a liquid glob. Shutting the door quickly, she immediately gagged at the smell and covered her nose.

"Oh damn! That is nasty," she said.

"Eww! That's disgusting," Wilcox said.

Wilcox recoiled as the rotting scent emitted from the door. They quickly left the kitchen and entered a dining room. Dim light came through the slider door and brightened the table and chairs, revealing a thick coating of dust. A cabinet of fine dishes sat against the far wall. Through the slider, the outside patio where they stood earlier could be seen as well as the distant Lake Methora. Another set of doors led out of the dining room and back into the hall. They crossed the hall and entered the master bedroom. A large bed was on their right, perfectly made with its white comforter tucked in. Next to the bed was a side table with a white lamp on it. Across from the bed, a large, tan dresser rested against the opposite wall. The round turret architecture of the mansion was located in the corner of the room, with windows at even intervals. Two other doors led from the master bedroom. One opened to a large walk-in closet. The other door opened to the master bathroom. White tiles decorated the bathroom floor. A hot tub was located in the back corner. The room reeked of stale water. Nancy looked at the side profile of Wilcox in the bathroom mirror and breathed in.

Will there ever be a good time to tell him how I feel about him? she thought.

"This place is pretty amazing" Wilcox finally said.

Nancy followed Wilcox back out into the hall.

"It's kind of creepy, if you ask me," she said.

"With no power here and all these shadows, there is bound to be a phantom lurking," Wilcox said.

"Yeah, right. That's not funny."

They continued to the end of the hall, which gave way to a sizable living room. Light came through the windows on either side of a large, stone fireplace. The fireplace hearth was raised slightly from the surrounding floor tiles. Wilcox walked over toward the fireplace, staring at a portrait that hung above the mantel. It was framed in gold with black matting. The portrait displayed Everett Quarton and an Axynnian woman, her sparkling, amber eyes expressing a genuine happiness. Nancy stopped beside Wilcox and looked up at the portrait.

"Was Everett married to her?" Nancy asked.

"I don't think so. None of the information I read indicated that he was married. Perhaps, they were good friends," Wilcox said.

"It looks like they were *very* good friends," Nancy said.

"Oh…that's sad," Wilcox said.

Wilcox noticed a small memorial plaque on the mantel.

"What?" Nancy asked.

"There is a memorial on top of the mantel that is a dedication to her. It *was* his wife and she died. He was a widower. Her name was Shandarr Quarton," Wilcox said.

"Aww. That *is* sad," Nancy said, noticing the memorial plaque.

"I wonder how long ago she died. He looks a little younger in that picture than the one I saw when I was doing the research," Wilcox said.

Soon, they turned away from the fireplace and toward the opposite side of the living room. An open stairway led up to a mezzanine on the second level that overlooked the entire living room. There was a door below the stairway. To their right, the living room opened up to a very large foyer. They walked out into the foyer, their steps echoing from the stone tile floor into the high arches. A chandelier hung high above them, covered in cobwebs. On their right was a long coat closet and to their left was a fountain. Similar to the fountain outside, the water was not flowing. The familiar scent of stale water lingered in the air. They stood before the front entry door of the mansion.

"So, here is the front door that's locked. Let's head back into the living room and up the stairs to the second level," Wilcox said.

"There was another door under the staircase," Nancy said.

They walked back into the living room. Wilcox headed for the staircase, while Nancy went toward the door underneath the stairs.

"Where are you going?" Wilcox asked.

"I just want to see what's in there," Nancy said.

Wilcox walked over to where Nancy stood at the door. She opened it. It was very dark inside. They both retrieved their flashlights and shined them into the doorway. The light revealed a stairway that led downward. A musty scent greeted them as they stared down the steps.

"Well, that must be the catacombs," Wilcox said. "You know, the haunted crypts…"

"Again, not funny. It's probably the wine cellar. It certainly is musty," Nancy said, closing the door.

They turned off their flashlights and headed up the open stairway. The steps were covered with dusty, burgundy carpeting. Dust also covered the wooden rail. When they reached the top of the steps, they both walked along the mezzanine and looked over the railing and down into the large living room. A dusty, black harpsichord sat on the far side of the mezzanine. Wilcox walked over to it.

"So, why is this place called North Harbor Mansion?" Nancy asked.

"I presume it is called North Harbor Mansion because the section of Lake Methora that is located in this area is called North Harbor, thus the name," Wilcox said.

"Oh, I see," Nancy said.

Wilcox opened the fallboard that covered the harpsichord keys. Standing next to the bench, he pressed several keys and the notes rang out across the upper living room area and echoed loudly. He closed the cover.

"You're quite the musician," Nancy said.

Wilcox laughed. Nancy followed him back across the mezzanine to a door that was on the right of the stairway. Entering the room, they found a lounge with several leather seats and a pool table in the center. The lounge was above the master bedroom and included the round turret section of the mansion. Wilcox walked past the dusty pool table and looked out the window into a courtyard below.

"Strange that beautiful flowers grow down there among the tall grass and weeds," Wilcox said.

Nancy walked over and peeked out the window at the colorful blue, pink, and yellow flowers.

"Wow. Those would make a nice arrangement," she said.

The sunlight dimmed considerably as dusk approached.

"Well, we need to find Everett's office to see if his case files are here…before we lose all of our daylight," Wilcox said.

"Yes. Remywl said it was on the second floor," Nancy said.

Leaving the lounge, they checked a couple of doors along the mezzanine. One led to a musty bathroom and the other led to a guest bedroom. A closet was located on the right of the bedroom entrance. On the left, there was a set of doors that led to an outside terrace. The surface of the terrace and stone railing were weathered with a black mildew. The bedroom furnishings included a bed, a dresser, a chair, and a side table. Leaving the guest bedroom, they walked around the corner of the mezzanine and into a long, dim hallway. To their immediate right was another stairway that led upward to the third level.

"The third floor looks pretty dark," Nancy said.

"Yes, it does. And it's dark enough now that we're going to have to use our flashlights. It would have been nice for Remywl to have the power turned back on for us, but I'm sure that would involve the hassle of contacting the utility company and would take a couple of days to schedule," Wilcox said.

"We could come back tomorrow at an earlier time," Nancy said.

"Well, we did leave early on Kesron's time, but that does not synch with Velassine's time. We would need to leave in the middle of the night to arrive here at an early hour," Wilcox said.

"No thanks," Nancy said.

Turning on their flashlights, the second-floor hallway came into full view. Brown, wooden flooring decorated the hall. Intriguing portraits hung on either side.

"That is absolutely beautiful!" Nancy said.

They both looked ahead at the far wall.

"Nice," Wilcox said.

On the wall, at the end of the hallway, an artist had painted directly onto the wall a picture of Lake Methora, its dark blue waters swollen with waves. On both sides of the painted water, a group of three wood pilings were painted, wrapped with rope. Lantern-style light fixtures were mounted on each side of the wall, at the top of the painting.

"I'll bet when the power is on and those lights brighten that wall painting, it is even more of a spectacular view," Wilcox said.

"Definitely," Nancy said.

There were two doors at the end of the hallway, on either side of the painting. Nancy opened the door on the right and shined her flashlight inside. It was a closet, located underneath the staircase. Wilcox opened the door on the left.

"Here we are! Everett's office..." Wilcox said.

They shined their flashlights around the room. A window was located on the right side of the office with drapes that were closed. The side of Everett Quarton's desk rested against the wall on the left. There were several filing cabinets on their left, across from the desk, a few of the drawers open. Above the filing cabinets, a taxidermied wolf was mounted on the wall. Behind Everett's desk, on the left, there was a small closet with its door left open. Jackets occupied two of the hangers. Wilcox walked around behind the desk and shined his flashlight onto its surface. There was a notepad and pen next to a picture. Wilcox focused his light onto the picture, revealing a portrait of Everett's late wife, Shandarr, the Axynnian woman that was with Everett in the portrait on the mantel above the fireplace. Wilcox looked in several of the desk drawers and noticed a small book. Nancy walked over to the open filing cabinets and noticed file folders lying on top of the drawer contents. She directed her flashlight from one drawer to the other.

"Look at this, Wilcox," she said.

Wilcox came from around Everett's desk and joined Nancy in front of the filing cabinets.

"The tabs on these file folders indicate they are for the Robert Hershall case," Nancy said.

Wilcox shined his light onto the tabs. Sure enough! Robert Hershall's case was labeled on several of the file folders.

"It looks like someone has been here at the North Harbor Mansion going through the very information that we're looking for," Wilcox said.

They looked at each other in the dim light.

"The case files are missing," Nancy said, walking over to the other cabinet with its drawer ajar. She thumbed through the files. "Here is one for the same case that contains a document."

"And this is why we keep our office disorganized…to purposefully throw off intruders," Wilcox said.

"Whoever was here must not have thought this was an important document…or they were careless in their work and missed it. That rumor that Everett's nephew, Remywl, heard about someone landing here at the mansion must be true. I'll bet he doesn't even know someone else was in Everett's office looking through these files," Nancy said.

Wilcox stepped over to the other filing cabinet where Nancy stood and looked at the document. It was the agreement that Robert Hershall signed when he hired Everett Quarton.

"This gives the details of the case. Robert hired Everett to help acquire the deed to the planet Staraliss. Apparently, Robert had paid Bryson Wieler, the real estate agent, for Staraliss and never received the deed. Welcome to a multi-generational investigation, with both Robert and Coradelle," Wilcox said.

Suddenly, a loud crash could be heard outside of the office and musical notes from the harpsichord rang out. It echoed throughout the hall and out over the mezzanine into the high ceiling of the living room. Nancy looked up at the mounted wolf as they quickly ran out of the office and down the hall toward the mezzanine. Shining their flashlights down the stairs and over the mezzanine railing, they did not see anyone or anything out of place. Wilcox shined his light toward the harpsichord and noticed the fallboard lying on an angle. One end had struck the bench and landed on the floor. The other end of the fallboard had landed against the keys, thus making the sound they had heard.

"You were right, Nancy, this mansion is creepy," Wilcox said.

"I know I was right."

Wilcox lifted the fallboard back up onto the harpsichord.

"Maybe this time, it will stay," he said.

"Let's hope so," Nancy said.

They returned to Everett's office.

"Well, obviously, someone was here and grabbed the files we need. Like you said, I guess the rumor that Remywl mentioned about someone coming here to the mansion was true. I mean, it's not real hard to miss from the air," Wilcox said.

"So, this is a dead end," Nancy said.

"Look through these other cabinets. I'm going to look at a book a saw in his desk drawer," Wilcox said.

Nancy continued looking through the other files. Wilcox opened the book he had found in Everett's desk. He paged through it and focused his flashlight on one of the pages.

"Um, Nancy, what do you make of this?" Wilcox asked.

As she walked toward him, Wilcox notice her beautiful silhouette on the wall as she passed through the beam of his flashlight. He immediately dismissed the thought and looked back down at the book.

"What is it?" she asked.

"This appears to be Everett's journal. The last few entries talk about the Robert Hershall case. He thought someone was after him ever since he took on the investigation. It says things started getting very strange and—although he brought the case files home from his agency each evening—he felt like he needed to be more cryptic. And then, it just has the number 42 listed," Wilcox said.

"What the hell is that supposed to mean?" Nancy asked.

"Good question," Wilcox said.

"Wait a minute. Turn to page 42 in his journal," Nancy said.

Wilcox turned back the pages to an earlier section of his journal. Two words were written along the page margin, followed by a number.

"Golden tome, 21." Wilcox read the text.

"Golden tome?" Nancy looked up at Wilcox.

"Perhaps, a book," Wilcox said.

"Turn to page 21," Nancy said.

Wilcox thumbed through the pages until he reached page 21. Along the margin was another word.

"Library." Nancy read the word this time.

"A golden book in the library?" Wilcox questioned.

"We didn't see a library in the mansion," Nancy said.

"We still haven't been on the third level," Wilcox said.

They both left Everett's office, shining their flashlights down the dark hallway. On their left, they looked up the staircase that led to the third floor. Starting up the steps, they could hear the old wood creaking beneath their weight. A landing was located at the top of the stairs. Wilcox and Nancy noticed the stairs continued up two more steps on the left side of the landing. Pausing in their tracks, they shined their flashlights all around the large room. The third floor was smaller than the second floor. As the beams of light scanned across the room, they saw a multitude of bookshelves, filled with books from floor to ceiling. Every shelf had a library ladder attached to a bar at the top. They made their way down an aisle. The overwhelming scent of books greeting them. Continuing around the corner of a bookshelf, they noticed even more bookshelves.

"Wow! The entire third floor is a library," Nancy said.

Moonlight shined through the curtains of a nearby window and brightened a section of bookshelves. The moonlight also revealed a small table and reading chair along one wall. As they walked along one of the aisles in the vast library, Nancy was a bit overwhelmed.

"Yes, it certainly appears to be the entire third level. This is quite impressive," Wilcox said.

"There are thousands of books in here. In the dark, it will take a while to find any golden colored books," Nancy said.

Wilcox shined his flashlight along the upper part of a shelf on his left. He walked through an opening between two shelves and onto another aisle. Books on a plethora of non-fiction subjects lined many of the shelves. A multitude of fiction novels in many genres were also present. In the corner of the library, bookshelves surrounded the round turret section of the mansion as it concluded its ascent at the third level. Making their way past a door, they stopped where a shelf was built into a wall near the door.

"Another room?" Wilcox questioned.

Nancy opened the door and shined her light inside.

"It's a stairway to the fourth level," she said.

The steps were unfinished wood, covered with a thick layer of dust. They followed the steps up to a landing that had two additional steps on the left, similar to the previous staircase one level below.

"Oh, it's just a small attic. It looks like he used it for storage," Nancy said.

Wilcox shined his flashlight onto crates and boxes covered in thick dust and cobwebs. The moonlight was much brighter in the attic since the window had no curtains. The night sky was filled with a spectacular display of northern lights. Green, purple, blue, and pink colors stretched across the night sky with pillars of light extending vertically across large sections of it. The shimmering colors danced around in waves of radiant beams.

"Wow!" Wilcox said.

"That is absolutely beautiful," Nancy said.

They both peered out the attic window for some time at the beautiful tapestry. Nancy looked up at Wilcox's handsome figure.

"Okay. We have a book to locate," Wilcox said.

Wilcox walked back down the stairs, followed by Nancy.

"I'll start on this side from top to bottom and you can start on the other side. We'll follow the shelves around in a logical manner and meet in the middle aisle," Wilcox said.

"This is for the birds!" Nancy said.

"I know it's going to be difficult, especially in the dark, but it's the only clue we have to go by at this point," Wilcox said.

Wilcox started looking at the top shelf along the round turret section of the room and worked his way toward the bottom shelf, carefully shining his flashlight across the color of each book. Nancy, began her search by shining the light at the top of the bookshelf near the stairway that led down to the second level. As they made their way along the shelves, they could feel the night temperature drop significantly. Slight gusts of wind could be heard as they blew against the metal roofing of the round turret section. Nancy thought she saw a golden colored book near the top shelf. She carefully climbed the library ladder to get a closer look. The book spine turned out to be yellow. As she made her way back down the ladder, she realized her palms had become dusty from the ladder rungs. Nancy held her flashlight between her knees and brushed her hands together to wipe off the dust. She continued searching for the golden colored book. Wilcox made his way around the corner onto the middle aisle where Nancy was. She stopped and held her flashlight steady on the spine of a golden colored book.

"I think I found it," Nancy said.

Wilcox walked over to where she stood and shined his light onto the book. Nancy set her flashlight down onto the floor.

"That certainly has been the only golden colored book we've seen," Wilcox said.

Nancy pulled the hardcover book from the shelf and discovered that it was a mystery novel.

"Isn't that ironic? At least Everett had a sense of humor," Wilcox said.

As Wilcox held his flashlight, fixed onto the book, Nancy opened the cover and flipped through the pages. On page 42, there was a small note inserted between the pages.

"White wine, 21." Nancy read the note. "What is that supposed to mean?"

"White wine, 21? Hmm," Wilcox said.

They both stood there in silence for a few minutes, thinking of an explanation.

"The wine cellar!" they said, simultaneously.

Nancy slid the book back into its spot on the shelf and grabbed her flashlight from the floor. They both left the library and headed back down the stairway to the second level. Passing the mezzanine, they went down the carpeted staircase and into the living room on the first floor. Nancy walked over and opened the door underneath the stairs, which they had peered down earlier.

"It's pitch black down there," Nancy said.

Wilcox took the lead as they started down the steps. At the bottom of the steps, they faced a cement wall. Shining their lights to the right, they discovered it opened to a small, one-room wine cellar. Across from the stairs, a furnace and water heater were located in the corner, both covered in dust. A shelf was located against the back wall with several supplies on it, including firewood, candles, and tools. Underneath the stairway was a diamond cube wine rack with the majority of the spaces filled.

"It is much colder down here in the wine cellar," Wilcox said, shivering.

"Yes, it is definitely chilly. I'm glad I brought my sweater. Look at all this wine. So, what do you think the 21 means?" she asked.

"Good question. With just two digits, a Marrithious Galaxy year the wine was produced doesn't make sense. Perhaps it is the location of the bottle with the counted number across or down," Wilcox said.

"How many bottles of white wine are here?" Nancy asked.

Wilcox removed a dark green glass bottle from the rack, its movement of liquid making a distinct sound. He looked at it as Nancy shined her flashlight onto the label. Wilcox returned the bottle to its slot.

"That bottle is a red wine. Traditionally, white wine will be in a light green glass bottle. There are a lot of them here," Wilcox said.

"Look! The rack is numbered underneath each slot," Nancy said.

"Those are tiny numbers," Wilcox said, shining his flashlight along the diamond cube rack.

Nancy began guiding her index finger along the rows until she came to number 21. Wilcox pulled the light green bottle from the rack and blew the dust from its surface. Particles of dust flew in front of the flashlight's beam. He inspected the label of white wine and immediately noticed that it was empty.

"There's no wine in this bottle," he said.

Wilcox pulled on the cork and it was easily removed from the bottle. He shook it and they heard something rattle inside.

"There's something in there," Nancy said.

"Yeah."

Wilcox turned the bottle upside down and shook it. A rolled-up paper fell out of the wine bottle and onto the cellar floor. Nancy reached down and retrieved it, handing it to Wilcox. He carefully unfolded the paper and looked at it as Nancy held her flashlight fixed onto the writing.

If you are reading this note, then you have successfully followed my clues. Unfortunately, it also means that something must have happened to me. I believe my life is in danger. My current case for Robert Hershall to find the deed to the planet Staraliss that he purchased has stirred some elusive figures. I'm convinced the real estate agent, Bryson Wieler, that my client used to purchase the planet is involved in fraud. I've been taking my case files home each night, but I believe they will come here looking for them. So, I left the clues that you obviously found in my journal, the golden book, and this wine bottle. I've never had to do this with any other case before.

I have found that the name of the planet Staraliss has been changed in the Marrithious Galaxy navigation database. Only someone with high authority would have access to do that. That is why Staraliss cannot be found in the navigation system. Someone changed it to Shext. I planned to confirm this by bringing my client to Shext, but if you found this note, then I did not get the chance to go there before they stopped me.

This case has been strange, to say the least.

Something is very wrong here and I hope it can be solved. I just have a feeling that someone is trying to stop me. And if they are after me, then they may also go after my client Robert Hershall. If you are finding this, then my worst fears have been realized. May you be more successful than I was in your endeavor. Godspeed.

—Everett Quarton

Wilcox and Nancy looked at each other. Suddenly, Wilcox felt a great anxiety in the pit of his stomach. As Nancy held her flashlight on the note, she could see his grim expression in the dim light. He folded up the note and put it into his pocket. After putting the cork back into the bottle, Wilcox carefully returned it to the diamond cube wine rack slot.

"Should we tell Remywl that someone may have murdered his uncle?" Nancy asked.

"I believe someone murdered both Everett Quarton and Robert Hershall. What in the galaxy did we stumble across with this case? Everett knew someone was after him. Until we can find out more information, we shouldn't trust anyone right now. So, no, we should not tell Remywl about this. This has me freaked out…a lot. I certainly hope no one is following *us*," Wilcox said.

"Well, you do have that laser pistol. I should have brought mine from my desk," Nancy said.

"Yup. It might come in handy," Wilcox said.

"Let's get back to the office. We have a lot of work to do," Nancy said.

"Actually, we're not going back to the office. We're going to the planet Shext. Or should I say Staraliss?" Wilcox said.

"Oh dear."

CHAPTER SEVEN

IN A SMALL military command post on Anneriss, a woman with short, blond hair stood near an overhead entrance. She was dressed in full military gear. Her brown eyes peered at a service vehicle as it approached the entrance. Once the vehicle was inside, she pressed a button on the wall and the overhead door closed. The warehouse was full of various military equipment. Two men stepped out of the vehicle, each wearing a maintenance uniform. They walked over to the woman who stood next to a metal container.

"Commander Stone… Commander Aolliam… What information do you have for me?" she asked.

"Things are definitely heating up," Commander Aolliam said.

Commander Aolliam had brown hair. His maintenance uniform was slightly dirty across the front.

"The plan for us disguised as maintenance personnel to service the environmental temperature control units at the Settlement Agency was successful. We were able to capture the conversation between the Settlement Agency director, Quinlan Zale, the settlement agent Chaslin Anders, and the real estate agent Bryson Wieler. There is a woman named Coradelle Hershall that is in danger and perhaps an investigator named Wilcox Brown as well. It appears this group has killed before," Commander Stone said.

Commander Stone had black hair. He was about the same height as Commander Aolliam.

"Also, they spoke of a boss they apparently report to," Aolliam said.

"Interesting… Keep your team surveilling. We need more information that our inside guys don't have access to," she said.

"Our internal agents are doing the best they can," Stone said.

"Understood," she said. "I want you both to protect Coradelle Hershall."

"Affirmative," Aolliam said.

"What exactly did they say about Wilcox Brown?" she asked.

"They said he may become a problem for them," Aolliam said.

The woman looked down and paced along the length of the container. She stopped before them and looked up.

"Have someone keep a protective watch on Wilcox Brown as well," she said.

"Yes, ma'am," Aolliam said.

Wilcox Brown sat at the controls of the *Enigma*. Nancy Louray sat in the seat next to him. As they drifted in orbit above Velassine, Wilcox programmed the ship's navigation for the planet Shext.

"It's a secluded planet that is part of the Tenebrous Region. It's a bit of a long flight," he said.

"I wonder who changed the name of the planet in the navigation database," Nancy said.

"I'm wondering that myself. What is so special about Staraliss that they needed to go through all this trouble?"

Wilcox cleared his throat several times.

"Are you okay?" Nancy asked.

"My throat is a little scratchy after being in that damp cellar. I'm fine," Wilcox said.

"You should go to the ship's lounge and gargle with salt water," Nancy said.

"I'll be fine."

As the *Enigma* made its way toward the Tenebrous Region of the Marrithious Galaxy at lightspeed-plus, silence filled the control area of the ship. The only sound that could be heard was the distant hum of the ship's engines.

Okay, I can do this, Nancy thought as she worked up the courage to talk to Wilcox about her feelings for him.

"Wilcox… I've been meaning to tell you something. I've—"

Suddenly, alarms started blaring as a few small asteroids came dangerously closed to their flight path.

"Shit! The nav system is supposed to avoid those," Wilcox said.

He scanned the space ahead of them and tracked two more asteroids that were already moving out of their path.

"That was a close call. And that's another reason why I don't like space travel," Wilcox said.

"Well, I did pray for safe travels," Nancy said.

"What were you going to tell me?" he asked.

"Oh, nothing. It's not important," Nancy said.

The *Enigma* came out of lightspeed-plus and a bright planet loomed before Wilcox and Nancy. Through the ship's observation window, they saw a planet with white clouds swirling across various shades of blue. Wilcox enabled the ship's anti-gravitational units. As he flew through the atmosphere, Wilcox wondered where Coradelle's father had taken her on the surface. Pondering on where Robert Hershall had planned to build his house, Wilcox leveled the ship and began flying above the forest. Endless white pine trees extended into the distance toward the sky blue horizon. Occasionally, the trees opened up to reveal clear blue lakes. Some of the lakes had small islands. It was a large planet and Wilcox knew he would have no way of knowing where Robert Hershall had landed before.

"What's that?" Nancy asked. She pointed to an object on the computer screen.

Wilcox looked at the screen and double-tapped on the object. Text was displayed on the screen next to it.

"It appears to be some type of shimmering energy field. Very interesting. Let's have a closer look," he said.

Wilcox maneuvered the *Enigma* toward the object. Passing exposed rock formations and outcrops, that were among the white pine trees, they flew onward. He initiated the landing sequence and settled the ship in a large clearing next to a tan rock wall. Noticing a shimmering field through the observation window, they looked at each other.

"That's interesting, indeed," Nancy said.

They made their way through the airlock door and onto the sandy soil. Clumps of grass and small stones could be seen scattered about the sandy clearing. As they walked through the sand toward the tan rock wall, they were startled by two wolves howling from a distant stone slab that overlooked the clearing where had they landed. Wilcox and Nancy turned their attention toward the distant rocks where the gray wolves lay. Peaks of the pine trees reached the height of the tan stone slab.

"Those wolves are beautiful," Wilcox said.

"Yes, they are, as long as they stay right where they're at," Nancy said.

They continued toward the energy field and Wilcox noticed something on the ground in the distance. As they approached, he stopped dead in his tracks. He saw odd skeletal remains protruding from the sand to the left of the energy field. They were partially covered with sand from the planet's weather of wind and rain. Nancy looked at the surprise on Wilcox's face at the discovery of the remains. The anxiety that Wilcox had felt in the pit of his stomach after reading Everett Quarton's note in the cellar suddenly intensified.

"Umm…" Wilcox managed.

"Those remains aren't human," Nancy finally said.

"Nor are they Axynnian. No…I've seen this type of skeleton before. I was just telling my Axynnian friend, Adamorr, that I had seen alien skeletons—just like this—on a previous case of mine. It was years ago, before you worked for me. I was hired by the old Space Agency to investigate an alien ship that had been discovered. There were skeletons on board the ship just like this. The alien crew had died. This is the exact same species, Nancy. Something happened here," Wilcox said.

He walked closer and knelt down next to the very tall skeletal remains. Examining the odd bone structure, he reached into his pocket for his comm. He immediately noticed three more alien skeletons in the sand. His eyes shifted from the remains in front of him toward the other three skeletons farther to the left. Standing up, he took several pictures of the alien skeleton in front of him with his comm device.

An occasional gust of wind broke the constant low humming frequency sound that emitted from the shimmering energy field.

"They must have been really tall. Do you still have your case files for that investigation?" Nancy asked.

"Yes, but it was never solved. The military took over the investigation and kicked us out. But I need to look at my notes. It was one of the strangest cases I've ever worked on. But I think this current case of ours has already surpassed the strangeness of that case," Wilcox said.

Nancy looked over at the shimmering energy field. It was located within a rough-edged, oval shape opening within the rock wall. The energy field had a wavy appearance at times and occasionally the shimmering field would sparkle. The low frequency sound emitting from the field peaked Nancy's curiosity. She walked next to the tan rock wall and looked closely at the energy field. Nancy reached her hand up and touched her fingertips to the shimmering light. The field sparkled brightly at each of her fingertips.

"It almost looks like a portal," Nancy said.

Wilcox was taking pictures of the other three skeletons. He looked up and saw that she was standing next to the field.

"Be careful, Nancy. If that is a portal, we have no idea what's on the other side," Wilcox said.

Wilcox pulled an old piece of cloth fabric from underneath one of the skeletons and examined it. Riilan was embroidered on the name patch. Wilcox took a picture of the fabric.

"I wonder who these people were," Wilcox said.

He looked up and Nancy was gone.

"Nancy? Nancy!" Wilcox yelled.

Frustrated with her, he put his comm into his pocket and ran toward the portal. Wilcox was reluctant to go through and hesitated. Abruptly, he stepped through to go after her. Wilcox disappeared onto the other side.

"Nancy?" he called.

Wilcox discovered that he was in a different world. It was not Staraliss. He found himself in a desert that stretched to the horizon. Large, reddish colored outcrops and rock formations protruded from the beige sands nearby. Wilcox immediately noticed translucent blue, purple, and black crystals scattered across the desert sands. As he stepped down a rocky slope and into the desert sand, he saw the colorful crystals sparkling brightly in the sunlight, which reflected beams of light in their respective colors. Wilcox observed Nancy near one of the outcrops to his right. He ran toward her as she picked up a light purple crystal from the sand. Its color was like a light amethyst, almost lavender.

"Don't touch anything!" he shouted.

But it was too late. After grabbing the purple crystal, Nancy fell to the ground. As Wilcox stopped next to Nancy, a strange feeling overwhelmed her. He looked down at the purple crystal that Nancy held in her hand and then he gazed into her green eyes. Wilcox could tell that something was wrong with her. Her eyes seemed dreamy. He rested his hand on her shoulder. The sudden emotions that ran through him took him by surprise. Wilcox leaned over, grabbed her arm, and helped her stand up from the sand. Suddenly, the strange emotions he was feeling intensified and he felt such an attraction toward Nancy that it was unbearable. They abruptly kissed with such a fiery passion, the likes of which neither had ever felt before. Their tongues merged and delicately danced around, playfully exploring. The love each of them felt engulfed them. Extremely aroused, Nancy dropped the purple crystal into the sand.

Like the snap of a finger, they both broke off the kiss, breathing heavily, and looked at each other in shock.

"Oh my! I am so sorry, Nancy. I have no idea what came over me," Wilcox said as he helped her steady her feet.

"I'm sorry as well. That was intense. Something happened when I touched that purple crystal. I fell madly in love with you," she said.

"I felt the same thing when I touched your arm to help you up. Again, I apologize for my behavior," Wilcox said.

"You don't have to apologize. I actually liked it. You see, I have had feelings for you for some time. I've tried to tell you before, but—"

"Nancy, that's just the effects of the purple crystal," Wilcox said.

A blue laser beam suddenly shot past them and impacted into the rock wall behind them. Looking up to see where the shot had come from, they saw two extremely tall alien military soldiers with laser rifles drawn. A second shot hit a rock next to them, sending a shower of debris over them. Brushing themselves off, they started running toward the portal. Another shot whizzed by Wilcox's head as they both jumped through the portal to the other side. They kept running toward the *Enigma*. At the ship's entrance, Wilcox grabbed his laser pistol from his inner pocket and turned around. The two alien guards did not pursue them through the portal. Wilcox and Nancy quickly stepped on board and closed the airlock door. Through the observation window, they both stared out at the portal for a long time. No one came through.

"Who were they? What was that place?" Nancy asked.

"With how tall they were, they are definitely the same alien species as those skeletons. Through that portal, it's a totally different planet," Wilcox said.

"It looks like they are guarding it well," Nancy said.

"I wish I would have taken a picture of those crystals," Wilcox said.

"I think our lives were just a little more important than the pictures," Nancy said.

"You're right," Wilcox said.

"I know I'm right," Nancy said.

"So, the portal may be why the Settlement Agency changed the name to hide this planet. I wonder who at the Settlement Agency is covering all this up and why," Wilcox said.

Wilcox engaged the ship's engines and they lifted from the surface of Staraliss.

Chapter Eight

After landing in the city of Kethan on Kesron, Wilcox sprinted along the sidewalk, past the shops, and toward the office. Nancy tried to keep up with him.

"Now, don't hurry," Nancy said. "You might fall and get hurt."

Wilcox did not respond. She finally caught up with him as he unlocked the office door. The familiar sound of the jingling bells rang as Nancy shut the door behind them. Wilcox quickly headed toward the back of the office.

"I need coffee. Do you want a cup?"

"Yes. Put some cream and sugar in mine, will ya?"

"I just want to hurry and look up my archived records from the old alien ship investigation. But I definitely need some coffee first," Wilcox said.

When the coffee was ready, he brought the cups back to his desk and set them down. Removing his hat, he put it on the rack next to his desk. Wilcox turned on the computer as Nancy moved her chair next to his. She sat down and sipped on her coffee. Wilcox took a long drink of his as the computer booted up.

"Thanks for the coffee," Nancy said.

"You're welcome. Okay, let's see what I have this filed under," Wilcox said as he typed a couple of words. "That's what I thought. It is filed under Space Agency. And since we have things purposefully disorganized in the office to keep any intruders confused, it's not under the letter S. It's under H since everything is backwards in the alphabet."

Nancy stood up and walked toward a filing cabinet against the back wall. She unlocked it and thumbed through the files until she found one titled Space Agency. Nancy pulled the file from the cabinet and walked it back to Wilcox's desk. She sat back down as Wilcox opened the file and looked over the paperwork.

"Well?"

"I was hired by the old Space Agency that used to manage all things space related in the Marrithious Government territory. That agency was eventually eliminated when the government took over that task. Anyway, I was hired to investigate a seemingly ancient ship that they had discovered on the edge of uncharted space," Wilcox said.

He flipped over a few papers and looked at one with notes on it.

"And was the ship ancient?" Nancy asked.

"No, not like the Space Agency thought. Our team went in and found the skeletal remains of an unknown alien species. Here are some pictures," he said, removing a paper clip.

Nancy looked at the pictures and set them back down.

"Those sure are the same skeletons we saw on Staraliss," she said.

"We didn't know the origin of their species. We believed their ship malfunctioned and they drifted in space for several years," Wilcox said.

"In one of the pictures of their ship, I saw a blue crystal. It's just like the crystals we saw from the other side of the portal," Nancy said.

"Yes. And there was one on the table in the waiting area of the Settlement Agency," Wilcox said.

"Oh yeah! You're right," Nancy said.

Wilcox flipped through the remaining papers.

"The military came in and took over the investigation. We were told to leave. I wanted to check the ship's computer to see if I could find an origin, but didn't get the chance. I'll bet the military knows where the aliens came from," Wilcox said.

"I wonder if you can find out about it from the military. I mean, your investigation was about sixteen years ago," Nancy said.

Wilcox organized the documents and put them back into the file folder. He put his finger to his lips in thought.

"You know, there is someone in the military that may be able to help me. There was a commander that I met during that investigation," Wilcox said.

"Any leads would help. Hopefully, he can give you some information," Nancy said.

"Umm, it's a she…" Wilcox corrected her. "And she's a general now."

Nancy stood up, grabbed the file folder from Wilcox, and strode to the back of the office to return it to the filing cabinet. Wilcox could tell Nancy was upset from learning the military officer was female.

"While I'm checking with Victoria to see if I can get any information from her, can you find out from Coradelle Hershall where her father's friend is located? I believe Coradelle said his name is Maxboro Lawson. I would like you to interview him and see if you can get some questions answered," Wilcox said.

Nancy walked back to Wilcox's desk and moved her chair back to her own desk.

"I guess so…" Nancy said.

Wilcox stood up and grabbed his hat.

"How do I look?" he asked.

"Really?"

"Never mind. I'll see you later. Good luck with Maxboro," Wilcox said.

He left the office and Nancy sat down at her desk and stared at the black computer screen.

Why am I jealous? I'm not even dating Wilcox, she thought.

The feelings Nancy had for Wilcox were getting stronger and she did not know what she could do about it. After the kiss on the other side of the portal, her emotions were intensified. She shook her head and decided to focus on the investigation. Nancy reached for the comm to contact the client.

"Hi, Coradelle. This is Nancy from the Wilcox Brown Agency. Hey, I'm wondering if you can give me some information about your father's friend Maxboro Lawson. Where can I find him? I'd like to interview him to see if I can get some more information regarding this investigation."

"Hi, Nancy. I was going to contact you and ask how the investigation is going. Maxboro Lawson lives here on Ryamesh. Let me grab my address book. I'll send you his address. I used to… he and I… You don't think he is involved in my father's death, do you?" Coradelle asked.

"Coradelle, this investigation has become very involved. We're not ruling out anything at the moment. There is so much information that we have already learned, but so much more that we don't know. I'm not at liberty to say anything at the moment because it may compromise the investigation. So, how are you doing?" Nancy asked.

"Honestly, not good. I think someone is after me. Yesterday, I was followed by two men, but I lost them. I'm scared, Nancy. I called the local authorities and they said they would look into it. Hopefully, it's nothing, but I'm going to go stay with my friend Alivia Bexley for a while," Coradelle said.

"Oh no! Being followed is not good. I think staying with your friend for a while is a good idea. I'll be heading to Ryamesh to speak with Maxboro. Do you need me to stop by and check on you?" Nancy asked.

"No. I'll be fine. I'll probably be at my friends by the time you get here anyway," Coradelle said.

"Okay. We will let you know when we have some solid answers with this investigation. Right now, there are too many unknowns," Nancy said.

"I understand," Coradelle said.

"I will say a prayer for your safety," Nancy said.

"Thank you. I'll send over Maxboro Lawson's address in a second. Talk to you later…" Coradelle said, looking down at her address book on the kitchen table.

"Okay. Take care," Nancy said.

Nancy set down the comm, looked back at the black computer screen, and sighed. She bowed her head for a long moment and said a prayer for Coradelle's safety. When finished, Nancy stood up, put the comm into her pocket, and headed for the door. After locking the office, she walked to her own ship, *Nellie*. Nancy didn't mind piloting on occasion, but preferred to ride as a passenger. At least she liked space travel better than Wilcox did. She hadn't started the ship in several days. When Nancy engaged the ship's engines, they started but made a strange clank sound.

"That didn't sound good. Come on, *Nellie,* don't give up on me now," Nancy said.

After strapping herself in, she enabled the ship's anti-gravitational units and it lifted from the surface of Kesron. As Nancy gained some distance from the city of Kethan, she focused on piloting through the clouds and into the darkness of space. She programmed the ship's navigation for the planet Ryamesh and engaged the lightspeed-plus engine. *Nellie* disappeared from Kesron with a streak of light.

Ryamesh was a bright planet, with swirls of white clouds against a brilliant blue sky. Nancy finished a prayer and sat for a long moment contemplating the case they were on. She programmed the navigation computer with Maxboro's address that Coradelle had sent her. *Nellie* flew toward the industrial town of Timber Wolf. Maxboro's house was located on the outskirts of the industrial area.

Suddenly, an announcement came over the ship's comm. "All non-authorized ship traffic coming into Timber Wolf must park at the landing area north west of town. We have shuttles from there. Please acknowledge," the voice said.

Nancy quickly replied, "Yes, sir. I am changing course and heading toward the landing area."

She changed *Nellie's* course. In the distance, Nancy could see several spaceships parked along a large landing area. She settled *Nellie* between two ships and disengaged the engines. After exiting the ship, Nancy looked toward the industrial town. Just as she looked in that direction, a shuttle stopped next to her.

The driver opened the door and looked at Nancy. "This is a free shuttle service provided as a courtesy by the town of Timber Wolf. We keep unauthorized ship traffic to a minimum, so there are no interruptions to the shipping logistics at any of our factories," the man said.

She stepped up into the shuttle and the driver closed the door. The shuttle had large windows, providing a panoramic view of the surroundings. No other passengers were on the shuttle at that moment.

"Where are you headed?" the driver asked.

Nancy gave the driver Maxboro Lawson's address.

"Okay. That is all the way on the other side of town, so you get to see the entire industrial area of Timber Wolf," he said.

Nancy made herself comfortable in one of the shuttle seats. The driver left the landing area and pulled onto a paved road that led toward the town. After looking back at *Nellie,* Nancy turned her attention to the road before them. The old, gray paved road crossed a small river ahead of them. A large, cement culvert under the road carried the river water from one side to the other. Nancy's gaze followed the river as it twisted its way underneath a wooden train trestle. White pine trees decorated the side of the road. To her left, Nancy noticed a sedimentary rock wall along the road with some foliage growing at a few spots along its vertical surface. To her right, she saw a set of power poles with a bank of three voltage regulators, high above the ground, resting on a platform between them. They were used to control some of Timber Wolf's power distribution lines. There was an older brick building across the tracks from the power lines. Ahead of them, the road curved slightly where it crossed the same railroad tracks that came from the trestle. Railroad tracks appeared on both sides of the road at that point. She noticed a sign that said: Welcome to Timber Wolf. The road crossed another set of tracks and turned toward the downtown area. Tall buildings were on either side of the street. The building on her right was very large and four stories tall. A small water tower sat on its roof. It was a large graphics company. The side of the building had a black, metal fire escape stairway mounted to the red brick wall. The brown brick building to her left was smaller with two stories. Many wooden pallets were stacked in the back of the building, next to a truck dock. The street was busy with semi trucks and cargo vans going to and from their destinations. As they traveled farther into town, she noticed the railroad yard. There were five storage rail lines filled with various train cars, including several covered hopper cars, flatcars, and boxcars. Nancy noticed two of the boxcars were painted ivory with burgundy doors. They both had the TWR acronym of the Timber Wolf Railway painted on them. Their open doors revealed wooden crates and lumber inside. Another railroad spur branched off from the yard and went into an opening in the large graphics building. Beyond the Timber Wolf Railway yard office, there were two diesel engines with the same ivory and burgundy TWR paint scheme on them. The yard office had a green bench outside its door with a man sitting there. A skid with several barrels on it sat next to the yard office building. As the shuttle moved along, Nancy saw that one of several large, metal containers was being lifted from a stack by a container handler. The operator could be seen at the controls of the immense, yellow machine. Most of the containers were gray with several numbers on them, but there were also a few burgundy containers with some large letters on them, and one white container on the ground with a circular, blue logo on it. The logo looked familiar, but Nancy could not recall where she had seen it before. Across the street was a blue terminal building with a few semi trailers parked in its docks. She noticed some pallets on the dock, ready for the next truck. Next to the truck terminal, there was an ink company in a red brick building. Outside of the building, a large tank was connected to the building with several pipes. A forklift could be seen, moving a pallet from the dock into the building. Nancy noticed a street sign that indicated they were at the corner of Robin Avenue and Industrial Drive. They passed another power pole with a large transformer mounted near the top of it. A few authorized freighter ships landed at a factory in the distance.

"This town sure is busy," Nancy finally said to the shuttle driver. "Where are all these containers from?"

"Most of these containers are headed for the warehousing planet of Noderell. Yeah, we are proud to be the largest industrial port on Ryamesh," he said.

Soon, the driver turned onto another street. They crossed two sets of tracks and went past a large electrical substation that was surrounded by a tall chain-link fence. It housed a large, rectangular bank of transformers that had cooling fans connected to them. An extra roll of fencing was tucked away in the corner of the substation. Some of the stones that covered the ground inside the fenced-in area were scattered out toward the road. A railroad spur with a couple of tank cars on it led off to the right toward a large refinery. As the shuttle approached the edge of the town, Nancy saw less buildings and more white pine trees. The driver, turned a corner into an old residential neighborhood. He slowly drove down a quiet street and stopped the shuttle.

"Here we are. When you need a ride back to your ship, contact us," the driver said.

After the shuttle driver opened the door, Nancy stepped out of the shuttle. "Thank you," she said.

The shuttle left and Nancy looked up and down the quiet street at the houses on either side. The sun was shining and its warmth felt nice, compared to the shuttle's air circulation system. As Nancy walked up to the front door, she saw an older man peek out the window. Before she could knock, the door opened. A man with gray hair stood on the other side of the door.

"Can I help you with something?" he asked.

"Hi. My name is Nancy Louray with the Wilcox Brown Agency. We are investigating a missing deed that belonged to Robert Hershall. Are you Maxboro Lawson?"

"Hi, Nancy. Yes, I am Maxboro Lawson. Robert was a good friend of mine," he said.

"His daughter, Coradelle, hired us to investigate this missing deed. She gave me your address so I could interview you and ask you some questions. Would you be willing to help with our investigation?" Nancy asked.

"Yes. I would like to help out my old friend. Come on in," Maxboro said.

Nancy followed Maxboro into his living room. He gestured her toward the couch.

"Have a seat and make yourself comfortable. Would you like something to drink? I have water, coffee, and cola," he said.

"I'll have a cola. Thank you," Nancy said.

Maxboro left the living room and returned with two cold bottles of cola. He handed one of them to Nancy and then sat in a chair adjacent to the couch. They both cracked open the colas, creating distinct pop sounds. Nancy took a long drink and set the bottle down onto the coffee table.

"Timber Wolf is quite a town," Nancy said.

"Yes. I've been here all of my life. Robert Hershall and I go way back. He lived in Emysh, the city south of here. That's where his daughter, Coradelle, currently lives," Maxboro said.

"Okay. So, how did you meet Robert Hershall?"

Maxboro laughed. "Oh, when I was a youngster, I used to hang around the rail yard. I know…it's dangerous and I don't recommend it. One day, I was over near the metal trestles and saw another boy sitting on a flatcar, dangling his legs over the edge. Naturally, I was curious to know who he was. He didn't go to *my* school. So, I walked over and asked who he was. It turned out that he also liked trains and hung around the rail yard from time to time. We were friends ever since."

"So—" Nancy was cut off.

"This one time, we climbed up the fire escape ladder and got onto the roof of the graphics company. From the top of the roof, there was another ladder that led to yet another level. On that higher level is where the water tower is located. I wanted to go up on the water tower, but Robert was too scared."

"Yeah, that probably would not have been a good idea," Nancy said.

"Robert would ride his bike all the way to Timber Wolf to hang out with me. As I said, he lived in the town south of here. We remained good friends through the years. I was there when he had problems with his girlfriend, Mercedes Brantt. Robert ended up getting custody of Coradelle. That was an ugly mess. He tried to make it work with Mercedes after that, but she was such a bitch. There *was* a spell where Robert and I didn't connect with each other for years. He was busy raising his daughter and working. I was busy with my own work."

"So, did Robert Hershall ever talk to you about the planet that he purchased?"

The old man looked at her and hesitated for a long moment. He stood up and paced the living room a couple of times and then sat back down. After taking a long drink of his cola, he shook his head.

"Yes. He told me about the planet he purchased. I mean, he could afford it. His income was a lot higher than mine. It would have been nice to have a planet all to yourself... Anyway, yes. He took me there once and showed me where he planned to build a house for him and his daughter. It's a planet called Staraliss. All he had to do was wait for the deed from the real estate agent. Marrithious Government law states that the real estate agent must transfer the deed to him within thirty days. But he never received it. He complained about it to me often. Of course, I couldn't do anything about it. I suggested he hire an investigator. We used to get together on occasion, but I hadn't seen him in several years. I did't even know he died until Coradelle contacted me."

"How much do you know about Staraliss?" Nancy asked.

"He used the same real estate agent that I used to purchase this house. His name is Bryson Wieler. I actually recommended him. But I didn't know he would turn out to be a piece of shit. I have my suspicions about Bryson. Every time Robert tried to contact him, Bryson was never available. The agent disappeared after receiving the credits from Robert, totally ghosting him. Apparently, Robert never received the deed."

"No, he never received it," Nancy said.

"Robert did hire an investigator and the investigator mysteriously died. Then about a year later, Robert mysteriously died the same way…without anything wrong with him," Maxboro said.

Nancy looked at the old man and narrowed her eyes.

"How do you know the investigator that Robert Hershall hired had a similar death? Who did you hear that from?" Nancy asked.

Maxboro was quiet for a long moment and stared into the distance. He stood up and paced the living room once more.

"There are things I cannot say. I'm sorry."

Nancy looked at him for a long moment. She became suspicious of him.

"You can't tell me? We are talking about the death of your friend. And possibly a murder of the investigator that he hired," Nancy said.

"I'm sorry…"

Nancy stood up from the couch and headed for the door. She stopped and turned around. "You are now a suspect in this investigation," she said.

"Wait! Please… Okay… I believe they were both murdered. Coradelle came here to Timber Wolf and told me about her father's death. Her and I…well we were seeing each other for a while. We aren't anymore. That was years ago and Robert did not know that his daughter and I were a thing. She was about twenty-three and I was old enough to be her father. I finally gathered up enough courage to go visit him and tell him. On that last visit with him—before I had a chance to tell him about Coradelle and I—he told me he finally hired an investigator named Everett Quarton to find the deed to Staraliss, but he said that Everett had mysteriously died without anything wrong with him. Robert's case died with Everett. He told me he was finally giving up on Staraliss. At that moment, I lost all the courage I had to tell him about Coradelle and I. If he knew, he would be rolling in his grave.

"Coradelle wanted me to know what happened to her father, so she stopped by to give me the news. It hit me hard…especially the guilt I felt of being in a relationship with his daughter and not telling him. And the fact that he died the same way as the investigator died just added to my anxiety. I don't believe he ever told Coradelle about the investigator that he hired. I was so shaken about Robert's death that I didn't think to tell her about it myself," Maxboro said.

Nancy thought for a moment about how much older Wilcox Brown was than herself.

"I'm not judging the age gap you and Coradelle had in your former relationship. It's none of my business. I'm just trying to solve a case. But you probably shouldn't feel guilty about an old relationship that you were in with another consenting adult. Anyway, I want to thank you for your time and your honesty," Nancy said.

She handed him a business card and turned back toward the door. Stepping outside, she said, "Contact us if you discover anything else about this case."

"Good luck," Maxboro said from the doorway.

Nancy turned around. "Thank you."

She walked along the sidewalk of the quiet street and reached into her pocket for her comm. Nancy contacted the shuttle service and waited for its return.

I'm still suspicious of that man, she thought.

Chapter Nine

"Thank you so much for letting me stay here for a while," Coradelle said.

She sat on a fluffy couch with her friend Alivia Bexley. The couch was an off-white color that matched the rest of the furniture in the large living room. The mirror mounted on the wall behind the couch revealed that both blondes had almost identical hair color.

"You are welcome here anytime, Coradelle. If someone is after you, I would not want you to be alone. Have you heard back from the authorities yet?" Alivia asked.

"Unfortunately, no. And the Wilcox Brown Agency is not telling me anything either. Maybe I should have just left this missing deed thing alone. I mean, who cares about some planet anyway?"

"Is that Coradelle Hershall talking? You know darn well that you want justice for your father getting ripped off. He would have wanted you to look into this. I'm sure the investigators will come up with something. You can stay here as long as you need to. I just want you to feel safe."

"Thank you." Coradelle reached into her pocket. "Here. This is

Wilcox Brown's business card, in case you need to contact his agency."

Alivia took the card and set it on the end table.

"No one followed you here, did they?" Alivia asked.

"I don't think so. I hope not," Coradelle said.

"So, you can sleep on the couch. I can get you a pillow and blanket later when we go to sleep. But for now, how would you like to play a board game? I just purchased this new one that looks *so* fun, but I haven't had a chance to play it yet," Alivia said.

"That sounds great," Coradelle said.

Alivia stood up from the couch and headed for her games shelf.

"Feel free to grab anything from the refrigerator or snacks," Alivia yelled from down the hallway.

Coradelle went into the kitchen and brought back two colas and some snacks, while Alivia set up the game on the coffee table.

"You know, I haven't had a chance to have fun and enjoy myself for a while now. Thank you for this, Alivia," Coradelle said.

"Anytime... That's was best friends are for," Alivia said.

Commander Stone and Commander Aolliam sat in a vehicle in the city of Emysh, watching Coradelle Hershall's house.

"She spotted us the other day and has not been home since," Aolliam said.

"She certainly did give us the slip. I didn't think we were that obvious," Stone said.

"We take our mission to protect her seriously and at this moment, we don't even know where she's at. That's a big fail," Aolliam said.

"Yes, it is. We need to—" Stone was cut off.

"Who the hell is that?" Aolliam asked.

They both looked across the street toward Coradelle's house as three men, dressed in black, stealthily walked from around the back of her house. One of them reached for a comm and spoke with someone for a brief moment. A minute later, a black van stopped in front of the house and the three men quickly stepped inside. The van sped away.

"They must have been in her house. Follow them!" Stone said.

Aolliam turned the vehicle around and accelerated toward the van. It was two blocks ahead of them and suddenly turned right, disappearing from sight. Once Aolliam reached the corner, he quickly turned and spotted the van. Ahead of them, the traffic light changed to red, but the black van had already gone through the intersection. Heavy traffic began to flow along the cross street. Eventually, they lost track of the van. Once the light turned green, they proceeded forward, but pulled off to the side of the street.

"We lost them," Aolliam said.

"Well, they were certainly after Coradelle. Let's head back toward her house. Perhaps they found something inside that told them where she went," Stone said.

"I feel like we are slightly behind on our mission," Aolliam said.

Aolliam pulled into the right lane of the busy street and headed back toward Coradelle's house.

Wilcox Brown sat at the controls of the *Enigma* as he flew through the darkness of space in the Sharmyra Star System. Distant blue stars could be seen through the observation window. As he passed a small, icy moonlet, the view of cold space sent a shiver down his spine.

The public relations headquarters and administrative offices for the military were located on the planet Sharmyra. It was a start to find General Victoria Ediira. Wilcox needed answers regarding the alien species that were found on the vessel years before and he knew she had the answers.

He saw the planet Sharmyra ahead of him as the *Enigma* exited lightspeed-plus. The security around the planet was intense and there were several levels of clearance that ships needed to go through in order to land.

Wilcox looked down at the comm as it crackled. "We have identified your ship as *Enigma.* Please confirm your identity and state the purpose of your visit."

Wilcox adjusted the comm. "This is Wilcox Brown of the *Enigma.* I am a private investigator and I am here to speak with General Victoria Ediira regarding my agency's current case."

After a few minutes, the comm sounded again. "Please proceed to the docking bay at the coordinates we are sending you now. You will be escorted down to docking bay P27A with an Angel Wing fighter ship that will fly behind you," the man said.

Wilcox received the coordinates and set a course for that specific docking bay. He noticed the Angel Wing fighter ship come in behind the *Enigma.* The sleek, white fighter ship had tapered delta wings and was one of the military's fastest, most maneuverable ships in its arsenal.

As Wilcox flew through the atmosphere of Sharmyra, the area below came into full view. Many ships approached and departed various locations in the distance. A hazy mist was seen against the sunlight. Docking bay P27A was just ahead of him. There were many buildings in the area. Once the *Enigma* entered the docking bay, the Angel Wing fighter ship departed.

Wilcox located an empty spot to park the ship. He disengaged the ship's engines and opened the airlock door. As he waited for it to fully extend, he looked at the sharp hinge that he had previously cut his arm on. It was just a reminder that he still needed to have it repaired. Wilcox wondered how his arm miraculously healed so quickly. He stepped out into the docking bay. Sunlight lit the area. Two military officers immediately walked up to him as he exited the ship.

"Wilcox Brown, we are here to escort you to the public relations office," one of them said.

Wilcox followed the officer. The second officer followed behind him. Wilcox was led to a set of doors within that level of the docking bay. As the doors slid aside, they entered a well lit corridor. The lights reflected from the shiny floor, but they intermittently blinked several times, as if something was wrong with them. As they walked along, the sound of their footsteps echoed. After being escorted by the officers for some distance, they finally came to a stop. The officer from behind stepped aside and entered a code into the door panel. The door opened to reveal the public relations office.

"Here we are. Have a good day," the lead officer said.

"Thank you," Wilcox said.

The two officers left. Wilcox entered the office. It was fairly busy. Many people sat in the waiting area. Wilcox walked to a short line in front of the reception counter. Two Axynnian men stood in line in front of him. He thought about Everett Quarton's Axynnian wife that he had seen in the picture at Everett's mansion and wondered what had happened to her.

A second reception counter opened up on the right. "I can help the next person," a woman said.

The Axynnians in front of Wilcox gestured for him to go ahead of them. He proceeded to the newly opened counter. "Hello. I am here to see General Victoria Ediira.

"Your name?"

"Wilcox Brown. I am a private investigator, working on a case and I have a few questions for her," he said.

"General Ediira is not currently on Sharmyra. She is on a special mission. The best I can do is give you her contact information to be reached by comm," the woman said.

"That will be fine. I just have a few questions to ask her," Wilcox said.

The woman gave Wilcox the information.

"Thank you," he said.

Wilcox left the public relations office. After exiting, two officers arrived to escort him back to his ship.

Once Wilcox Brown was back in space above Sharmyra, he let the *Enigma* drift. Wilcox adjusted the ship's comm and entered General Victoria Ediira's contact information. Before he transmitted the signal, he hesitated for some time, thinking about the relationship he had with Victoria over the years. Like he had recently explained to his Axynnian friend, Adamorr, the relationship Wilcox had with Victoria was not for love, but a mutual exchange of sexual needs. He was not interested in those needs at the moment, but needed to get more information for his current case. He abruptly hit the send button.

"General Victoria Ediira speaking."

"Victoria, this is Wilcox Brown. It's been a long time since I've seen you. I am hoping that you can help me with my current investigation," Wilcox said.

"It *has* been a while since we've been together. How are you doing?" she asked.

"I am… Well, the case I'm currently on has me very concerned. We were hired to find the missing deed to a planet. It appears that the client's father and a former investigator that he had hired have both been murdered. I believe we have stumbled upon some dark stuff. My assistant, Nancy, and I have been to the planet that the missing deed corresponds to. We saw skeletal remains of the same alien species that was discovered on the derelict ship sixteen years ago," Wilcox said.

There was a long moment of silence before Victoria responded. "I am currently on a special operation. I am going to send you a set of confidential coordinates. I want you to follow the coordinates and then we can discuss this in person," she said.

. . .

Wilcox discovered the confidential coordinates that Victoria gave him led to a location on the planet Anneriss. He thought it strange to be returning to the same planet that the Settlement Agency was on. The area Wilcox was headed for was far from the Settlement Agency, however. There were many industrial buildings in the immediate vicinity. He slowed the ship down to maneuver along raised piping that ran parallel to the ground. Wilcox began to wonder where exactly the coordinates were taking him. Ahead of him, he spotted the destination. He landed at the precise location that General Victoria Ediira had instructed. The building was concealed within the large industrial area. Wilcox flew into the bay and the large bay door automatically closed behind him. After disabling the ship's engines, he stepped out of the ship and looked around the small docking bay. There was one other ship off to one side as well as a large amount of military equipment. There didn't seem to be anyone around to greet him. He noticed the faint smell of hydraulic fluid in the air.

"Wilcox Brown… How are you doing, my friend?"

Wilcox turned to his right. Victoria stood next to a metal container. She looked stunning with her short, blond hair. The General's high-ranking insignia was affixed to the left front of her uniform. Wilcox hadn't seen her in several years.

"Victoria! You've become a general since the last time I saw you. Congratulations on the promotion. It is a pleasure to see you. You look absolutely beautiful," Wilcox said.

They walked toward each other and hugged. She kissed him passionately. Wilcox smiled at her.

"I'm glad I was able to get your contact info from the military public relations on Sharmyra," he said.

"I'm glad you were able to contact me. I was thinking about you recently. I can't say much, but you need to watch your back with the current investigation you are on," Victoria said.

"Interesting… I know the military has a lot of intel resources. I actually wanted to contact you to get some information on that old ship that we discovered sixteen years ago. I know it's probably classified, but in my current investigation, I have discovered the same species as the ones I found on that old ship," Wilcox said.

"The military's investigation regarding that ship *is* classified, but it's interesting that you have discovered more of the species. Where exactly were your findings?" Victoria asked.

"And I want to know more about why I need to watch my back," Wilcox said.

There was an awkward silence. Victoria turned and stepped toward the *Enigma.*

"How fast is she?"

"The *Enigma's* lightspeed-plus engines probably aren't as fast as anything the military has, but she gets me where I need to go," Wilcox said.

"You always did hate space travel," Victoria said.

"Yes. It certainly is not my favorite thing to do," Wilcox said.

She turned around, walked over to Wilcox, and leaned in to kiss him again. Her tongue felt warm against his.

"It's been a long time, Wilcox. Would you like to rekindle an old memory?" she whispered.

"I think that would be nice," he said in a soft voice.

Victoria began to unbutton her uniform.

"I'm the only one here at the moment. It's been a minute since I've had you, Wilcox Brown," she said.

Victoria removed his hat. She knew they were both at a stalemate with exchanging information. Perhaps afterward, he would loosen up a bit.

As the *Enigma* exited the docking bay of the military base, the large door automatically closed. After adjusting her belt, Victoria reached for her comm.

"Hi, Commander Ashten. This is General Ediira. I have just learned from a source that more Sharrixian skeletons were discovered. However, I do not have an exact planet location. I will contact the Sharrixians and inquire about it. I just wanted you to document the information. When I know more, I will contact you," Victoria said.

"I will record the info. We're starting to put this puzzle together. Perhaps, if this source you speak of could actually join in our investigation, it would be helpful," Commander Ashten said.

"Roger that. I will give that some thought. I'll talk to you soon," Victoria said.

She looked at all the military equipment in the warehouse and put her finger to her chin in thought.

Asking Wilcox to join in our investigation...not a bad idea, she thought.

Victoria entered a small corridor and walked into a communications room. There were several pieces of radio equipment fixed along a curved console. A group of large cables joined together and ran along a conduit into the ceiling. She sat down in one of the chairs and enabled a long range radio transmitter.

Hopefully, there won't be galactic interference this time, Victoria thought.

"High Commander Shirom, do you read?"

Victoria stared at the comm for several minutes, waiting for a response.

"This is High Commander Novish Shirom."

"Commander Shirom. This is General Victoria Ediira. I have a question for you regarding our investigation."

"I'm glad your signal was able to get through. What question do you have?" Novish Shirom asked.

"I have recently heard from a trusted source that four Sharrixian skeletons were found on a planet. I currently do not know where this planet is, but I plan to find out. This could be part of what took place twenty years ago, but I'm not positive. I'm hoping that you may know something about it," Victoria said.

Silence followed for some time.

"Ah... I am aware of those four Sharrixians. One of them was my uncle Riilan. Yes, they are from the same incident where the humans came through the portal and later killed our Gatherers on your side of the portal. There were actually five Gatherers that were killed. One of them made it back through the portal and told our people what had happened. He later died of his injuries. Unfortunately, we do not know where the portal leads to on your side. It is forbidden for us to go through it since the incident.

"There has been recent activity at the portal, however. Our guards recently spotted two humans come through the portal, a man and a woman. The woman had picked up a purple crystal, which apparently affects love emotions in humans, as our guards witnessed. As a result, they kissed. When our guards began firing at them, the woman quickly dropped the crystal and they ran back through the portal," Novish said.

"Really? They kissed? Well, I think I may know exactly who they were. If they are who I think they are, then I can assure you they are conducting their own investigation into this and meant no harm. Let me confirm that is the case and I will be in contact with further details," Victoria said.

"I see. Well, our guards will shoot to kill, so I don't recommend they go through the portal again," Novish said.

"Understood."

On the planet Ryamesh, the night sky became dark over the city of Emysh as rain poured down. A storm quickly approached in the distance. Commander Stone and Commander Aolliam made their way through Coradelle Hershall's backyard toward the door with flashlights in their hands.

"This is where those three men must have busted in through the back door," Stone said.

Aolliam gently pushed the ajar door open and splinters of wood from the frame fell onto the floor. They entered the house, their wet boots squeaking on the entry floor. Splitting up, both men began to search for any clues of where Coradelle may have gone. Stone walked through the dark living room, shining his flashlight around. Nothing seemed to be out of place. Aolliam walked down a hallway toward the kitchen. Stone looked around the bedroom. He noticed large and medium sized suitcases next to the dresser. There was a stack of clothes on the bed. Stone made his way to the kitchen where he found Aolliam looking down at the table.

"It looks like she packed her clothes and took the smallest suitcase of the set. She left some outfits behind that she must have thought were not necessary. I don't think she plans to stay away for very long," Stone said.

"I think I just came across where she's at," Aolliam said.

Stone walked over to the kitchen table, where Aolliam stood shining his flashlight onto an open address book.

"What did you find?" Stone asked.

"She left her address book open. The only entries on this page are Maxboro Lawson, whose address is in Timber Wolf, north of Emysh, and Alivia Bexley, whose address is here in the city of Emysh," Aolliam said.

"I would bet she is staying at this Alivia's place here in town. She should have closed this address book. Those men that were in here have probably come to the same conclusion," Stone said.

"And they have a major head start on us," Aolliam said. He documented the address.

"Let's go!" Stone said.

Chapter Ten

Coradelle Hershall was trying to get comfortable on Alivia's couch as she tossed and turned. Powerful crunches of thunder and bright blue bolts of lightning rolled through that area of Emysh, making it very difficult to fall asleep. She wished she would have changed out of her clothes and into something more comfortable. Coradelle looked over at her small suitcase next to the couch. She sat up on the couch and shifted her attention toward Alivia's closed bedroom door.

I wonder if she is sleeping through this storm, Coradelle thought.

After another loud crash, Coradelle decided to get up and head to the kitchen.

That one didn't really sound like thunder, Coradelle thought.

Half asleep, she staggered into the kitchen and opened the refrigerator. The beaming light from the open door revealed a man, dressed in black, staring at her from the other side of the refrigerator door. Coradelle began to scream and backed up against the kitchen island, knocking over a set of cutlery onto the tile floor. Another man quickly put something over her face that made her pass out. She fell limp into the man's arms. A third man came through the broken back door and shined a flashlight onto Coradelle's face.

"That's her. Let's go," he said.

They carried Coradelle out the back door and disappeared into the night.

Alivia's eyes opened wide when she heard the metal cutlery hit the tile floor. She quickly jumped out of bed and ran to her bedroom door in her underwear.

"Coradelle! Are you okay? Coradelle?"

Alivia turned on the lights. She saw the knives on the kitchen floor. A gust of wind blew the back door open and she felt a mist of rain blow into the kitchen and onto her bare skin. She shivered. Walking over to the door, she noticed it had been kicked in from the outside, the door frame totally destroyed.

"Coradelle!" Alivia yelled out into the dark backyard. "Coradelle!"

A loud crash of thunder made her jump. After wedging the door shut, Alivia slid down the kitchen counter to the floor and began to cry.

How did they find you here?

After a moment, Alivia quickly stood up and went to the end table in the living room. She picked up Wilcox Brown's business card that Coradelle had given her and reached for her comm.

Wilcox kept seeing another ship appear and then disappear on the edge of his long-range scanners.

Interesting... I wonder who is following me, Wilcox thought.

He remembered that Victoria told him to watch his back. Adjusting the *Enigma's* lightspeed-plus engines, he increased his speed and continued to recalculate and change trajectories. After multiple vector changes, Wilcox was confident that he lost the ship that was trailing him. Suddenly, the comm sounded.

"Wilcox, this is Nancy. We have a problem."

"What's wrong?"

"Our client has gone missing. I just received a communication from Coradelle's best friend, Alivia Bexley. Coradelle was staying at Alivia's house. Apparently, someone broke into her house and took Coradelle. Alivia is really upset. She called the local authorities, but they left when two military officers showed up and took over the scene," Nancy said.

"What? I'm on my way back to Kesron now. Be at the landing pad. I'm going to pick you up. We're going to Ryamesh," Wilcox said.

"I'll be waiting for you when you get here," Nancy said.

Nancy put the comm into her pocket and began praying for Coradelle's safety. She remembered the strange vision she had of Coradelle. Nancy grabbed her white sweater and put it on as a chill ran through her. Locking the office, she headed for the landing pad to wait for Wilcox.

Victoria walked down a corridor in the military base and entered her small office. The military base of operations was only supposed to be temporary, but the military's investigation into who killed the Sharrixians had been going on for years. Had she known at the time, she would have picked a larger office. Her comm sounded.

"General Ediira. We have lost Wilcox Brown. He increased his speed and performed several changes to his flight trajectory," the woman said.

"What do you mean, you lost him? How hard is it to keep a watchful eye on Wilcox Brown for his safety? I need you to find him and watch his back," General Victoria Ediira said.

"Roger that."

Victoria ended the transmission and sighed.

First Stone and Aolliam failed to protect Coradelle Hershall. Now, the team has lost track of Wilcox Brown. Victoria shook her head.

Coradelle suddenly woke up and opened her eyes, taking a deep breath. She found herself on a cot in a small room. The only light emitted from underneath the door. Nothing else was in the room. Coradelle stood up from the cot and walked toward the door. It was locked from the outside.

Remembering the incident from Alivia's kitchen, Coradelle became distressed. She was hungry and she also had to pee.

Those must have been the people who were after me. Where am I? she thought.

Coradelle bent down onto the concrete floor and looked underneath the door where the light was emitting from. Squinting her eyes at the bright light, she noticed rows of racks, filled with pallets.

She could not be certain, but it looked like white containers were fixed along one of the walls.

This is definitely a warehouse, she thought.

Suddenly, a pair of boots blocked her view. She heard a sound from the lock and the door swung open to the outside. Coradelle looked up at a man dressed in black.

"Well, it looks like you're awake now," the man said.

He stepped into the room and closed the door as Coradelle stood up.

"Where am I? Why are you people after me?" Coradelle asked.

"I cannot answer your questions. I just need to report if you're awake," the man said.

He stepped back outside and closed the door. She heard him tell someone on his comm that she was awake. Coradelle heard the lock turn and then his footsteps walking away.

"I have to use the bathroom," Coradelle shouted.

The footsteps stopped. She heard the man return. He unlocked the door and opened it.

"The last thing I want to do is clean up your mess. I'll take you to the bathroom. Hold out your wrists," he said.

The man grabbed a zip tie from his pocket. Coradelle held out her wrists and he wrapped the zip tie around them. He grabbed her arm and led her out of the room. They walked across the warehouse floor. Coradelle looked in all directions. The small room they kept her in appeared to be meant for storage. The warehouse was massive, with aisle after aisle of racks that went as far as she could see. She confirmed that there were white containers along the back wall. Each of them had a circular, blue logo in the center. Several yellow forklifts were parked along one side. They were the same shade of yellow as the large container handler next to them.

The man led her toward an opening underneath the racks. It opened to a small hallway with several offices. They passed a lunch room that appeared to have a glass door that led outside. Finally, they reached the bathrooms. No one else seemed to be around. He brought her into the women's bathroom and led her to a stall. He opened the stall door and pushed her inside.

"There. Use the bathroom," he said.

"How am I supposed to with my wrists tied?" she asked.

The man pulled out a knife, flicked it open, and cut the zip tie.

Coradelle shut the stall door, rubbing her wrists. She saw him waiting outside the stall. Coradelle inspected the seat, pulled her pants down and was finally able to pee. After the noise from her stream hitting the water finally trickled to a stop, she could hear the man become impatient. Coradelle quickly finished up, but hesitated before flushing the toilet. Her mind raced. Coradelle sighed, flushed the toilet, and opened the stall door. The man was waiting with another zip tie.

"May I wash my hands?" she asked.

He motioned her toward the sink. Coradelle walked to the sink, washed her hands, and grabbed paper towel from the dispenser. Then, with a rush of adrenalin, she ran past the man and out the bathroom door as fast as she could.

"Hey!" he yelled.

The man chased her down the hallway. Coradelle turned into the lunch room and headed for the glass door that she had noticed earlier. Pushing it open, she ran outside of the warehouse. The sunlight was bright and warm. Coradelle ran along green grass next to the building. The massive white, metal building stretched far into the distance. A small, paved service road ran along the side of the building. On the other side of the service road was a forest. Unfortunately, it was separated with a tall chain-link fence. Coradelle noticed three men, all wearing black outfits, now chasing her. There was a large distance between her and them. She ran faster than she thought possible. Looking up at the tall white building, she saw the same circular, blue logo that she had seen on the containers inside the warehouse. She looked back and screamed as the three men gained on her.

"No!"

Coradelle quickly jumped over a guard rail and ran past a set of truck docks. As she neared the back corner of the building, she heard their footsteps behind her. She dodged around the back corner of the building and ran straight into a chain-link fence. Through the fence, Coradelle saw many other warehouse buildings in the distance. Unlike the warehouse she had found herself in, the ones in the distance were actively busy with semis backing into docks and forklifts visible through the overhead doors. She began to climb the fence and felt a set of hands grab her shirt and pull her down. She fell hard onto the grass, hitting her head. The three men pinned her face-down, put her arms behind her back, and wrapped a familiar zip tie around her wrists. Coradelle felt the pain of a knee against the middle of her back.

One of the men, grabbed her blond hair just above her left ear and pulled her head up. As she tried to catch her breath, Coradelle strained her blue eyes, looking sideways up at the man, her hair partially covering her vision.

"You bitch! There will be no more bathroom breaks for you. Go in the corner of the room next time," he said.

The man slammed her head back down to the grass. After the three men recovered from the chase, Coradelle felt the pressure of the knee against the middle of her back being released. Two of the three men stood Coradelle up and she was led back around the corner of the building toward the truck docks. They walked toward the nearest warehouse entry door and up several concrete steps that had a yellow railing on either side. One of the three men entered a code into the panel next to the door and it opened. It was much dimmer inside the warehouse.

Coradelle could feel a dull headache begin as she adjusted her eyes. They moved her along one of the long aisles and back toward the room they had held her in.

"Once the black crystals arrive, we won't have to put up with you anymore," the man on her right said.

"Then you will die, just like your father. And there will be nothing to pin it on us," the man on her left said.

Black crystals? she thought.

Coradelle realized they had murdered her father. She began to cry.

Chapter Eleven

Novish Shirom strode down the brightly lit corridor of the Sharrixian Government Building at a quick pace, his burgundy cape flowing behind him. He passed a government worker and she turned toward him with a questioning look. Clearly, he was pissed off. The overhead lights glistened off from the crystals that decorated the long corridor, casting blue, purple, and black reflections in beautiful patterns against the walls and ceiling. Novish turned a corner and entered the briefing room. Commander Gedlo Othan and Commander Covlan Prilston both turned toward him as he came to a stop in front of them.

"I need to have a word with you two in private," Novish said.

Only one officer sat at the computer display in front of them.

"Please excuse us for a moment," Gedlo said to the officer.

"Yes, sir," the officer said. He stood up and left the briefing room.

Once the tall door closed behind the officer, Novish took a deep breath.

"Queen Empress Aminarra Vistona has let that damn council get to her. The council has run out of patience with the human military investigation and wants to declare war against the humans. Aminarra gave in to them," Novish said.

"Oh. Well, that changes things up," Covlan said.

"The queen empress has full authority over the council and doesn't have to do this. Yet, she let them influence her. It doesn't make sense. I am *not* happy about this. We've been working with General Victoria Ediira and the humans are getting closer to finding all the people who murdered our Gatherers. This war declaration is just going to cause chaos and the murderers will get away with it when the human military focuses their efforts against us and away from the investigation," Novish said.

"I understand your frustration. As two of your highest commanding officers, we've been with you through this journey. It does seem like we are close to having justice for our Gatherers with General Ediira's investigation. It doesn't exactly make sense to me either," Gedlo said.

"I've been tasked with gathering a fleet of our battleships and proceeding to the planet Rafith Astonn. It is the half-way point across the galaxy where our special operations military officer Versill had met with General Victoria Ediira previously. We are to stage our offensive assault against the humans from Rafith Astonn. I was told that if the Axynnians get in our way, we are to fire on them as well," Novish said.

"How long do you estimate the logistics will take for the fleet to launch?" Covlan asked.

Novish sighed and thought about it for a moment. "I estimate we can have four battleships for the fleet ready in three days. I will be commanding the *Credence Revenge*. Covlan, I need you to command the *Arcinaris*. Gedlo, I need you to command the *Lhasariss*. Commander Jafer will be on the *Shartannis*. I need all of our personnel involved in the logistics. I am assigning that task to both of you, effective immediately. Those battleships need to be stocked with supplies, be fully powered, and fully staffed. Our other battleships will stay here in Sharrixian territory to protect our people. If we need reinforcements, they will be attached to the fleet as needed," Novish said.

"We will get right on this, sir," Covlan said.

"It's not like I want this, but I must follow Queen Empress Aminarra's orders," Novish said.

"Understood," Gedlo said.

"While you two get started on that, I will inform our fighter pilots with the task they'll be facing. I want forty Stormrider fighter ships in the docking bays of each battleship," Novish said.

"Yes, sir," Gedlo said.

Novish Shirom left the briefing room. As Gedlo and Covlan watched him disappear behind the door, they quickly began the massive task ahead of them.

As the military high commander, Novish Shirom was responsible for giving a speech to the fighter pilots who would be risking their lives in this offensive assault. After making an announcement for the pilots to meet in the Sharrixian Government Building's large hall, he stood on the platform of the hall and waited. He stood there and watched as the chairs began to fill up with Sharrixian military fighter pilots. While he waited for all the pilots to arrive, he stepped to one side of the platform for privacy and picked up his comm.

"Hi, Versill. This is High Commander Novish Shirom. I have a special mission for you," he said.

"I heard about our active duty alert and I would be honored to be a fighter pilot. I'll be in the hall in just a few moments," she said.

"I appreciate you volunteering, but your mission will not be as a fighter pilot. You are a special operations military officer and your mission will be vitally more important than any of these fighter pilots. In fact, you have the most important mission in this entire campaign. I'll go over the details after my speech with the pilots. Meet me in my office afterward," Novish said.

"Yes, sir," Versill said.

Novish turned from the privacy along the side of the platform and walked back over to the front of the hall, standing near a microphone. A few more pilots trickled into the hall and found some available seats that remained. The walls were lined with crimson red drapes to dampen the sound of music and plays that were held in the hall. The drapes contrasted the color of Novish's cape. As the murmur died down, Novish turned on the microphone that was fixed in the center of the platform. He looked out at all the fighter pilots, dressed in their military uniforms. Some wore caps that covered the bumpy, uneven surface of their heads.

"Thank you all for coming on such short notice. As you may have already heard, we will be preparing for war against the humans that will take place on the other side of the Marrithious Galaxy. Queen Empress Aminarra Vistona has declared war. We are currently preparing a fleet of four battleships for this offensive operation. Each battleship will house forty Stormrider fighter ships. Many of you will be selected and assigned to a shift on one of the battleships. Those who are not selected will be on call in case we need to bring in reinforcements.

"You are all excellent pilots and will be chosen randomly. This campaign is to bring long-awaited justice to our Sharrixian people for the Gatherers who were murdered. I have confidence that each of you will use your piloting skills for all the precision targets that are assigned to you. The human military's Angel Wing fighter ships are very maneuverable, but I am confident that you can outmatch them in a dogfight with our Stormriders. Once our fleet reaches the planet Rafith Astonn, assignments will be given to you and we will await Queen Empress Aminarra's order to launch this offensive.

"Commander Gedlo Othan and Commander Covlan Prilston will contact the pilots who are chosen and they will tell you the battleship you will be assigned to. Good luck and thank you for your commitment to our Sharrixian people," Novish said.

After turning the microphone off, Novish watched as the pilots slowly dispersed from the hall, the tall figures disappearing through the exits. He left the hall and made his way toward his office in the upper levels of the Sharrixian Government Building.

There was a ring at the office door. Novish stood from his desk and walked over to answer it. The electronic door swiftly slid aside.

"Versill, please come in," he said.

She entered the large office, the tall door sliding shut behind her. She wore a special forces, black military uniform.

"Have a seat," he said, gesturing toward an office chair.

Novish sat down across from her.

"Versill, you are one of our best special officers. That's why I had previously chosen you to fly half way across the galaxy to meet General Victoria Ediira. I'm very happy that your meeting with her went well. She has actually been in contact with me since then and is getting very close to solving their investigation. Unfortunately, Queen Empress

Aminarra has been persuaded by the council into declaring war. So, I must follow her orders, even if I disagree. But I cannot do this, knowing there will never be true justice for our Gatherers…for my uncle Riilan. That's why I need you to go on a special mission. Your role is so vital, so important, that it may very well prevent a disastrous war.

"Our fleet will be gathering at Rafith Astonn, where you had met Victoria Ediira. Queen Empress Aminarra will be monitoring fleet communications, so I needed to speak with you before the fleet is outbound for Rafith Astonn. You will actually be using a Stormrider fighter ship, but your mission is much different. You will be going through the portal and using your comm to contact General Victoria Ediira once you're on the other side. I have the frequency you need to use in order to contact her," Novish said.

"Queen Empress Aminarra forbids us to go through the portal, sir," Versill said.

"I understand your concern. If there is any fallout over this, I will accept full responsibility. Besides, she did inquire about our fighters fitting through the portal. If I didn't think this mission was of the utmost importance, then I would not have you do this. You will be an envoy of good intentions. I cannot promise there won't be dangers on the other side. The portal is a natural phenomenon and we don't quite understand it. The portal guards will be dismissed and picked up by a shuttle for a briefing here in the Sharrixian Government Building. They will be gone before you arrive in the fighter ship. Be careful flying through, as there is not much clearance for a Stormrider. Here is a drive with General Victoria Ediira's comm frequency. Once you are through, you are to contact her, meet with her, and explain that time is quickly running out. They need to conclude their investigation quickly. Once I have the order from Queen Empress Aminarra, it's too late. I will be with the fleet at Rafith Astonn on monitored communications…monitored by Queen Empress Aminarra herself," Novish said.

He handed her a small storage drive. Versill looked at the device in the palm of her hand for a moment before closing her beige-green fingers and putting it into her pocket.

"I will do my best, sir," Versill said.

"When it's time for you to return, take the long way home," Novish said.

"Roger that."

"Hi, Avalaur. It's just your old friend Nancy. How are you?"

"Nancy! It's been a little while. I'm doing great. How are you?"

"We've been working this really complex case. We've been running to *this* planet and *that* planet. I am glad to have a day off," Nancy said.

"Wow. It sounds involved. So, what are you doing on your day off?" Avalaur asked.

"Actually, I'm on a date. He's not here yet, though," Nancy said, looking out the cafe window.

"Wilcox?"

"No. It's an old friend that I haven't seen in years. I'm not even sure what to expect," Nancy said.

"Well, what happened with Wilcox? I thought you were going to tell him how you feel," Avalaur said.

"Believe me, I have. But it does not seem to matter. I even kissed him…but I can't get into why because it is part of our investigation. However, I can tell that Wilcox is interested in this military woman, just by the way he acts when he mentions her. I must say, I'm a bit jealous. I'm just trying to move on by dating again," Nancy said.

"Well, don't give up on Wilcox," Avalaur said.

"I'll keep trying, but…I don't know," Nancy said.

"I'll say it again. Don't give up on Wilcox," Avalaur said.

A gleaming, purple light shined through the cafe window and reflected onto Nancy's booth. She looked across the street to the source of light and saw a man holding a translucent purple crystal in a dark cloth. It was the exact same type of purple crystal that she had picked up on the other side of the portal when they visited Staraliss. The man wore a black jacket with a hood covering his head. He handled the crystal with black gloves and appeared to be showing it to a tall human woman. The woman wore a long, tight, blue dress. She had shoulder-length, black hair. They stood in front of an intoxication joint, which was a popular drinking establishment along the main thoroughfare. After speaking a few words with the woman, he wrapped the purple crystal back up inside the dark cloth. She handed the man a large amount of credits and he gave her the bulky cloth. The woman put it inside her bag, turned around and walked away, disappearing from Nancy's sight.

Nancy gasped. "Oh shit!"

"What? Is your date there?" Avalaur asked.

"No. I just witnessed something across the street that is very important to our case. I'll talk to you later. I have to take a picture of this guy," Nancy said.

"Okay. Call me later," Avalaur said.

"Will do."

Nancy ended the transmission and looked across the street. She held up her comm to take a picture of the man who had sold the purple crystal to the woman. Before she could take the picture, a vehicle pulled up in front of the intoxication joint. The driver stepped out and walked over to the man on the sidewalk. Nancy recognized the driver as Bryson Wieler, the real estate agent she had seen at the Settlement Agency. She took a picture of Bryson receiving the bundle of credits from the other man, after the man took a few for himself. After what looked like a slight argument, Bryson Wieler got back into his vehicle and left the scene. The man that did the transaction turned and went inside the intoxication joint.

I have got to show this to Wilcox, Nancy thought.

"Nancy!"

Nancy turned and looked up at her old friend. Her date had finally arrived. He was a tall man with dark hair and brown eyes.

"Hi, Jim. It's been a long time. How are you doing?" Nancy asked.

She stood up and gave him a hug. They both sat down in the booth across from each other.

"You look absolutely beautiful. I am doing fine. I've just been keeping myself busy, working in the aerospace tech field with spaceship designs. Thank you for reaching out to me for this date. I appreciate it. So, what are you up to these days?" he asked.

"I'm still at the investigative agency, working cases. We're actually on one of our biggest cases to date right now," she said.

"Interesting. Well, I hope they pay you well," Jim said.

"I can't complain. But I certainly am glad to have a day off," Nancy said.

A waitress stopped at their booth with two glasses of water.

"Welcome to Knablean's Cafe, one of the oldest food establishments on Sarloh's World. What drinks can I get you two started with?" she asked.

"I'll have a cup of coffee with creamer," Nancy said.

"Sugar and creamer are both on the table," the waitress said.

Nancy looked over to the side of the table and spotted them.

"I'll have an ale," Jim said.

"Got it. I'll be right back with those. The menus are there behind the creamer."

After the waitress left, Nancy looked out the window at the intoxication joint across the street for a long moment.

"You seem distracted. Are you okay?" Jim asked.

"Oh, I'm just thinking about work," Nancy said.

"It's supposed to be your day off. You need to leave that stuff at the door when you go home," Jim said.

"I suppose you're right. Sorry," Nancy said.

"No worries."

They both grabbed a menu and looked through it.

"Do you know the name of that intoxication joint across the street?" Nancy asked.

"Yeah. That's Falpherr's Place. I used to go in there once in a while. These days, it's just a haven for criminal activity," Jim said.

"Well, that's not good. So, what made you pick this place?" Nancy asked.

"It's not far from my house here on Sarloh's World. I'm sorry. I should have picked something more fancy," Jim said.

"No. This is fine. Actually, I'm glad you did. I got a chance to look at the scenery while I waited," Nancy said.

"Scenery? I know sarcasm when I hear it," he said.

"It's fine…really," Nancy said.

They continued looking at the menus and made their selections just in time for the waitress's return. She set the drinks down onto the table and took their orders.

"You can just put the menus back against the wall there," the waitress said as she left.

After putting the menus back, Nancy looked across the table at Jim. She did not find him attractive like she had years before and began to wonder exactly what she was doing. She thought about Wilcox for a long moment.

I wonder if Wilcox Brown will ever be more than just my boss, she thought.

As Nancy turned and looked across the street at Falpherr's Place, she noticed the man that she had seen earlier exit the intoxication joint. He walked down the sidewalk and disappear out of sight.

"You seem distracted again," Jim said.

"Damn it, Jim, I'm sorry, but I need to leave. You're right. I am distracted. Just before you arrived, there was some very important information that was discovered regarding our current case and I really need to get back to the office. It's an urgent matter. I hope you understand," Nancy said.

"Oh, I get it," Jim said.

Nancy stood up from the booth. "I'm really sorry," she said as she headed for the door.

"Yeah, me too," Jim said to himself.

The waitress returned with a plate in each hand and had a puzzled look when she saw Nancy leave the cafe.

"I'll just take both plates," Jim said.

Chapter Twelve

Alivia Bexley opened her front door.

"Hello. I presume you are Alivia, the one who contacted us. I am Wilcox Brown and this is Nancy Louray. We came here as quickly as possible."

"Yes. Thank you for coming. Come on in," Alivia said.

They stepped into the living room.

"I'm glad the sun is out today. It rained pretty hard here last night. Have a seat on the couch," Alivia said. "Don't mind the folded blanket and pillow. Here, let me move those. Coradelle was sleeping there last night."

After moving the pillow and blanket, Alivia sat in a chair next to the couch.

"So, tell us what happened," Wilcox said.

"Coradelle is my best friend. She came over here to stay because she noticed that someone was following her. Someone was after her. She was afraid. We played board games and talked a lot, until it got late. I know that she hired you to find the deed to her father's planet that he had purchased. I'm glad Coradelle gave me your card. She mentioned that she was told by you, Nancy, that the case was getting very involved," Alivia said.

"Yes. This is a very involved case. The last time I spoke with Coradelle, she told me that she was being followed and planned on coming over here," Nancy said.

"In the middle of the night, I heard my set of knives fall onto the kitchen floor. I ran out here from my bedroom and found that she had been taken. There must have been a struggle in the kitchen. The back door was busted open and the rain was coming in."

"When you contacted us, you said two military officers came here and took over the investigation from the local authorities. Can you tell me about that?" Wilcox asked.

"Yeah. Right after I called you, I called the local authorities. They arrived pretty quickly. Their sergeant talked with me and before I could finish explaining what had happened, two military officers showed up and spoke with the sergeant. The sergeant told me that the military was taking over the investigation. All of the police left. I explained to the military officers what had happened. When those two departed, I was left with no answers," Alivia said.

"Well—" Wilcox was cut short from a knock at the front door.

Alivia stood up and walked over to answer it. A man stood there in a work uniform.

"Hi. I'm here to repair a door," the man said.

"Hi. I'm Alivia. Right this way," she said.

Alivia led the man past Wilcox and Nancy, heading for the kitchen.

"Here is the damaged door. The frame is broken on the side and the door is destroyed," Alivia said.

"Okay," he said, looking at the damage. "I'll replace the entire door and frame. Let me get some measurements and then I will go pick up a matching door."

"Okay. I'll just be in the living room with my guests if you need me," Alivia said.

She walked back into the living room.

"Thanks for patiently waiting. I couldn't leave my door like that," Alivia said.

"That's understandable. I was going to say that you probably won't have any more answers when we leave either. But I can assure you, we will be working relentlessly on solving this case," Wilcox said.

The repair man walked past them to the front door. "I'll be back with a new door shortly," he said.

"Thank you," Alivia said as he left.

"The odd thing about this incident is the military's involvement," Wilcox said.

"I thought that was strange as well," Alivia said.

Wilcox recalled Victoria telling him that he needed to watch his back. He wished that she would have elaborated with more information on the reason why.

"I'll see if I can find out more information from the military," Wilcox said.

"I hadn't seen Coradelle that anxious since we were kids. This incident has really bothered her. She normally didn't stay here at my place like that," Alivia said.

"What happened when she was a kid?" Nancy asked.

"We've been friends since childhood. When her parents split, Coradelle became very stressed. Robert Hershall and Mercedes Brantt were not married. Coradelle confided in me with everything. Her mother was very difficult to be around. Coradelle was caught in the middle of a vicious legal battle for custody. Her father won, but there was a lot of bitterness and animosity between Coradelle's parents for years. She told me that after the custody battle, her dad tried to make it work with her mom. Unfortunately, he just could not win with her. Coradelle seems to think that her father had proposed marriage to her mother once at a special place—possibly that planet—in order to make things work. Coradelle is not close to her mother at all. On occasion, she tries to visit her mom on Adanarr, but Mercedes is never home or too busy for Coradelle," Alivia said.

"Coradelle had told us during our initial meeting with her that she thinks her father proposed marriage to her mother on Staraliss. Do you know if that is true?" Nancy asked.

"That's what Coradelle seems to think. There is a friend of Coradelle's father named Maxboro Lawson who may know more about that. Coradelle and Maxboro were in a relationship years ago. She didn't want her dad to know about it, but she tells me everything," Alivia said.

"I have interviewed Maxboro. He didn't mention anything about Mercedes being on Staraliss, but he did say that there was a length of time where him and Robert did not contact each other," Nancy said.

"Perhaps, we should interview Mercedes Brantt," Wilcox said. "You said she lives on Adanarr?"

"That is correct. Here, let me give you her address," Alivia said.

Alivia wrote down Mercedes Brantt's address on a piece of paper and gave it to Nancy.

"Thank you, Alivia. Please be assured that we will do our best to located Coradelle," Nancy said.

"I appreciate it. Thank you for coming to Ryamesh. Good luck," Alivia said.

The three of them stood up and walked toward the front door.

"Good luck with your door repair," Nancy said.

"Oh. Thanks," Alivia said.

Wilcox and Nancy left Alivia Bexley's house and walked toward the landing pad where the *Enigma* was parked.

"You may want to contact your General friend, *Victoria,* and ask her why the military is involved here," Nancy said.

Wilcox looked and Nancy as they walked along the sidewalk.

"You really have a problem with Victoria, don't you?" Wilcox asked.

Nancy did not respond.

Versill sat in the cockpit of a Stormrider fighter ship, flying across the desert of Lairdain Tannis at a low altitude. The sleek ship had a dark gray, metallic look. She gazed out the canopy window on the port side of the ship at a city in the distance. She could make out the faint details of the tall buildings against the horizon. The city of Leti was just one of many cities on Lairdain Tannis.

Unlike the humans and Axynnians, most of the Sharrixians lived on one planet only, Lairdain Tannis. However, they did use several of the nearby planets in Sharrixian territory for resources and military bases, including the planets Rassioth, Ryth Oparrian, and Narross Selontious.

As Versill looked ahead of her toward the Crystal Field, she began to see sparkling crystals littered along the desert sand. She always thought their black, blue, and purple hues were beautiful. Versill remembered a storybook called *The Legend of the Green Crystal* that her mother had read to her when she was a child. It was a story about a green crystal with special powers for whoever possessed it. Even though she realized there were no green crystals, Versill enjoyed her mother reading the story to her. She smiled at the memory.

"I miss you, Mother…" she said to herself as a tear rolled down her patterned face.

Versill wondered if her mother would have been disappointed in her for going through the portal against Queen Empress Aminarra's rule.

Red rock outcrops began to appear as she flew along. Versill saw a reddish colored rock wall in the distance. It was part of a small range of mountains on which the other side was just more desert. However, the rock wall had a shimmering portal that stretched across it. She was amazed at the sight of it. As Versill flew closer, she noticed a shimmering effect emitting from the portal. She trusted that High Commander Novish Shirom had dismissed the portal guards for a briefing at the Sharrixian Government Building, like he said he would. Versill looked at the computer screen and adjusted the throttle, slowing the fighter ship down. It was going to be a tight squeeze. One miscalculation and she would be consumed in a ball of fire and twisted metal. She felt strange going against Queen Empress Aminarra's orders, but she trusted that Novish was correct about the human military's investigation almost being complete.

Here I go, Versill thought.

The Stormrider fighter ship plunged through the portal with perfect clearance from the rocky sides. Bolts of blue static danced along the ship's hull as it disappeared to the other side. Versill looked at the back screen display. The portal looked similar to the Lairdain Tannis side. She circled around and landed the ship near the portal. Versill was thankful for the Sharrixian military gathering data from across the galaxy over the years to program their ship navigation systems with correct maps, space charts, and planet names that humans and Axynnians referred to them as. After a long moment, the computer indicated that she was on the planet Shext.

The area around the portal had desert sand, similar to Lairdain Tannis. However, it was only near the opening of the portal, as if the sand had blown through from the other side. It quickly gave way to a forest that stretched far into the distance. A rock cliff could be seen in the distance of the forest with a slab of gray stone across the top of it. Versill opened the canopy and stepped out of the ship. She was greeted by the fresh scent of white pine trees. She immediately noticed footsteps in the sand.

Someone was here recently, she thought.

She looked around and rested her hand on the laser pistol at her side. The portal was located within a tan rock wall with green shrubs scattered about its vertical surface. It looked much different than the red rock wall on the Lairdain Tannis side. Walking toward the portal, she saw the four, tall Sharrixian skeletons partially buried in the sand. A grim expression came across her patterned face, her light orange, beige, green, and black tones becoming slightly flush as she filled with anger. She walked closer and noticed that one of the skeletons was recently disturbed, the bones pulled up from the ground slightly. That's when Versill saw the name tag of Novish's uncle. She squatted down with her long legs and inspected the piece of fabric that was once his Gatherer uniform.

"Riilan," she said. "We will soon have justice for you, Riilan."

Versill realized the war that Queen Empress Aminarra had declared on the humans would destroy many, many more lives than the five Gatherers that were murdered. That realization made her mission to contact General Victoria Ediira that much more important. She walked back to her ship and stepped inside, closing the canopy. Removing the storage drive that Novish had given her from her pocket, she plugged it into the ship's console. A specific comm frequency populated onto the computer screen. She switched the ship's comm system to that frequency.

"General Victoria Ediira, do you copy?" Versill asked.

Moments later, her comm lit up.

"General Victoria Ediira speaking." A voice came over the speaker.

"Hi, General Ediira. This is Versill. I'm the Sharrixian special operations military officer who met with you on Rafith Astonn."

"Versill? This is an unexpected communication. Is...there a problem?" Victoria asked.

"Actually, there is a massive problem. High Commander Novish Shirom has sent me on a special mission to meet with you in person regarding an urgent matter. So, I am wondering if we could meet somewhere for a discussion. I am on your side of the Marrithious Galaxy, so it should not take long to meet at whatever location you want."

"I see... Well, I'll send a set of coordinates to your comm and we can talk as soon as you arrive," Victoria said.

"Just so you know, I'm in a fighter ship. It's the only thing that would fit through the portal. It would be appreciated if your military doesn't fire at me," Versill said.

"Ah, the portal that Novish mentioned. I am very interested to know where that is. I'm sending the coordinates now. I'll talk to you soon," Victoria said.

"Okay. I just received them. I'll see you soon," Versill said.

Versill ended the communication and programmed the coordinates that she received into the ship's navigation system. She engaged the Stormrider's engines and lifted from the surface of Shext. As Versill flew past the rock cliff, she noticed two beautiful wolves carefully watching her ship from atop the gray stone slab. She had never seen an animal like that before. One of them howled.

That's cool, she thought, smiling.

Admiral Novish Shirom peered out the observation window on the bridge of the *Credence Revenge*. In the distance, he saw the bright planet of Rafith Astonn. Next to the *Credence Revenge* were three other battleships, *Arcinaris*, *Lhasariss*, and *Shartannis*. Novish was acting as both High Commander and Admiral for the operation. Stormrider fighter ships could be seen practicing maneuvers in the distance of space.

Novish reached for the comm and opened a channel for the entire fleet. "Commander Othan, Commander Prilston, and Commander Jafer, my team is still compiling the assigned target lists. As soon as the computer is finished, I will send each of you a specific list," Novish said.

"Roger that," Covlan Prilston said.

"Thanks for the update," Jafer said.

"Roger that," Gedlo Othan said. "The *Lhasariss* has sent our Stormrider fighter pilots out for practice runs on the planet Rafith Astonn. They are joining with the fighters from *Arcinaris*. I understand the *Credence Revenge* and *Shartannis* fighter ships are scheduled on the next shift."

"That is correct. I just saw the group of fighters in the distance," Novish said. "How are you three coming along with my request to stock up the supplies in the your battleship's medical facilities?"

"The *Shartannis* sick bay is stocked, as requested, sir," Jafer said.

"I have the *Arcinaris* sick bay stocked as well," Covlan said.

"Thank you for the reminder, sir. I will have my team get right on that," Gedlo said.

"Okay. Now that the group of Stormriders has reached Rafith Astonn for their practice runs and we have a clear path, I need the battleships of the fleet to go through the testing sequence of all forward and aft laser cannons," Novish said.

"Acknowledged, sir," Covlan said.

"Roger that," Gedlo said.

"Yes, sir," Jafer said.

Novish instructed the team on the bridge of the *Credence Revenge* to test fire both the forward and aft laser cannons. The officers at the bridge console could be seen flicking banks of switches and adjusting intensity levels. Soon, intense, blue beams of laser fire emitted from all the battleships in the fleet, brightening the darkness of space.

"Okay. I have further instructions for laser cannon testing. Each battleship is to separately reposition above the rest of the fleet and test port and starboard laser cannons. I will begin with the *Credence Revenge*. Once I'm back into position, next will be *Arcinaris*, then *Lhasariss*, followed by *Shartannis*," Novish said.

Novish gave the instructions to his crew. The *Credence Revenge* moved above the other battleships and began testing their port and starboard lasers. Once the battleship was back into position with the fleet, each of the other battleships performed the same test.

"I'm glad to see that our weapons are functioning as expected," Gedlo said.

"Yes. The computer just finished compiling the target lists for assignment," Novish said. "I will send each of you your specific list. When the Stormriders return from their practice later, we'll send out the other two groups."

"Roger that," Gedlo said.

"And then we wait for Queen Empress Aminarra's launch command for this offensive," Novish said.

A new voice came over the comm. "This is Queen Empress Aminarra Vistona. As you know, the fleet is on monitored communications. I want to thank each of you for your service and dedication to the Sharrixian people. I have one more meeting with the Sharrixian Council to review the details of this Marrithious Galactic War. Stand by. I will contact you later."

The comm fell silent and Novish looked out the window at the darkness of space. He sat down in the central chair of the bridge, put his hand on his forehead, and sighed. Novish hoped Queen Empress

Aminarra's council meeting and response to the fleet would be delayed. He thought about Versill's secret mission and he wished her great success.

A man in a black hoodie sat in the waiting area of the Settlement Agency on Anneriss. He picked up the blue crystal that decorated the table, examined it, and set it back down. He had sold hundreds of the blue crystals. Ever since he had been assigned to the purple crystals, he was making more credits. At that moment, Bryson Wieler came from a back office and met him in the waiting area.

"Hey, Merritt," Bryson said.

"I received your message and got here as soon as possible. I left the rest of the purple crystals in my ship," the man said.

"Yes. Come on back to the office. There are some questions the team has for you," Bryson said.

Merritt stood up from the white couch and followed Bryson through a door and into the back. After a maze of turns, Merritt noticed they were in a secluded area of the building. They entered a small room and Bryson shut the door. The settlement agent Chaslin Anders sat at a table with the Settlement Agency director, Quinlan Zale.

"Have a seat," Bryson said.

Merritt sat down at the small table, followed by Bryson Wieler.

"Hi, Merritt. We have appreciated you selling our crystals on the black market. You did well with the blue crystals, but you made a serious mistake with the last sale of the purple crystal on Sarloh's World," Chaslin said.

"Mistake?" Merritt questioned. "Listen, I took my cut and gave the rest of the credits to Bryson."

"Yes. But according to Bryson, you sold a purple crystal on a main street in broad daylight. You've always sold our crystals inside the intoxication joint. What changed?" Chaslin asked.

"The woman did not feel comfortable going inside Falpherr's Place. I didn't think much of it. Bryson was arguing with me about it when he picked up the credits. People sell stuff on the street all the time on Sarloh's World," Merritt said.

"Unfortunately, we *do* think it's a big deal and you will no longer be selling crystals for us," Chaslin said.

"In fact, you won't be leaving this room," Quinlan Zale said. He pointed a laser pistol at Merritt's head.

"Wait a minute. I—" Merritt was cut off.

"Hold out your palms," Quinlan ordered.

Merritt held out his hands with a questioning look. Another man entered the small room. He wore gloves and held a dark cloth. Opening the cloth, he carefully removed a translucent black crystal and placed it in Merritt's palms.

"I've only seen blue and purple crystals. What is this black one?" Merritt asked.

"Close your hands," Quinlan said. He continued to point the laser pistol at Merritt's head.

Merritt closed his palms and suddenly everything went black. He slumped over dead onto the table. The man with the gloves carefully picked up the black crystal, returned it to the cloth, and wrapped the cloth around it. As the man with the black crystal exited the room, Quinlan returned the laser pistol to his side.

"Chaslin, have someone from our team put his body in his ship, program it to fly to a remote part of space, and just let it drift. Then have the team member retrieve the remaining purple crystals from Merritt's residence," Quinlan said.

"There is no need to retrieve the crystals from his residence. I asked him to bring them with him. They are on his ship," Bryson said.

"Perfect. In that case, Chaslin, I need you to get the crystals from Merritt's ship. Have one of the other members take care of the body and program the ship," Quinlan said.

"Yes, we need all the crystals we can get. Our supply is running low. If we can just go back to Staraliss to harvest more crystals, we won't have an inventory problem," Bryson said.

"We have been told by the boss that there is a moratorium on harvesting more crystals at the moment. We are not to go to Staraliss until further notice. We still have plenty of crystals to sell. Bryson, perhaps you could remind our sellers to be more discreet during their transactions," Quinlan said.

"I will do that, right after our meeting here," Bryson said.

"Good luck with Merritt here, Chaslin. Bryson and I have an appointment with the boss," Quinlan said.

• • •

A ship entered the secret military base on Anneriss. The docking bay door automatically closed as a man exited the ship. Victoria had received the communication for his arrival just moments before. The man was one of the military's undercover operatives within the Settlement Agency.

"Hi, Agent Marshall. Thanks for contacting me regarding this situation," Victoria said.

"Yes, ma'am. Why are the defense weapons for our base here at full alert?" Marshall asked.

"Just in case a visitor that I'm expecting isn't so friendly," Victoria said.

"I see…"

"So, from what you told me, Chaslin Anders took purple crystals from this ship? You were tasked with programming this ship to fly to a remote location in space and letting it drift with the body left inside?" she asked.

"Affirmative. I overheard Chaslin talking on his comm to someone about killing this guy with a black crystal," Marshall said. "Also, Quinlan Zale and Bryson Wieler are meeting with their boss shortly. Our operatives have installed a tracking device on Quinlan's ship. I have the signal info for you."

"Nice! So, they have black crystals that cause death. Interesting… I am going to have one of our medical examiners check the body. Nice work, Marshall. We can enter the tracking info from Chaslin's ship into the computer. Discovering who the boss of their operation is will bring a resolution for all the murders of the Sharrixians and some humans, including the guy in this ship," Victoria said.

"Definitely," Marshall said.

"I need you to move this ship off to the side of the docking bay. I'm expecting another ship to arrive soon. After that meeting, we can track Quinlan's ship," Victoria said.

Marshall went to move the ship and Victoria reached for her comm.

"Hey, this is General Ediira. I need a medical examiner at the base here on Anneriss as soon as possible."

Chapter Thirteen

Wilcox sat in his office chair with his feet up on the desk. He held the top of an ink pen up to his lips as he contemplated their current case of the missing deed to Staraliss. Nancy also sat at her desk with her hands against her forehead. Silence filled the office for some time. Busy street traffic could be seen out the front window.

"Nice work on getting the pictures you took of that crystal transaction. We have confirmed Bryson Wieler is a major player in this. You said you were on Sarloh's World for a date when you saw this?" Wilcox asked.

"Yes. His name is Jim. He's an old friend from years ago," Nancy said.

"What line of work is he in?" Wilcox asked.

"He designs and works on the technical side of spaceships," Nancy said.

"Hmm. I wonder if he designed the door hinge to my ship," Wilcox said.

"The one that cut your arm? Smart-ass! Now who's jealous?"

"I'm not jealous. Although, he probably did design it."

Nancy shook her head and smiled.

Perhaps there is hope in this relationship yet, she thought.

"This case has become very involved," Nancy said.

"So, what do we know? We know where they got these crystals from. We know what the purple ones do. Sorry again about the kiss at the portal. We know they are selling them for large amounts of credits…apparently to individuals who use them as aphrodisiacs, like a love potion. We don't know what the other crystals do. We do not know how many individuals are in their group nor who their boss is. But they are willing to murder and abduct people over the crystals," Wilcox said.

"Don't forget, they also changed the name of the planet Staraliss to Shext in the Marrithious Galaxy's main navigation database," Nancy said.

"That too," Wilcox said.

"By the way, I happened to like the kiss we had at the portal," Nancy said.

It became awkwardly silent.

"There are so many loose ends that I'm starting to lose hope in finding our missing client and solving this case. Things seem to get exponentially worse by the day," Wilcox said.

"So, let's broaden the investigation and go over motive," Nancy said.

"We know the motive. It's all about crystal avarice," Wilcox said.

"Yes, but we were hired to find a missing deed. And we still haven't done that," Nancy said.

"This deed mystery has turned into a murder mystery on a grand scale. I wasn't expecting the mess we are in. I think I need to retire," Wilcox said.

"I was looking through some files earlier that I would like to show you," Nancy said, grabbing a file folder from the cabinet on her left. "Damn!"

"What?"

"Paper cut…" she said.

Wilcox noticed blood running down her hand.

"Oh, that one's a gusher. Let me grab the first aid kit," he said.

Wilcox quickly sprinted to the back of the office and grabbed the first aid kit from the bathroom.

"Hand me a sterile wipe and a bandage…please," she said.

Nancy wiped the blood from her finger. Wilcox opened the

bandage for her and she applied it over her finger.

"That looks worse than a paper cut," Wilcox said.

"It was the edge of the manila folder," Nancy said.

"Ouch. No wonder it's a gusher," he said.

"It will be fine," she said.

Wilcox held her bandaged hand for a moment and looked into her eyes. "I enjoyed the kiss at the portal too. I just… So, what were you going to show me in this dangerous folder of yours?" Wilcox asked.

Nancy smiled and opened the folder.

"These are my notes from the interview with Maxboro Lawson on Ryamesh. The town of Timber Wolf has a no-fly zone for non-industrial ships. So, I had to park *Nellie* and take a shuttle to Maxboro's house. When we passed the rail yard, I saw a white container with a circular, blue logo in the center." She pointed at the notes. "The shuttle driver said most of the containers were being shipped to the planet Noderell. Well, you know how I told you that I have visions sometimes? I had a vision that Coradelle was running from someone along a warehouse with that same circular logo on it. I think she might be on Noderell."

Wilcox sat back in his chair and contemplated what Nancy had said. "Do you realize how many warehouses are on Noderell? If you are right, she could literally be in any of them. The last thing we need right now is to chase a dead end. I think our next step is to interview Coradelle's mother, Mercedes Brantt. We need to know if she was on Staraliss. Coradelle seems to think that her father proposed marriage to Mercedes on Staraliss," Wilcox said.

"Also, we should tell Mercedes that her daughter has been abducted," Nancy said.

"I agree. And after we interview Mercedes, I think we need to pay another visit to the Settlement Agency and really push them with some questions," Wilcox said.

Nancy closed the folder and returned it to the filing cabinet next to her desk. She stood up and grabbed her white sweater from the back of her chair.

"Let's go," she said.

"Do you have Mercedes Brantt's location?" Wilcox asked.

"Yes. Coradelle's friend Alivia Bexley gave it to me," Nancy said.

"After you," Wilcox said, grabbing his hat from the top of the coatrack.

As they proceeded toward the door, Wilcox's comm sounded. He looked at it. Nancy stopped at the door and turned around to wait for him to answer.

"Hi, Victoria. What's up?" he asked

"Wilcox, I'm hoping you have reconsidered giving me the location of the planet that you discovered the skeletons on. It would really help in my investigation of these aliens," she said.

"Well…it is interesting that you are still investigating them after sixteen years. Have you reconsidered telling me why I have to watch my back? Who is after me? I noticed a ship following me recently. It's a little stressful…especially since there are some murders involved in our current case," Wilcox said.

"So, we are still at a stalemate, then?" Victoria asked.

"Look, Victoria, the military came in and took over my investigation on that alien ship and had us leave with no answers whatsoever. I assume that the military will do the same thing on the planet we discovered the alien skeletons on. I don't want to interfere with your alien investigation, and I don't want you to interfere with my missing-deed investigation," Wilcox said.

"Well, I cannot promise the military won't take over the planet when it's discovered, but I do wish you the best on your investigation," Victoria said.

The communication ended. Wilcox sighed.

"Let's go," he said.

Sensors on the Stormrider indicated heavy weaponry was present at the destination ahead. Versill guided the fighter ship toward the secluded docking bay. The coordinates that Victoria had given her were odd to say the least. The planet Anneriss was not what she was expecting. Versill slowed the ship down and gently landed in the docking bay. As the docking bay door closed, Versill slid the canopy open and climbed out of the ship. The sound of her black boots hitting the metal floor echoed into the heights of the docking bay. Versill had her special operations, black military uniform on. She removed her black helmet and tossed it up onto the cockpit seat. General Victoria Ediira was standing on one side of the docking bay, waiting for her arrival. Versill noticed a few other personnel performing various tasks. When two medical examiners rolled a stretcher across the docking bay with what appeared to be a dead man, Versill had a grim expression on her alien face. She began to question High Commander Novish Shirom's mission for her. The medical examiners looked up at her extremely tall figure, patterned skin, and bumpy head and had a grim expression of their own.

Victoria walked over to meet her. "Hi, Versill. It's nice to meet you again. Rafith Astonn was such a desolate place to meet. It's nice to meet in a more comfortable setting," Victoria said.

"Comfortable? I thought you were going to fire on me," Versill said.

"Did you pick up the laser cannons on your sensors?" Victoria asked.

"I did."

"No, that was just a precautionary measure. There was no intention of firing," Victoria said.

"I am concerned about my confidentiality of being seen here. Other than you, no human nor Axynnian has ever seen a live Sharrixian before...until now," Versill said. "Except for the murderers at the portal, of course..."

"I did see their expression at the sight of you. The military personnel here, including the military medical examiners, keep things confidential. So, there is no need to be alarmed. That man on the stretcher was recently killed by the same people who killed the five Sharrixian Gatherers at the portal," Victoria said.

"So, it's not just Sharrixians they have targeted?" Versill asked.

"No. I want to bring this group down so badly. And we are close. This military base was actually built here on Anneriss because of that group. They are working through an estate settlement agency, simply known as the Settlement Agency, some distance from here. We've been gathering information about them for some time now and have even infiltrated their organization," Victoria said.

"Yeah, I was expecting a fully militarized planet with security clearance and strict course guidance," Versill said.

"Oh. Our military headquarters is on a different planet. We have military outposts at many points across this sector of space...well, at least on this side of the Marrithious Galaxy. So, you were saying that there is a massive problem. Can you elaborate on that?" Victoria asked.

"As I had said over the comm, I have been sent here by High Commander Novish Shirom for a special mission to give you a message in person.

"Our council persuaded Queen Empress Aminarra Vistona to declare war on the humans because there has been no justice for the five murdered Gatherers. I am here to tell you that your investigation needs to be concluded quickly," Versill said.

Victoria stared up at Versill for a long moment.

"I see… We are doing everything we can to expedite this investigation. It just takes time," Victoria said.

"In the council's viewpoint, you've had twenty years to figure it out. Personally, I know that is not the case," Versill said.

"No, that is not the case. The Gatherers were murdered twenty years ago. Your people sent a ship here to investigate, but the ship malfunctioned and the crew died. We only discovered the ship sixteen years ago. For many years, we were just trying to figure out where this alien ship came from and what species these tall skeletons were. It wasn't until recent years that we realized there was a connection with this organization that has been harvesting crystals through the portal. That's when we decided to build a secret base here on Anneriss.

"There is a private investigator friend of mine who is also working this case, except from a different angle. I am considering asking him to join my team and help solve this once and for all. He has been to the portal, but he will not tell me what planet it's on. Since you have gone through it, please tell me what planet it's on," Victoria said.

"According to the nav system, it is the planet Shext," Versill said.

"Shext… Thank you. That will help in our investigation. Can you tell me about this war declaration?" Victoria asked.

"We have a fleet of battleships that are loaded with Stormrider fighter ships, just like this one I flew into your docking bay, waiting near Rafith Astonn. They await Queen Empress Aminarra's orders to proceed. If I could just convince them that you are concluding your investigation into the murders of our people, I would hope it would avoid an ugly war. Novish Shirom does not want war either. He sent me here as an envoy of sorts to try and avoid it. Unfortunately, he must obey Queen Empress Aminarra's orders. The fleet is on monitored communications with Queen Empress Aminarra. Novish told me not to go back through the portal when I return home. The queen empress does not know about my secret mission here, nor would I want her to. It is forbidden for us to go through the portal and she would probably have me killed," Versill said.

"I appreciate your bravery…as I'm sure Novish does too," Victoria said.

"For whatever it's worth, the fleet at Rafith Astonn consists of four massive battleships that are equipped with heavy laser cannons. Each battleship has two docking bays with twenty Stormrider fighter ships in each bay. So, there is a total of one hundred and sixty fighter ships. Also, there are other battleships on call to attach to the fleet if necessary. Victoria, I am very concerned," Versill said.

"You and me both."

"Basically, my mission of delivering the message is finished. Is there anything else I can do here to help speed up your investigation?" Versill asked.

"I'm not sure. You are welcome to stick around so we can figure that out together. I need to go monitor a ship that we are tracking. Supposedly, it will lead us to the boss of this organization," Victoria said.

"Sure. Whatever I can do to help," Versill said.

"You just don't want to return home because you might be killed," Victoria said as they walked toward the offices.

"Is it that obvious?" Versill asked.

"Yes. But hopefully, you will return a hero," Victoria said.

They both walked down a small corridor and entered the communications room. Agent Marshall sat at the control console. He looked up and gasped at the sight of the tall alien officer.

"Agent Marshall. This is Versill. She is a special officer for the Sharrixian military. She will be joining us indefinitely," Victoria said.

"Sorry about my initial shock. It's just that I've never seen a Sharrixian before…only the tall skeletons from the alien ship." He stood up from the chair and looked up at her tall figure, holding out his hand. "It's a pleasure to meet you," he said.

Versill reached out her gloved hand and shook his.

"It's nice to meet you as well," she said.

Marshall sat back down in the chair and flicked a switch.

"There hasn't been any movement on the ship yet. It's very odd. I'm not sure what their delay is," Marshall said.

"Contact one of our undercover operatives in the group and see what the delay is," Victoria said.

"Yes, ma'am," Marshall said.

He contacted another inside agent over the comm.

"We haven't seen any movement on Quinlan's ship. Is there a delay in them taking off?" Marshall asked.

"They already took off. They used Bryson Wieler's ship, not Quinlan's," the man said.

"Shit!" Marshall exclaimed.

"And you guys didn't think to put a tracking device on both ships?" Victoria questioned.

"No… I'm sorry about this setback," Marshall said.

"We are on the brink of galactic war and we cannot afford any setbacks," Victoria said.

"Understood," Marshall said. He could see her frustration.

"Versill, I need to call for an emergency meeting with our commanders regarding this war declaration. I would like you to join me at the meeting," Victoria said.

"Whatever I can do to help prevent war…" Versill said.

The flight to Adanarr was quiet. Wilcox programmed the *Enigma* along an alternate route after the computer indicated heavy ship traffic along the main route.

"You look tired," Wilcox said.

"I *am* tired," Nancy said.

"This investigation has been exhausting. Plus, you cleaned the entire interior of the *Enigma* with a bucket of soap and water. You can lie down in the back lounge area," he said.

"Yeah. Maybe after a nap, I'll get a second wind," Nancy said.

She stood up from the seat next to Wilcox and made her way back to the *Enigma's* lounge area. There, she lay down on the soft, white leather bench and closed her eyes.

Wilcox checked the computer to see how close they were to Adanarr. The *Enigma* was traveling at lightspeed-plus, which was a general term used when referencing speeds beyond that of light. Many ships were capable of traveling much faster than the speed of light. Wilcox was proud of the *Enigma's* speed. He was thankful he was able to lose the ship that had followed him recently. Fortunately, he had not noticed anyone else following him. It still bothered him that Victoria would not tell him who was after him…especially after they had been intimate together.

Very odd… I'm sure she has her reasons, he thought.

After some time, the computer began to beep and Wilcox looked at the display. They were approaching Adanarr. He noticed the white sphere in the distance of space quickly become larger as the *Enigma* automatically exited lightspeed-plus. The blue and white planet loomed before him. He stood from his pilot's seat and walked toward the lounge to wake up Nancy.

"Nancy, we're at Adanarr," he said as he rounded the corner to the lounge.

She was already sitting up on the leather bench staring into the distance.

"Are you okay," Wilcox asked.

"Yes. I had another vision," she said.

"Coradelle, again?" Wilcox asked.

"No, it was not Coradelle again. Sometimes, I wonder if these occasional visions are a curse or a blessing," Nancy said.

"Any gift from God is a blessing," Wilcox said.

She gave him a side stare and sighed. "I had a vision of a galactic war. We were under attack by the aliens, like we had seen the remains of on Staraliss. There was intense laser fire and explosions. People were screaming. It was just awful, Wilcox," she said.

"I'm sorry. Maybe it was just a bad dream," he said.

"No, it wasn't a dream. I was awake. That scared the hell out of me."

"I'm sorry... Well, I came back here to tell you that we have arrived at Adanarr. What are the coordinates that Alivia gave you to Mercedes Brantt's house?" he asked. "By the way, did I tell you that I was being followed the other day?"

"I overheard you mention something about it to Victoria over the comm. Who do you think it was?" Nancy asked.

"Probably the same people who abducted Coradelle and murdered her father and Everett Quarton," Wilcox said.

"That's all we need..." she said.

"Yeah..."

Nancy stood up and walked toward the front of the ship with Wilcox behind her. Being careful with her bandaged finger, she reached into her pocket and retrieved the piece of paper that Alivia had given her with the address on it. She handed it to Wilcox.

"Here, program this into the computer," she said.

Wilcox sat down and entered Mercedes Brantt's address into the navigation system.

"Okay, let's buckle up and head to the surface," Wilcox said.

Nancy sat down and they both fastened their seat belts. After the *Enigma* pierced a thick layer of white clouds, they saw a brilliant blue sky. As the ship flew closer to their destination, a city became visible. The large city spread far into the distance. Ship traffic became noticeably heavy as they approached the city, which stretched to the horizon and faded into the sun's shimmering haze. Wilcox turned on a local communications channel.

"Welcome to Torontarr, one of Adanarr's largest cities." The automated voice came over the ship's comm. "If you're visiting for the first time, we recommend staying at one of our luxurious—"

"Oh, turn it off!" Nancy said.

Wilcox flicked a switch on the ship's console.

"That was a highly annoying advertisement," he said.

They both gazed out the *Enigma's* observation window in amazement at all the intricate details of the city as they flew along the programmed route. Nancy looked down and saw a group of people exiting a public bus, each person going in a different direction. One woman and her two children headed for a large department store in the downtown area. Farther along, they noticed people in line for what looked like a movie or concert. The city stretched for kilometers. They passed an industrial area before entering a fancy residential area. The programmed coordinates led them toward houses that were more secluded and spread farther apart. Finally, the *Enigma* hovered over a landing pad in front of a luxurious home. Wilcox manually landed the ship and disengaged the engines. They unfastened their seat belts and peered out the window at the house. They saw another spaceship parked on another landing pad near a building behind the house. Wilcox assumed it was Mercedes Brantt's ship.

Brown and tan stone decorated the home's exterior. Many levels and roof angles could be seen. The landscaping was immaculate, with various shrubs and beautiful, flowering trees against a flawless, green lawn. A wide sidewalk led from the landing pad to the house. They exited the ship and took a deep breath of fresh air. Together, they followed the sidewalk up the stone steps to the front door. Wilcox rang the bell. After a short time, the door opened to reveal an older woman with blond hair and blue eyes. It was like they were seeing an older version of Coradelle.

"May I help you?" she asked.

"Hello. I am Wilcox Brown and this is Nancy Louray. We are private investigators and we're hoping to speak with Mercedes Brantt regarding our current investigation."

There was a lengthy, awkward pause.

"I'm Mercedes Brantt. I hope this is quick because I'm expecting guests to arrive any time now," she said.

"It shouldn't take long. We just have a few questions," Nancy said.

"Can we come in?" Wilcox asked.

"No. I don't know who you are. You can ask your questions right here at the door," Mercedes said.

"Fair enough. We were hired by your daughter, Coradelle, to find the missing deed to a planet that her father, Robert Hershall, had purchased. It was supposed to be part of his estate to her, but the Settlement Agency has indicated that there is no such planet nor document. Coradelle seems to think otherwise. She thinks that perhaps her father had taken you to the planet Staraliss and proposed marriage. We are trying to gather all the information we can so we can locate this deed. Were you on Staraliss with Robert Hershall?" Wilcox asked.

Mercedes squinted her eyes and then looked down at the threshold of the door. She tightened her jaw and looked back up at them.

"Robert and I were never meant to be together. I was out of his league. He won custody of our daughter and lit a raging fire in me that has yet to be extinguished. He had this grand dream to build a house for him and Coradelle on this new planet that he purchased. What an idiot! What child would want to be stranded on some desolate planet with no friends? Between the wolves and other…dangers, her safety was at risk," Mercedes said.

"Other dangers? How do you know about the wolves?" Wilcox asked.

"Yes, Robert did take me there once. It was right after he won custody of Coradelle. He wanted to make things work out and thought that proposing marriage to me and promising a beautiful house on that planet would fix the fact that he stole my daughter from me. When I declined his marriage invitation, he got pissed off, went to his ship, and took off. I was left stranded there. He didn't come back for hours. I had plenty of time to explore the area and discover interesting things. That is how I know about the wolves," Mercedes said.

"So, do you know where the deed to Staraliss is?" Wilcox asked.

There was a long pause.

"I think this conversation is over," Mercedes said, stepping back into the door.

"Wait! Mercedes, your daughter has been abducted. She's our client and she has gone missing. Someone broke into her friend's house and there was a struggle in the kitchen. Coradelle was taken during the night. We are also hoping that you can help us find her," Nancy said.

Disbelief covered Mercedes face and she suddenly became angry.

"I don't know where Coradelle is, but when I find out who did this to my daughter, they will have a very bad day," Mercedes said.

"We understand your frustration. If we locate her, we will let you know," Nancy said.

"Thank you," Mercedes said.

After stepping back into the house, she closed the door with a loud thud. Wilcox and Nancy turned around and proceeded back down the stone steps.

"Well, that didn't go as expected," Wilcox said.

They entered the *Enigma* and lifted from the surface of the landing pad. Wilcox flew the ship back toward the city of Torontarr. A ship passed them, going in the opposite direction. The *Enigma* ascended toward the clouds.

Mercedes came back out and stood in front of her house, watching their ship disappear into the sky. Suddenly, a new ship arrived and lowered to the front landing pad.

Ah, my guests have arrived, she thought.

"I think she knows something that she's not telling us," Nancy said.

"She's definitely hiding something. The fact that she was on Staraliss and was left to explore when Robert left in anger means that she could have discovered the portal and the crystals on the other side," Wilcox said.

"That's possible. She was very upset about Coradelle, however. So, I'm not certain there is a connection," Nancy said.

Wilcox programmed the navigation computer to set a course for Anneriss.

"I'm hoping that we can get more answers when we arrive back at the Settlement Agency," Wilcox said.

Nancy fiddled with her bandaged finger.

"We need to be more pushy," she said.

"Why don't you let air get to it. It will heal faster," Wilcox said.

"What?"

"Your finger."

"Oh. Yeah, it probably has stopped bleeding by now," Nancy said.

She pulled off the bandage and looked at the deep cut. Wilcox grabbed a small trash can from underneath the console and held it up toward Nancy. She discarded the bandage and he returned the trash can.

The ship became quiet as they both stared out the observation window, studying the fascinating tapestry of space. The distant blue stars created the perfect backdrop.

A short time later, the computer beeped to indicate they were approaching Anneriss. The *Enigma* soon switched to sub-lightspeed and slowly reduced its speed until it drifted above Anneriss. They felt the anti-gravitational units automatically engage as the ship flew through the atmosphere toward the Settlement Agency. Wilcox landed the ship in a large docking area. Several other ships of various models were parked on the concrete surface.

"It looks like they are busy," Wilcox said.

Nancy observed the other ships as they exited the *Enigma*.

"Well, some of them are leaving," Nancy said.

As they approached the building entrance, Wilcox and Nancy passed a few people who were leaving. They made their way down the corridor to the black doors they had gone through previously. The doors slid aside and they entered the hall. The familiar sound of flowing water greeted them as it continuously flowed in the hall's center fountain.

They noticed a woman at the counter speaking with the secretary. Beyond the fountain of flowing water, a man sat on one of the white couches in the waiting area. Wilcox and Nancy walked across the marble floor and waited in line behind the woman at the counter. After the woman received an envelope containing important estate documents, she left. Wilcox and Nancy stepped up to the counter at the large, rectangular opening in the wall. It was not the same woman who had been there on their previous visit.

"Is Chaslin Anders available?" Wilcox asked the secretary.

"Do you have an appointment?" she asked.

"No. You can let him know that Wilcox Brown and Nancy Louray are here to ask some further questions regarding our investigation," Wilcox said.

"Okay. I will let him know. It may be a while as he is currently with a client. Feel free to have a seat in our waiting area," she said.

"Thank you," Wilcox said.

They walked across the marble floor, passing the fountain. Making themselves comfortable, they sat on the couch, across the table from the client they saw when they arrived. Nancy gazed up into the high ceiling of the hall and was amazed at the interesting architecture.

A side door opened to reveal an Axynnian man. He walked over to the man who waited on the couch across from them. The Axynnian's light brown fur looked very well groomed. Wilcox and Nancy looked up at his amber eyes as he addressed the client.

"Thank you so much for waiting. If you want to follow me back, we can go over your settlement from the estate," the Axynnian man said.

The man across from them stood up and followed the Axynnian to the side door. Holding up his badge to an access control panel the Axynnian settlement agent opened the door. They went through the door and disappeared. Nancy looked around the room and focused her eyes on the blue crystal that decorated the table in front of her.

"Wilcox, this is the blue crystal we saw the last time we were here. They must have gotten this from the other side of the portal on Staraliss," Nancy said.

"They must have," he said.

She picked up the translucent blue crystal and observed its many angled surfaces. Suddenly, her finger began to tingle. She looked at the deep cut in her finger and watched as it healed completely within seconds. Her eyes became wide.

"Wilcox, my hand tingled and I just watched this blue crystal heal my finger. The blue crystals are for healing!" she said, excitedly.

Wilcox thought back to when he picked up the same crystal the last time they visited the Settlement Agency.

"You're right! After I picked it up last time, I felt tingling in my arm where I had cut it on the ship door. That explains how my arm healed so quickly."

"We know the purple crystals are for love and the blue crystals are for healing," Nancy said.

"There were also black crystals on the other side of the portal. I wonder what those do," Wilcox said.

"Good question," Nancy said. "If purple crystals are being sold on the black market, then I'm sure these blue crystals are as well."

"The fact that these crystals have specific properties is a major clue in this case," Wilcox said.

Nancy looked in awe at her healed finger and rubbed at its tingling sensation. They waited a very long time for Chaslin Anders.

"Perhaps, he doesn't want to see us," Nancy finally said.

They both looked up as the door opened to reveal Chaslin Anders. He walked past the flowing fountain of water and proceeded to the waiting area.

"Wilcox Brown… This is an unexpected visit. Is there something more that I can help you with?" Chaslin asked.

Wilcox and Nancy stood up from the couch.

"Yes. We've come to ask a few more questions regarding Coradelle Hershall's inheritance," Wilcox said.

The question seemed to throw him off a bit. He hesitated slightly before answering.

"Okay. What additional questions do you have?" Chaslin asked.

"What is your relationship with Bryson Wieler?" Wilcox asked.

Chaslin was taken aback by the question. His posture shifted slightly.

"Bryson Wieler is a real estate agent who does business with the Settlement Agency on occasion when he is selling estates. What does that have to do with Coradelle Hershall?" Chaslin asked.

"Bryson was the real estate agent who sold Coradelle's father, Robert Hershall, the planet Staraliss. You know, the planet with the missing deed that was supposed to be part of my client's inheritance? I've been to Staraliss… Or should I say Shext? I know that is where you are getting the crystals from through the portal. You know, the crystals like this blue one here on the table that has the power to heal…and like the purple ones that make people fall in love, which were recently sold to one of your clients on Sarloh's World? Chaslin, where has Coradelle Hershall been taken?" Wilcox asked.

"I don't know what you are talking about. This is ridiculous! I don't have to put up with your accusatory statements," he said.

Chaslin walked over to the secretary at the counter.

"Did I hit a nerve?" Wilcox asked.

"Call Security!" Chaslin told the secretary.

Wilcox and Nancy looked at each other. They both walked past the center fountain to where Chaslin stood at the counter.

"So, you call your Security Department when you can't answer our questions? That's not suspicious at all," Nancy said.

Suddenly, the side door opened and several security officers burst into the hall.

"Chaslin, you called for security. What seems to be the problem?" the lead officer asked.

"These two are harassing me. This is their second time here and they need to leave. If Quinlan was here, I'm sure he would concur," Chaslin said.

Wilcox recognized one of the security officers in the back.

"Okay. You two need to leave now. Since this is your second time doing this, you are both permanently banned from the Settlement Agency," the lead officer said.

"First of all, we did nothing wrong. We only had a few questions for Chaslin. The first time, we were helping our client Coradelle Hershall with her estate," Wilcox said.

"I do recall Coradelle," the security officer said. "She came in here and told us to fuck ourselves. Yeah, I have no doubt that you two are also causing issues. You both need to leave now. Start walking toward the door. Let's go."

The group of officers escorted Wilcox and Nancy out of the hall. Wilcox turned back and, once again, looked at the security officer that he recognized. They proceeded toward the hall exit. The security officers walked them down the corridor and all the way to the front entrance of the building. Once outside, the officers waited while the two of them boarded the *Enigma* before they returned into the building.

"Well, that went real smooth," Wilcox said.

"This is bullshit! Chaslin got all hostile because everything we said was true," Nancy said.

"I recognized one of the security officers," Wilcox said.

"Really? From where?" Nancy asked.

He is Commander Mawtesh Corbinn. He worked closely with General Victoria when they took over the alien ship investigation. Very strange..." Wilcox said.

"Why would a military commander switch careers and become a security officer? It seems like a bad career move to me," Nancy said.

"I don't think he would, especially as high-ranking as he was. I am going to contact Victoria. We need some answers," Wilcox said.

Chapter Fourteen

"What do you mean, there was nothing wrong with him?" Victoria asked the medical examiner.

"There was absolutely nothing wrong with the man," the medical examiner repeated.

"Okay. Thank you," Victoria said, ending the communication.

"Nothing wrong with whom?" Versill asked.

"Apparently, your black crystals kill and leave no trace of anything wrong with the victim," Victoria said.

"Interesting… Us Sharrixians can touch the blue, purple, and black crystals without them having any effect on us. We use them for decorations, mostly in buildings," Versill said.

"So, they affect humans, but not Sharrixians… I wonder what the blue and purple crystals do," Victoria said.

"Good question," Versill said.

"I wonder if any of the crystals affect Axynnians," Victoria said.

They sat in a mess hall within the military base on Anneriss. Agent Marshall walked in and handed Victoria a report.

"This is a report from Commander Mawtesh Corbinn that just

came in," Marshall said.

Victoria read the report and looked at Marshall.

"So, Wilcox Brown has been banned from the Settlement Agency. Apparently, Mawtesh thinks Wilcox recognized him from the alien ship investigation. I'm glad Wilcox didn't blow his cover," Victoria said.

"The alien ship you speak of is ours. It's called the *Credence.* Where exactly is the ship?" Versill asked.

"It currently resides in one of our shipyards, located in the Celtarenia Star System. When the investigation concludes, we plan to return it to your people. The skeletons that were on board have been respectfully preserved and will also be returned," Victoria said.

"Thank you," Versill said.

"Thank you for the report, Marshall," Victoria said.

"Yes, ma'am," Marshall said, leaving the mess hall.

"Are you sure you're okay with attending the commander meeting with me?" Victoria asked.

"Yes. I'm sure they will have questions for me. I really don't want to come across looking like a traitor to my people. I'm on a special mission. High Commander Novish Shirom really doesn't want war. He believes in you and trusts in your ability to wrap up this investigation. I do not understand why Queen Empress Aminarra is pushing this so hard now…especially when you are so close to a resolution," Versill said.

"I don't think you will come off looking that way in the meeting. If any of the commanders get out of line, I will straighten that shit out immediately," Victoria said.

"Thank you," Versill said.

Military personnel were left to manage the base on Anneriss, while General Victoria Ediira and Versill left on a military shuttle for the planet Sharmyra. The shuttle was piloted by two officers. Victoria and Versill sat in the back of the shuttle. The trip was quick. Before long, they found themselves going through Sharmyra's security clearance protocols and landing in a large docking bay. Soon, the shuttle's airlock door opened and a set of three steps automatically lowered downward to the concrete floor.

"Welcome to the Marrithious Government's military public

relations headquarters and administrative offices. Are you ready for this?" Victoria asked.

"I sure hope so," Versill said.

As they exited the shuttle, Versill had to duck way down to avoid hitting the doorway. They proceeded along a sidewalk toward the building entrance. Behind them, the shuttle steps retracted and it lifted from the concrete surface, exiting the docking bay. After passing through the glass doors, they continued down a brightly-lit corridor. Versill was careful with her height clearance at every junction. As other personnel passed them in the corridor, Versill received many surprised looks. They passed two maintenance robots that were repairing a section of lighting in the ceiling of the corridor. Versill looked at the robots with curiosity.

"We can take the stairs because you are too tall for the elevator," Victoria said.

She led Versill through a doorway and into the stairwell. Once again, Versill ducked through the doorway. They proceeded up the stairs to the fifth level before exiting the stairwell. After several other turns along a corridor, Victoria came to a stop in front of a closed door. She looked up at Versill.

"Here we go," Victoria said.

She opened the door. Beyond, was a large conference room with a long, oval table in the center. Several commanders sat at the table in their military uniforms. They looked up as Versill ducked through the doorway and walked in with General Victoria Ediira.

"Ladies and gentlemen, I present to you Versill. She is a Sharrixian special operations military officer from the planet Lairdain Tannis. She will be joining us in this meeting," Victoria said.

They walked over to two open chairs and sat down. Versill found the leg height of the table a bit difficult to get comfortable, so she moved her chair backward slightly. A barrage of greetings came from commanders, welcoming her to the meeting.

"Thank you all," Versill said.

"I called this special meeting of commanders because of the message that Versill brings. She was sent on a special mission through the portal as an envoy by the Sharrixian high commander, Novish Shirom, to contact me directly. Novish is the Sharrixian that we've been in contact with regarding our investigation into the murders of their people and the alien ship that was discovered.

"The message she brings is grim. Unlike our leader, Essir Phensaa, who is voted into power, the Sharrixians are ruled by the queen empress of a monarch. Unfortunately, their queen empress has run out of patience with our investigation. They have assembled a fleet of battleships and fighter ships at Rafith Astonn, a planet at the half-way point in the Marrithious Galaxy between our two civilizations. That is actually the planet where Versill and I first met. Their fleet awaits the order of their queen empress to launch an assault against us. High Commander Shirom wants us to complete our investigation and bring justice for their murdered people. However, Novish must listen to their queen empress once she gives the order. He sent Versill to urge us to expedite the investigation and try to avoid a war," Victoria said.

"This is actually going to make it more difficult to focus on the investigation when we need to shift our resources into a defense position," Commander Ashten said.

Commander Ashten was an older man with whitish-gray hair that was parted on his right side. One longer strand of gray hair hung lower along his forehead.

"I understand. I agree that we need to take immediate measures for a defense position and stand at high alert. But I will also continue with this investigation because we are so close to finding out who is behind this," Victoria said.

"It's basically a race between completing the investigation and their queen empress's command," Commander Stone said.

"If I may speak… Our Queen Empress Aminarra Vistona, who has ruled Lairdain Tannis since before I was born, is very strong-willed. Yet she has let the Sharrixian Council—which she has full control over—coerce her into a war declaration. It seems strange to both High Commander Shirom and myself. The closer you get to bringing justice to those involved with the murder of our people, the less patience Queen Empress Aminarra and the council have. I apologize for this pressing news. There are some of us Sharrixians who have more patience. Apparently, Queen Empress Aminarra is not one of them. Also, she now has open communications with the fleet. So, anyone contacting High Commander Shirom will be monitored by the queen empress," Versill said.

"So, this portal that Versill was sent through is the portal that High Commander Novish Shirom has communicated to you about when you first contacted him?" Commander Aolliam asked.

"Yes, it is. We were trying to find its location for the longest time. I was really close to finding out from Wilcox Brown, but he has yet to disclose that information to me. Fortunately, Versill here has been through the portal and has now revealed that it is located on the planet Shext. Commander Stone and Commander Aolliam, I want a military crew sent there immediately to guard the portal and prevent anyone from going through to get more crystals.

"Speaking of Wilcox Brown…I have decided to take Commander Ashten's advice and bring his agency on board with us, instead of us doing this investigation independently. That may help expedite things.

"As far as the high alert and defensive positions go, I want those done immediately as well. Commander Ashten, contact all of our bases and outposts and put them on high alert…and contact our leader, Essir Phensaa, on Ovlarr to give him the news. As the Marrithious Government leader, it will be his decision to make a public announcement or not. But we must protect Ovlarr, as it is the seat of the Marrithious Government. Let Essir Phensaa know that we can inform him if and when battleships do approach before he makes any announcement. I would hate for him to make the announcement that will cause prejudices against the Sharrixians, when the war may not happen. Commander Morphus, be sure our battleships and Angel Wing fighter ships are prepared for an assault. Let's hope and pray that we conclude the investigation first," Victoria said.

"And what will become of Versill?" Commander Ashten asked.

"She has offered to stay and help me with the investigation, but she is free to go home at any time," Victoria said.

"Understood," Ashten said.

"Commander Stone and Commander Aolliam, have either of you had any progress at locating Coradelle Hershall?" Victoria asked.

"I'm afraid not," Stone said.

"Well, let's focus on guarding Shext at this point. You can assign another commander to Shext once an outpost is set up there," Victoria said.

"Yes, ma'am," Aolliam said.

"Okay, we are finished with the meeting. Godspeed, Commanders. Keep me posted on any updates," Victoria said.

Each of them stood from their chairs and said a few kind words to General Ediira and Versill before leaving the conference room. Once everyone had exited, Victoria looked at Versill.

"That wasn't so bad for you, was it?" Victoria asked.

"No, it went better than I expected. Thank you," Versill said.

Victoria called for the shuttle to return as they left the conference room. Immediately after she ended the connection with the shuttle pilot, her comm went off. She looked at the device.

"Wilcox Brown, how ironic that you are contacting me. I was just about to contact you," Victoria said.

"Hi, Victoria. Nancy and I are not getting anywhere with this investigation about the missing deed. When I saw Commander Mawtesh Corbinn as a security officer at the Settlement Agency, I wanted to contact you because he was very much a part of the alien ship investigation years ago. Why is he at the Settlement Agency?" Wilcox asked.

"Actually, I can now fill you in on everything. So, I need you to meet with me at our base on Anneriss…you know, the one you've been to before," Victoria said.

"We just left Anneriss, but I will turn around and head back there. We've been permanently banned from the Settlement Agency," Wilcox said.

"So I've heard… See you soon," Victoria said.

Victoria and Versill continued walking through the corridors and down the stairwell to the front entrance. The shuttle was waiting for them.

"Who is Wilcox Brown?" Versill asked.

Victoria smiled.

Wilcox turned the *Enigma* around and returned to Anneriss.

"Exactly when were you on Anneriss before?" Nancy asked.

"I went there to ask her if I could get more information about the alien ship we discovered sixteen years ago. She wanted me to tell her what planet the portal is on, but I didn't tell her, because she wouldn't tell me any more information about why I need to watch my back," Wilcox said.

"Do you have feelings for Victoria?" Nancy asked.

"Ah…not exactly. I mean, we had sex, but there are no feelings between us. It's not like this was the first time we were together. We connected on multiple occasions over the years. It was only sex. We're not in love with each other. She's just an old friend," Wilcox said.

"With benefits, apparently," Nancy said.

"Are you jealous?"

"Damn it, Wilcox, yes, I am!"

Nancy stood from the seat next to Wilcox and stormed off toward the lounge. Wilcox checked the ship's heading and stood up to follow Nancy to the ship's lounge area. She was sitting on the bench with her arms crossed.

"Nancy, there is no need to be jealous. We don't need to quarrel over this nor put a strain on our investigation," Wilcox said.

"I've tried on multiple occasions to tell you how I feel about you. The kiss at the portal really just confirmed my feelings. It's none of my business who you've been with, but please, please, just acknowledge me. I've tried dating other people. I have feelings for *you*, Wilcox. If you can't at least discuss it with me, then perhaps I should find another job. I'm really sick and tired of being marginalized," Nancy said.

"Wow… I'm a bit shocked. I remember you mentioned something before about your feelings, but I've been trying to focus on this investigation," Wilcox said.

"Except when you wanted to fuck Victoria…then you had time to focus."

Wilcox breathed deeply. "I don't want to lose you as an employee. I will talk to you about this in depth after we solve this mystery."

Nancy looked at Wilcox for a long moment. "You have a deal."

Novish Shirom walked along an empty corridor aboard the *Credence Revenge*. At a corridor intersection, he turned right, opened a panel, and entered into a narrow service aisle. He put the panel back into place behind him. Through the grated, metal flooring, he could see countless conduit channels running along parallel with the aisle. The aisle jogged to the left and ended at a narrow, grated, metal stairway that led to an upper level. Novish proceeded up the stairs to a catwalk that ran along a large section of the ship's communications system. Since the *Credence Revenge* was the lead battleship in the fleet, it was modified with the open communications module. He stopped and read the numbers on the panel to his left. Opening the panel revealed a complex group of cables and circuit boards. Novish located a blue wire harness and followed it to a small, black box mounted to the inside wall of the panel. He reached into his pocket and retrieved an even smaller, gray box that had a short cable connected to it. Novish set the small, gray box next to the black box inside the panel. He unplugged the blue wire harness from the black box, plugged it into the gray box, and plugged the short cable from the gray box into the black box.

Now, I can remotely disconnect the fleet's open communications with Queen Empress Aminarra. The humans need more time," Novish thought.

The *Enigma* landed in the docking bay of the military base on Anneriss. Wilcox and Nancy exited the ship and began to walk across the docking bay when they both stopped in their tracks at the sight of the tall alien who towered over Victoria. After a moment, Wilcox and Nancy continued forward toward them.

"Wilcox Brown, this is Versill. She is a Sharrixian special operations military officer from Lairdain Tannis on the other side of the galaxy," Victoria said.

Seeing one of the Sharrixians alive was fascinating. To Wilcox, Versill's patterned skin looked mottled, almost camouflage. He reached out to shake her hand.

"Nice to meet you, Versill. Victoria and Versill, this is Nancy Louray, my investigative assistant in solving mysteries. She's been with my agency for many years now. So, this is quite a surprise seeing a species that I'm not familiar with," Wilcox said.

"I get that a lot on this side of the Marrithious Galaxy," Versill said.

Nancy also shook Versill's hand.

"So, you are the same species of the skeletons that we found by the portal and also the ones from the ship?" Nancy asked.

"Yes. Those were all Sharrixians," Versill said.

"Let's head to our make-shift conference room and have a discussion," Victoria said.

They all followed Victoria out of the docking bay and down the small corridor. They passed the communications room and the mess hall before entering a small room set up with a table and several chairs.

"Have a seat," Victoria said.

She closed the door and sat down with the others.

"Wilcox, I know where the portal is now. It's on the planet Shext. Versill actually flew the fighter ship that you may have noticed in the docking bay through the portal to find me. I've been in contact with High Commander Novish Shirom of the Sharrixian military over several years during our investigation of the murdered Sharrixians that you discovered on Shext. It's very complicated and involves the portal, crystals, and the Settlement Agency. I'm divulging this information because I would like us to collaborate our investigations to expedite and resolve this as soon as possible, before..." Victoria said.

"Before?" Wilcox inquired.

"We are on the verge of war, Wilcox. Versill said they have a fleet of battleships half way here, waiting for their queen empress's command," Victoria said.

Nancy immediately recalled the vision she had regarding a war and had a grim expression on her face.

"By the way, the planet Shext was called Staraliss until someone with high authority changed the name in the galactic navigation database. That someone is most likely working at the Settlement Agency. We've learned that they are selling these crystals on the black market for a lot of credits. They have gone through the portal, gathered the crystals, and sold them over the years. That's why they changed the name of the planet. Our client's father had purchased the planet and he never received the deed for it...most likely because a portal was discovered on the planet that led to the crystals. We also know that this group has murdered our client's father, the investigator that he had hired, and probably others. In addition, they have abducted our client Coradelle Hershall," Wilcox said.

"Interesting about the planet name change. We have learned the black crystals will kill humans if we touch them and it will show no signs of anything wrong with the victim. I'm not sure what the purple and blue crystals do," Victoria said.

"Versill, you don't know what these do? Aren't they from your planet?" Nancy asked.

"The crystals do not affect us in any way. We use them for decorations in our buildings and architecture," Versill said.

"Well, the purple ones make you fall in love and the blue ones heal," Wilcox said.

"They had to have used black crystals to kill Everett Quarton, the late investigator, and also Robert Hershall, our client's father and owner of the planet Staraliss. Neither of them had anything wrong with them when they died," Nancy said.

"Yes, and this group has killed others using the black crystals. I had our military medical examiner confirm that with one of the victims. I know we have various types of different colored crystals and stones here on this side of the Marrithious Galaxy, but those are nothing like these unique crystals from Lairdain Tannis," Victoria said.

"It is strange that Staraliss is on one side of the portal and Lairdain Tannis is on the other side, yet they are across the galaxy from each other," Wilcox said.

"Yes. The portal is some type of natural phenomenon that creates a shortcut in space. We are not sure how it got there nor for how long it's been there," Versill said.

"And the skeletons you discovered on this side of the portal were Sharrixian Gatherers, who would harvest crystals on their side to be used for their building decorations. When this group of people we are investigating discovered the portal, they went through and found the crystals. There was a confrontation and the humans were chased back through the portal to this side. That is where four of the Sharrixians were killed by the humans, including High Commander Novish Shirom's uncle Riilan. A fifth Gatherer was injured, but he made it back through to tell his people what had happened. He later died of his injuries," Victoria said.

"I took a picture of Riilan's name tag while we were investigating Staraliss," Wilcox said.

"The alien ship you were investigating all those years ago was, in fact, a ship called the *Credence*. They were sent out on a mission to investigate what had happened to those Gatherers. Unfortunately, the crew had become lost and eventually died," Victoria said.

"Do you happen to know where our client Coradelle Hershall is located? She was abducted from Ryamesh," Nancy said.

"I do not know where she was taken. I had two of our commanders watching her and they screwed up and were unable to stop the abductors. And I no longer have the resources to search for her with everything going on," Victoria said.

"Since we're divulging information, who was following me?" Wilcox asked.

"We have undercover officers working inside the Settlement Agency—as you had seen with Commander Mawtesh Corbinn—and we received word that this group would be coming after you and Coradelle. That's why I said to watch your back. We also had our people watching Coradelle…and you," Victoria said.

"Well, I was being followed at one point, but I lost them. I'm not sure who it was," Wilcox said.

"That was us. You lost us. I was only trying to help protect you, Wilcox," Victoria said.

"You must really care about him," Nancy said.

Victoria looked at Nancy and then at Wilcox and opened her mouth slightly, but didn't speak. It became awkwardly silent.

"I have an idea," Versill said. "How about we focus on what's next."

"Yes, that would be great," Wilcox said.

"I have a plan that involves you—" Victoria was cut off.

"I'll bet," Nancy said.

Victoria looked at Nancy and frowned.

"She knows…" Wilcox finally said.

Victoria smiled. "Nancy, I'm not ashamed of meeting my needs, but it sounds like you care for Wilcox a lot. So, if that's the case, I certainly can meet my needs from someone else," Victoria said.

"You are correct. I do care for Wilcox a lot," Nancy said.

"Consider Wilcox and I finished with that aspect of our relationship, then," Victoria said.

Wilcox rested his hand against his forehead. "Please continue with the discussion," he said.

"I have a plan that involves you becoming a player in the military's investigation and going back to the Settlement Agency. I understand you are banned for life, but it won't matter. You will go in and make an announcement. We will be coming in right behind you with a team of officers to confront them and make arrests," Victoria said.

"Two things… First, it's not just the military's investigation, it's my agency's as well. Second, what announcement am I supposed to make?" Wilcox asked.

"We have to come up with something creative to draw all of them out into the hall. I will have Commander Mawtesh Corbinn take care of the security team so they don't become involved," Victoria said.

"Okay. So, when do we get started?" Wilcox asked.

"As soon as I confirm that Quinlan Zale and Bryson Wieler have returned. I want them and Chaslin Anders present. Hopefully, there are more of them there," Victoria said.

"We still need to know who their boss is. I mean, we have a few suspicions, but cannot prove anything," Wilcox said.

"Perhaps, when we confront them, we'll find out. I was going to wait until they led us to their boss, but time is running out, so we will just take out the lower portion of the organization and worry about the top afterward," Victoria said.

"Sounds like a plan," Wilcox said.

"If I'm not involved in this plan, perhaps I can try to locate Coradelle Hershall. No one else is doing that at this point. I'll contact her friend Alivia Bexley and see if she's heard anything," Nancy said.

"Yes, please do. We certainly don't want to forget about our client," Wilcox said.

"Do I have a role in this plan," Versill asked.

"In fact, you do. I have a great idea for your involvement," Victoria said.

Chapter Fifteen

Admiral and High Commander Novish Shirom looked across the console of the bridge on the *Credence Revenge*. Through the ship's observation window, the crest of the planet Rafith Astonn could be seen, its whitish-tan surface bright against the darkness of space.

"Sir, we have an incoming message from Queen Empress Aminarra," one of the officers at the comm said, turning around toward Novish.

"Put her through," Novish said.

I didn't have a chance to cut off the communications yet, so I hope it's not too late, Novish thought.

"This is Queen Empress Aminarra Vistona, addressing the entire fleet at Rafith Astonn. I just met with the Sharrixian Council and we can now proceed with an offensive assault against the humans *and* the Axynnians. I have made my choice to include the Axynnians as well. I will give the permission to launch the assault once I'm back at the Lythinarr Palace. From there, I will monitor the Marrithious Galactic War. Stand by until I contact you again shortly."

"This is Admiral Novish Shirom. We will be standing by to

proceed. Please keep in mind that we are experiencing some heavy communications interference from the supernova in the Pixellis System," Novish said.

The communication went silent. Novish sighed deeply and removed his hand from the remote control device in his pocket. He placed his hand over his forehead for a long moment, hoping he had made the right decision.

The officer at the console in front of Novish turned around.

"Sir, the communications are dead. How did you know...?" He trailed off and turned back toward the console, knowing not to question the admiral.

Novish stood up and left the bridge.

Nancy Louray needed a lift back to the office. She called for a shuttle and was picked up from a public area on Anneriss, some distance from the military base, and transported to Kesron. The shuttle settled on a landing pad in the city of Kethan. Nancy paid the pilot credits due and walked toward the office. When she arrived at the door to unlock it, she noticed a note shoved into the side of the door. She pulled it free while unlocking the door. After entering the office, Nancy closed the door, the bells jingling. She read the note as she walked to her desk. It was a request to hire the Wilcox Brown Agency to solve another mystery.

Well, they're just gonna have to wait, she thought.

Nancy set the note on the middle of Wilcox's desk and noticed the office needed a good cleaning. Grabbing a dust rag from the back closet, she began to clear the dust from the desks and cabinets. Nancy grabbed a broom and swept the floor, putting the particles into a dust pan. Afterward, she inspected the ceiling for cobwebs and only found one. Reaching up with the broom, she removed it and put the cleaning items back into the closet. Stopping in her tracks, she noticed that some things were out of place in the office. She quickly opened her desk drawer, moved some items, and checked to see if her laser pistol was still there.

Good, she thought.

Nancy grabbed the small laser pistol and put it into her pocket. She stood up and looked around. Walking to the back of the office, she noticed several filing cabinets were open. Apparently, someone had been looking through them. Nothing seemed to be missing. Nancy walked past the bathroom and down a narrow hallway to a small back window. Sure enough, someone had pushed the window up from the outside and entered. There was no broken glass, but the lock was bent and needed to be replaced. She closed the window and walked back to her desk. Sitting down, Nancy grabbed her comm.

"Wilcox, this is Nancy. Someone broke into our office. It appears that nothing was taken. They looked through some files, but probably gave up because they couldn't understand our scrambled filing system. The lock on the back window needs to be fixed."

"Okay. I'll fix it when I return to Kesron. Let me know if Alivia Bexley has heard anything about Coradelle. We'll be planning our strategy for the Settlement Agency," Wilcox said.

"Okay. Be safe," Nancy said.

"You too, Nancy. I'll keep you posted," Wilcox said.

Nancy ended the communication, made herself a cup of coffee, and sat at her desk for a long time just staring at the dark computer display. The coffee was delicious. She knew Alivia Bexley would not have an update on Coradelle. Nancy never intended to contact her in the first place. Instead, she was thinking about the white container with the circular, blue logo on it that she had seen in Timber Wolf on Ryamesh. The logo matched the one from her vision of Coradelle running from someone. The shuttle driver had said that some of the containers were shipping to Noderell. Wilcox said the planet was filled with warehouses and that it would be a dead end. Nancy disagreed.

She closed her eyes and began to pray to God for help. Nancy prayed for Coradelle's safety and that she would be able to find her. She also prayed for her own safety and that of Wilcox. Nancy continued to pray that the vision of war she had seen would not come to pass. She was very faithful in her prayers and trusted in God.

Even if Wilcox seemed to think it was a waste of time, Nancy knew what she had to do. She stood up from the desk, finished her coffee, turned off the coffee pot, and headed for the office door. Nancy adjusted the laser pistol in her pocket as she closed and locked the door. Walking around the block to the landing pad, she climbed aboard *Nellie* and engaged the engines. After enabling the anti-gravitational units, she lifted the ship above the city of Kethan and toward the white clouds. Once she was above Kesron, Nancy set a course in the navigation system to the planet Noderell and engaged the lightspeed-plus engines.

Upon reaching Noderell, *Nellie* automatically exited lightspeed-plus and drifted toward the planet. Nancy switched to manual control when she noticed many different space freighters in the shipping lanes above the planet. Most of the freighters rivaled the size of a battleship. She gazed at all the intricate details along their hulls, each a slightly different shade of gray. Through one of the docking bay openings, Nancy caught a glimpse of a few light gray containers stacked high in the bay. She assumed they were all waiting in line to load or unload via the cargo shuttles that could be seen flying between the large ships. Nancy maneuvered *Nellie* away from the shipping lanes to a different trajectory and descended through the atmosphere of Noderell. When the misty, white clouds parted, Nancy saw countless warehouses that extended all the way to the horizon. Against the bright blue sky, several cargo shuttles could be seen ascending and descending from various warehouses.

Wilcox was right. This is going to be near impossible without exact coordinates, Nancy thought.

She was not going to give up that easy. Nancy flew *Nellie* lower and looked for a white building, like in her vision. She knew it shouldn't be that difficult because most of the buildings were yellow, blue, and gray. A white building should be easy to spot from her vantage point. Nancy continued to fly back and forth, her eyes carefully scanning the myriad of buildings in the distance. She was careful to avoid any cargo shuttle that crossed her path. On occasion, she would spot a white building and looked for the circular, blue logo from her vision.

So far, none of the white buildings have the logo on them, Nancy thought.

She continued to fly along the countless warehouses for hours and started to get very tired. Ready to give up, Nancy turned *Nellie* around for one more pass along a group of warehouses that ran near the edge of a large forest area. As she flew along the edge of the forest, she saw another white building ahead of her. To her amazement, she saw the circular, blue logo on the side of the building and gasped.

"Holy shit! I found it," she said to herself.

There was another ship parked at the landing pad near a set of front offices. Nancy flew toward the rear of the building and gently landed

Nellie near some truck docks. There were no semis parked there at that moment. She disabled the ship's engines and exited.

Nancy squinted at the bright sunlight. Looking at the side of the building, she recalled her vision of the logo and seeing Coradelle running. Removing the laser pistol from her pocket, she carefully walked along the grass near the building's foundation. Beyond the truck docks, a set of steps led up to an entrance door. Holding the laser pistol in her right hand, she grabbed the yellow railing with her left hand and quickly ran up the steps to the entry door. It was locked and required a code on a keypad. Nancy aimed the laser pistol at the control panel and fired. An intense blue beam destroyed the panel. She tried the door. It still would not open. Nancy shot the locking mechanism on the door itself twice, sending a shower of sparks back at her. She quickly shielded her face. The door became ajar. Nancy opened it and stepped inside the warehouse. Adjusting her eyes to the dimmer lighting, she peered down the long aisles at the extensive rack system.

"Where are they keeping you, Coradelle?" Nancy whispered to herself.

Nancy didn't see anyone in the warehouse, which she thought was unusual. Of course, if it was being used by a group of criminals, she didn't expect to see normal warehouse activity. As she made her way along the aisle, she kept ducking underneath the racks to keep out of sight. When she reached the end of the rack at an intersection, she carefully peered around the corner. Turning left, she entered into a cross aisle. From there, she was able to see in both directions down the full length of the longer, perpendicular aisles. Nancy slowly made her way down the cross aisle as she looked up at the tall racks. Most of them were full of pallets that had silver, metal crates on them. However, there was an occasional silver crate with a red lid, located randomly in higher bays of various racks. She wondered what product was inside the crates. Ducking underneath one of the racks and into its bay, she crouched down next to a silver, metal crate and put her laser pistol back into her pocket. She carefully removed the crate's lid. To her surprise, it was empty. Nancy checked several other silver crates and all of them were empty. She stepped back out into the aisle and continued walking. Eventually, Nancy came to the end of the cross aisle where it stopped at another longer, perpendicular aisle. Half way down the long aisle, Nancy spotted one of the silver crates with a red lid, located up on the third shelf of the rack to her right. She carefully climbed up the rack, gripping its metal column. Nancy placed her footing carefully along the beam and grabbed the column on the next level. When she finally reached the bay containing the silver crate with the red lid, she crouched down and rested for a moment.

Usually, I'm *the one telling people to be careful and not do stupid things,* she thought.

She looked down at the red lid and noticed a set of numbers printed along the edge. Nancy removed the lid and gasped.

Holy shit!

The metal crate was filled with blue crystals, just like the one on the table at the Settlement Agency and like she had seen on the other side of the portal. She quietly returned the lid and looked across the warehouse to see if she could spot any more of the crates with red lids. She had already seen several of them along the way. Another one was located across and down the aisle quite a ways. They were always located on an upper rack. She leaned over and opened the lid to a plain silver crate in the bay next to her, just to confirm her suspicions. It was empty.

Well, this is interesting, Nancy thought.

Nancy climbed up one more level of the rack to the top so she could get a better view of the warehouse. From that vantage point, she was able to see several yellow forklifts parked to one side. Against a far wall, she spotted a few of the same white containers with the circular, blue logo on them that she had seen in the town of Timber Wolf.

I wonder if Maxboro Lawson has anything to do with Coradelle's abduction. Why would one of the containers from this company's warehouse be in Timber Wolf? she thought.

Nancy noticed a storage room and some offices in the far distance. She carefully climbed back down to continue her search for Coradelle. Once Nancy reached the floor, she saw a man in the distance of the aisle. He didn't notice her. She quickly ran to the next cross aisle and turned a corner, running straight into another man who was walking through.

"Well, what do we have here?"

"Hi. I think I might have the wrong warehouse. I'm looking for ship service parts," she said.

"You are trespassing on private property. How did you get in here?"

"The door—"

"It doesn't matter. This is a highly confidential operation and now you cannot leave," he said.

"Say! Don't you talk to me that way," Nancy said.

She took her comm and began to contact Wilcox. The man knocked it out of her hand and it slid across the concrete floor, breaking apart. He grabbed her arm and she struggled to break free, but he was able to zip tie her hands together.

"Stop it. What are you doing?" Nancy asked.

He pulled her along the aisle toward the other man, who turned around when he heard the commotion.

"We have ourselves a trespasser," the man said as he pushed Nancy along.

"Interesting… Well, we have just the spot for her," the other man said, reaching into his pocket for a set of keys.

Nancy was led to the small storage room. The second man unlocked the door, cut the zip tie, and shoved Nancy inside. She could hear him locking the door behind her. It was much darker inside the storage room, but there was some light coming from underneath the door. She saw Coradelle sleeping on a cot. Nothing else was in the room. Nancy walked over to the cot and kneeled down on the floor next to Coradelle. Suddenly, Coradelle awoke and gasped. Nancy held her finger up to her mouth for Coradelle to be quiet. Although the men walked away, Nancy didn't want them coming back any time soon.

"Nancy!" Coradelle whispered.

She sat up on the cot and gave Nancy a hug.

"I found you. They think I just wandered into the wrong warehouse," Nancy said.

"How did you find me?" Coradelle asked.

She started crying and hugged Nancy once again.

"It's a long story. I'll have to explain it in greater detail some other time, but I have visions. That is how I found you," Nancy said.

"I heard those men talking. They killed my dad with black crystals. And I heard them say they are waiting for some black crystals to arrive here to kill me with them. I'm scared, Nancy," Coradelle said in a low tone.

Coradelle brushed the tears away from her eyes and looked at Nancy.

"Don't you worry, Coradelle. We're not going to stay in here,"

Nancy said.

She pulled the laser pistol from her pocket and showed Coradelle. With a fresh glimpse of hope, Coradelle smiled.

"One of the—"

"Shhh," Nancy whispered. "I hear them talking. Listen."

There was a faint mumbling between three different men. It sounded like one of them had just arrived back to the warehouse. Two of the voices got louder.

"And now we have to deal with some woman that wondered in here," one of the men said.

"That's unfortunate for her. I've retuned with the black crystals from the container on Ryamesh. These should take care of our guests. Let's go to the storage room and get this over with," the man said.

Nancy and Coradelle saw the shadows of the two men blocking the light that emitted from underneath the door. Nancy aimed her laser pistol at the door. One of the two men unlocked the door and opened it. He jumped back in surprise when he saw the laser pistol pointed at them. The other man was standing next to him with black gloves on. In his gloves, he held a cloth that contained the black crystals. Neither of them had time to react. She fired the laser pistol. A Blue beam of intense light sliced through the upper torso of the man holding the crystals, immediately killing him. He slumped over and slammed hard against the metal door. As he hit the door, the black crystals fell to the ground. The door swung back with great force and hit the other man in the head. He lost his balance and fell to the warehouse floor, landing on the black crystals. The crystals punctured through his shirt, instantly killing him.

"Come on!" Nancy said.

Nancy and Coradelle both leaped over the two bodies and out of the storage room. The third man came running after them when he heard the disturbance.

"Hey!" he shouted.

"Follow me," Nancy said to Coradelle.

Coradelle was right behind Nancy as she ran down a familiar aisle of racks. The man ran after them.

"I remember this guy. He's the one that I saw in my friend Alivia's kitchen," Coradelle said as they ran.

Nancy turned back and saw that he had drawn a weapon. He fired. A blue beam whizzed by Coradelle.

"Duck under here into an empty bay," Nancy said.

Nancy and Coradelle took shelter in the rack bay as more blue beams zipped past them in the aisle. Nancy fired back. Surprised by the return fire, the man dove for cover. It gave them the opportunity to further distance themselves from the man. As they approached the cross aisle, another shot hit an upper rack, sending a shower of sparks that rained over them. They turned left onto the cross aisle. Nancy fired back around the corner, her shot missing the man by centimeters.

"Where are we going?" Coradelle asked as they ran down the cross aisle.

"Out the back door," Nancy said.

They turned the corner to the right and onto another long aisle. Nancy recognized the racking system along the wall. It was the aisle that led to the door she came in. As they rushed toward the dock area, the man fired a barrage of blue laser beams at them. A beam slightly singed Coradelle's leg as it flew by. She ducked underneath the rack across from the truck docks. Nancy dashed behind a metal beam next to the door she had entered through. She saw Coradelle across the aisle, underneath the rack. As the man ran closer, he did not let up on the intense laser fire. The beams of energy continued to fly past them in the aisle. Nancy peeked around the corner at the man and looked up at the racks high above him. She swung around and concentrated her laser pistol on the rack above his head. It was enough energy to shower him with hot shrapnel. He ducked into the bay of a rack. It gave Coradelle enough time to run across the aisle to where Nancy was, near the entry door.

"Let's get out of here," Nancy said.

She fired around the corner a few more times and they both ran for the door. It was still ajar from earlier. Coradelle ran down the concrete steps, recognizing them from when she tried to escaped the first time. Nancy hesitated before going down the steps. She knew they would not reach *Nellie* before getting shot and killed. There was absolutely no place to take cover between the building's door and the ship. There was only one way to save their lives. She turned around and held her pistol up at the door. As soon as the man opened the door, Nancy fired. A single blue laser beam sliced through his head, melting his brain. He stood there motionless for a moment before dropping his pistol and falling forward, past Nancy, and headfirst down the concrete steps. Smoke rose up from the gaping hole in the back of his head. She

walked down the stairs and stepped over him.
"Does that hurt or is it sore?"

Chapter Sixteen

Victoria looked at Wilcox as he put the comm back into his pocket. He had tried to contact Nancy twice, but she did not answer. That wasn't like her.

"She's not answering again?" Victoria asked.

"No," he said.

"You care a lot about her, don't you?" Victoria asked.

"Hey, about earlier… I'm sorry. She—"

"She's in love with you. It was totally obvious to me. And it seems that you care a lot about her as well. Our little thing we have once in a blue moon needs to be over. You need to focus on Nancy," Victoria said.

Wilcox looked at Victoria for a long moment and sighed.

"You're right, Victoria," he said. "I just didn't want it to get in the way of our investigations."

"Only if you let it…" she said.

Wilcox stared into the distance.

"I certainly hope she's okay," Wilcox said. "I left a message on her ship's comm that we will be going to the Settlement Agency."

"Are you ready?" Victoria asked.

"I am. I have my wire attached," Wilcox said.

"Remember the plan. Our team will be close behind you, waiting for the cue," Victoria said.

A group gathered behind Victoria and Wilcox that included Versill, Commander Stone, Commander Aolliam, and Agent Marshall among others.

"Understood," Wilcox said.

Wilcox landed the *Enigma* in the docking area of the Settlement Agency. He knew the military ships would not be far behind him. As he exited the ship, he corrected himself from walking too close to the airlock door hinge again. Staring down at the sharp piece of metal, he was reminded that he still needed to have it repaired. Stepping outside, he took a deep breath and proceeded toward the glass doors. After the long trek down the corridor, Wilcox stopped in front of the black doors that led into the Settlement Agency's customer service hall. Victoria had said the security would be taken care of with the military's inside agents. He had never been banned from anywhere before, so the situation was a bit uncomfortable for him. He gathered his thoughts for a moment before entering.

"Here we go," he said to himself.

Wilcox walked into the hall. The waiting area had no clients. He immediately noticed that the blue crystal from the table was gone. He attributed that to the fact that he pointed it out to Chaslin Anders the last time he was there. The flowing water in the center fountain broke the silence of the hall. For a brief moment, Wilcox studied the fountain's sculpture of an animal jumping over the stream of flowing water. He walked over to the counter and noticed that the same secretary who had called security for Chaslin the last time he was there was once again working. He was hoping it would have been a different secretary.

Shit! he thought.

"Hi. Is Chaslin Anders available?" Wilcox asked.

When she noticed that it was Wilcox Brown, the secretary immediately called security again as well as Chaslin.

"You are banned from this Settlement Agency. I will have security escort you out again," she said.

The side door opened and Chaslin Anders walked into the hall.

"Wilcox Brown, you are not supposed to be here. You are banned from the Settlement Agency. Security will be out here in a moment to escort you off the premises. It looks like they may need to rough you up this time," Chaslin said.

Wilcox noticed Chaslin's conceited smile.

"Actually, I need to talk to you about something," Wilcox said.

"I don't want to hear anything you have to say," Chaslin said. He turned toward the secretary. "Where the hell is security?"

"I'll check," she said.

The secretary could be seen contacting a few different people.

"Chaslin, unfortunately, security is tied up at the moment with a different urgent matter and they are unavailable. I've contacted the agency director, Quinlan Zale. He will be out shortly," she said.

At that moment, the door opened to reveal several people. Among them was Quinlan Zale, Bryson Wieler, and a few others that Wilcox did not recognize. One of the men that he did not recognize wore a pair of black gloves. Quinlan walked over to where Chaslin stood.

"Security is tied up at the moment, Chaslin," Quinlan said.

"I heard," Chaslin said.

"Wilcox Brown, you have been banned from the Settlement Agency. Why are you here?" Quinlan asked.

"Well, I was trying to tell Chaslin, but he didn't want to hear anything I had to say," Wilcox said.

Quinlan folded his arms and stared at Wilcox.

"Well, we're listening. Why are you here?" Quinlan repeated.

"I was recently on Staraliss for my investigation into the missing deed and just happened to notice one of your agency's men taking crystals from the portal," Wilcox said.

Chaslin immediately unfolded his arms, turned around, and looked at Bryson Wieler. Bryson looked surprised and looked at Chaslin and the others.

"Well, don't look at me. I haven't been there recently," Bryson said.

"You know the boss has a moratorium on any more harvesting!" Quinlan said.

"I wasn't there!" Bryson said.

"Bryson, you are the one who kept talking about needing more crystals…as if the warehouse on Noderell isn't enough," Chaslin said.

"I said that the crystal inventory from twenty years ago is getting low. I didn't say that we should go against our boss," Bryson said.

"So, who was it, then?" Quinlan asked, looking at the others next to Bryson.

"Quinlan, the last time I went to Staraliss is when you wanted more black crystals to store in the container in Timber Wolf on Ryamesh. You know how I hate handling them," a woman among the group said.

"I think we need a black crystal for Wilcox here," Chaslin said.

"You mean, like you used for Everett Quarton when he was close to solving his case about you? Or like you used on Robert Hershall so he wouldn't keep asking for the deed to Staraliss that he paid Bryson for? Those black crystals? What about the aliens you killed at the portal? Your crystal avarice has caught up with you," Wilcox said.

"I wasn't going to let those aliens from the other side of the portal get in our way of making millions of credits," Chaslin said.

"Where is the deed to Staraliss?" Wilcox asked. That was the cue Victoria was waiting for.

Quinlan Zale pulled out a laser pistol and pointed it at Wilcox.

"You know too much," Quinlan said.

"Well, apparently, so does your secretary and others who actually do real work to settle estates around here. I'm surprised none of the other employees who work here haven't figured out your criminal activity within the agency yet. Or maybe they did and you killed them with your black crystals too," Wilcox said.

Overhearing the entire conversation, the secretary and an Axynnian employee quickly left their seats, disappearing into the back offices. Victoria heard enough evidence from the wire that Wilcox wore. Moments later, the hall door opened and a team of military officers swarmed in with laser rifles drawn.

"Don't move! Drop your weapon!" Commander Stone shouted.

Quinlan set the laser pistol onto the marble floor.

"Put your hands in the air!" Commander Aolliam shouted.

General Victoria Ediira stepped past the officers with Versill behind her. Victoria walked over and picked up Quinlan's laser pistol from the floor. The group from the Settlement Agency looked up at the height of Versill.

"Thank you, Wilcox. It appears that the plan worked. It caused infighting and has revealed many things to us that we have now captured on record.

"Quinlan, you and your group are responsible for murders of five

Sharrixians at the portal on Shext—Staraliss—as well as Everett Quarton, Robert Hershall, and Merritt. You are all also responsible for many other crimes, including selling the crystals on the black market, changing a planet name in the galactic navigation database, and abducting Coradelle Hershall. A Marrithious Government military trial would have been nice, but Versill here has requested something different. After speaking with our leader, Essir Phensaa, he has given me the authority to fulfill Versill's request. I hereby assign all justice for your group to the Sharrixians. I'll let Versill give you the details," Victoria said.

Victoria handed Quinlan's laser pistol to one of the officers behind her. Versill stepped forward, towering over them, and they recoiled in fear. From the uneven bumps on her head to the light orange, beige, green, and black patterned skin, they were certainly shocked to see an alien that was alive on their side of the portal.

"My people have been waiting for justice for twenty years. You don't realize what you've done. Our queen empress ran out of patience and has declared war on the humans because of what your group has done to our people at the portal. There are four battleships waiting for the queen empress's orders to launch an assault. After discussing justice with General Ediira here, it has been determined that your group will stand trial in a Sharrixian court. That is not going to end well for any of you," Versill said.

The man who wore the black pair of gloves tossed a black crystal at Versill. It hit her in the arm and fell to the marble floor, rolling across the black and white tiles. She looked at the man and then reached down with her bare hand and picked the black crystal up from the marble floor. She walked over to the man who threw it and held it up to his face. He recoiled backwards.

"Black crystals cause humans to die, but they have no affect on us Sharrixians, nor do the purple or blue crystals. It was a nice try, however," she said, putting the black crystal into her pocket.

"The others in your organization, including your boss, will soon be brought to justice as well," Victoria said.

"That's funny. So, you lied about one of us getting more crystals from Staraliss? You are also lying about this queen empress declaring war," Chaslin said.

"Is that so?" Versill asked.

Suddenly, Bryson Wieler leaped over the counter at the rectangular wall opening, where the secretary had sat, and he ran into the back offices, disappearing from sight. Commander Stone fired a burst of blue beams from his laser rifle at the counter. The charred holes emitted a few glowing embers that quickly faded, smoke rising up from them.

"Restrain them," Commander Stone said.

Several military officers walked over and put handcuffs on all of them.

"You are all under military arrest," Victoria said.

Abruptly, Nancy and Coradelle ran through the door and stopped when they saw the military officers with their weapons drawn. The criminal group acted surprised to see Coradelle alive.

"Wilcox, I got the message you left me on my ship's comm. My mobile comm was destroyed in a warehouse on Noderell. So, this is the group responsible for all the bullshit?" Nancy asked. She gazed upon them with shame and contempt.

"Yes, except for their boss and Bryson Wieler—who just conveniently escaped—and a few other stragglers. We also have their security officers rounded up," Wilcox said.

"Well, there are three dead stragglers at your warehouse on Noderell. They planned to kill Coradelle and I with black crystals, so I had no choice but use self defense," Nancy said, addressing the group.

"I was worried about you, Nancy," Wilcox said.

She looked at Wilcox and smiled.

"If you'll excuse me, Victoria, I need to contact Novish Shirom immediately regarding this situation," Versill said.

She walked outside the hall and into the corridor with her comm in hand.

"Admiral Shirom, this is Versill. Open communications or not, I have news," she said.

"Hi, Versill. At the moment, the open communications have been disabled. Queen Empress Aminarra was going to go back to Lythinarr Palace and give the order from the comfort of her own home, so I had to do what I had to do by temporarily circumventing open communications. What news do you have?" Novish asked.

"We have captured the bulk of their crystal harvesting operation. These are the humans who are responsible for murdering the

Gatherers, including your uncle Riilan," Versill said.

"Good. So, you stayed?" Novish asked.

"Yes. I was just trying to help in their investigation. One of the men from this group escaped, but that was the military's plan. He should lead them right to his boss. I plan to bring these people back to Lairdain Tannis to stand trial in a Sharrixian court," Versill said.

"That should be interesting," Novish said. "Listen, Versill, I'm not sure how long I can use the supernova at Pixellis as an excuse for the open communications issue. At some point, I'm going to have to turn it back on. When I do, I will need you here with your prisoners who are responsible for the deaths of our Gatherers. How close are you to achieving that?"

"I can leave soon with everyone except their boss and a man named Bryson Wieler. There may be a few other, less significant, people involved, but they are not big players in this and did not murder our Gatherers. The people who have been arrested will have to suffice for now," Versill said.

"Sounds like a plan. Why don't we meet here at Rafith Astonn?" Novish asked

"Yes, sir."

"How do you suppose you will transport your prisoners in a Stormrider fighter ship?" Novish asked.

"I'll be flying the *Credence*, sir."

Chapter Seventeen

The prisoners were transferred to the military base, some distance from from the Settlement Agency. They were to be temporarily held until the *Credence* could be prepared for transport across the galaxy.

General Victoria Ediira, Commander Ashten, and Versill stepped aboard a shuttle in the docking bay at the military base on Anneriss. They each settled into the back of the shuttle and fastened their seat belts. Soon, the pilot closed the airlock door and slowly exited the docking bay.

"I appreciate you taking me to the *Credence*," Versill said.

"No problem. Let's hope the engines still fire. It's been in the shipyard for approximately sixteen years and hasn't operated for close to twenty," Victoria said.

"I'm not sure about Sharrixian technology, but if our battleships sit for long periods of time, it generally has no impact on the engines firing," Ashten said.

"I'm sure it will be fine," Versill said. "I've only piloted a ship that size in training years ago. Large scout ships are usually manned by a small crew, like the crew you found aboard the ship when you first discovered it. But I think I can manage. I may need to run back and forth between the bridge and the engine area in certain circumstances. The auxiliary power should still be working with the ship off, like the air system, the docking bay entrance airlock field, artificial gravitation, and low-level lighting."

"The shuttle will land in the docking bay of the *Credence* when we arrive at the shipyard. Once we're there, we will load the preserved Sharrixian skeletons of the original crew back on board the *Credence*. They are currently being stored in a climate-controlled environment on the planet Celtarenia. They deserve a proper burial on Lairdain Tannis. Commander Ashten, our shuttle pilot, Tauren, and I will stay aboard the *Credence* to help you with what we can as you fly it back to Anneriss. Once we're back, you can retrieve your Stormrider from the base. We will have a modern nav system installed on the *Credence*. Also, we will load the prisoners aboard for your return trip to Lairdain Tannis so they can stand trial. I would like to be informed when the trial occurs so that I can be present for it," Victoria said.

"Thank you for your help. At some point, my people will need to retrieve the skeletons on Shext—Staraliss—as well. However, we can do that from our side of the portal, if need be. Right now, I'm in a time crunch to avoid war. As with all of our large ships, I'm certain that there is a brig on the ship where we can place the prisoners. It is usually on level two, near the docking bay," Versill said.

"I expect the shuttle with the skeletal remains of the original crew to arrive on the *Credence* approximately the same time as us," Victoria said.

Silence filled the shuttle as they flew along through the darkness of space toward the Celtarenia Star System. Versill closed her eyes for a long moment, mentally exhausted from her special mission. She had been so anxious about getting back in time before Queen Empress Aminarra was able to contact Novish that she felt physically drained. She fell asleep.

"Versill! Versill, we're here," Victoria said.

Versill opened her greenish-gray eyes and focused on Victoria and Ashten.

"Sorry. I must have been tired."

Versill unfastened her seat belt and joined Victoria and Ashten, who already stood in the aisle of the shuttle. Crouching down to avoid hitting the ceiling, she exited the shuttle after them and stepped into the docking bay of the *Credence.* Versill looked around at the dim docking bay and over toward the far wall. The shuttle lights shined onto the metal floor of the dark docking bay, revealing designated parking areas that were indicated with yellow tape.

"When I first saw this ship, I thought the rounded edges were quite an interesting design," Victoria said.

"I agree. They don't design large scout ships like this anymore. Excuse me a moment, I'm going to go enable the full docking bay lighting just over there by the wall," Versill said.

Versill walked in the dim light toward the far wall of the docking bay. Opening a panel, she flicked several breakers to enable the full docking bay lighting. Squinting at the change in brightness, Victoria looked around the docking bay and up high at the metal beams above. Victoria reached for her comm.

"This is General Ediira. How far out are you with the Sharrixian remains?"

"Actually, we are coming around the starboard side of the *Credence* now," the pilot said.

"Roger that," Victoria said.

Moments later, a second shuttle came through the docking bay airlock field, a blue static appearing around the ship's hull as it passed through. The sight of the blue field reminded Versill of her experience going through the portal with the Stormrider fighter ship. The second shuttle settled into one of the designated parking areas. The pilot, Tauren, exited the first shuttle and stood next to Victoria, Ashten, and Versill as they watched the second shuttle's airlock door open. An officer exited the second shuttle, went down a ramp, and walked over to Victoria and the others.

"General Ediira… Commander Ashten… And you must be Versill," the officer said, looking up at the tall alien woman.

"That, I am," Versill said.

"It's nice to meet you. We have the preserved remains of the original Sharrixian crew from this ship aboard the shuttle and ready to transfer to the *Credence*," the officer said.

"Your timing was perfect," Victoria said.

Two additional, younger officers appeared in the doorway of the shuttle. A young male officer and a young female officer moved a hovering, silver preservation chamber down the ramp, maneuvering it into the docking bay by its metal handles on either end. The anti-gravitational preservation chamber was air sealed and had a curved window on its front top portion. The officers moved it to one side and went back up the ramp to retrieve more. Versill walked over and looked into the chamber. Seeing the skeletal remains, a feeling of great sympathy flooded her emotions. The others joined her next to the chamber.

"They died of starvation?" Versill asked.

"We presume that is the case. When the *Credence* became lost and they could not communicate back to Lairdain Tannis, the ship records show that they had sent a distress signal out. The crew drifted until they ran out of supplies. Originally, Wilcox Brown, who you've recently met, was hired by the old Space Agency to take on this case. I was put in charge by our military to take over his investigation. I was a commander back then. Our team tested this distress signal and found that it was not a type that we would have picked up on our scanning systems. We have since modified our systems to pick up such signals," Victoria said.

"We did not receive the signal either. There may have been galactic interference. I know you've had issues with that when trying to contact High Commander Shirom," Versill said.

The two young officers moved a second silver chamber down the ramp and positioned it next to the first one. They disappeared back up the ramp and into the shuttle. After a third and fourth chamber were lined up next to the first two, the two younger officers returned to the shuttle.

"Thank you for delivering the remains," Victoria said to the older officer.

"You're welcome, General Ediira," the older officer said, returning to the shuttle.

Once the airlock door closed, the shuttle maneuvered around toward the exit and flew from the *Credence*.

"We respectfully preserved the skeletal remains all these years and I'm happy they can finally be returned home," Victoria said.

"I am honored by the care that you've taken for both the crew and the ship. If you all can help me maneuver these preservation chambers over to the storage facility off from the docking bay, I would appreciate it," Versill said.

"Yeah. Lead the way," Victoria said.

Versill grabbed the metal handle at the head of the first preservation chamber and Victoria walked over and grabbed the handle at the foot of it. Commander Ashten and the shuttle pilot, Tauren, took the second preservation chamber and followed Versill and Victoria. The four of them moved the hovering chambers across the smooth, metal docking bay floor toward the back wall. Versill opened a large door that led to a storage facility. The room was fairly large with cluttered shelves on the left and old equipment on the right.

"This will be fine for the trip back to Lairdain Tannis," Versill said.

They moved the chambers into the storage facility and went back to retrieve the other two chambers. Once all four were moved into the storage facility, Victoria opened a panel on each of the preservation chambers and adjusted the anti-gravitational modules to disable transport mode. Versill made a mental note on how to re-enable the modules for their arrival across the galaxy. Versill closed the door to the storage facility and sighed.

"Perhaps you will return a hero," Victoria said.

"We'll see. Now, let's head to the bridge and see if I can get the engines started," Versill said.

They followed Versill up a yellow, metal stairway to the docking bay's second level. From there, they went through an automatic door, which struggled to open, and they entered a long, dim corridor. Tauren was amazed at the height of the doors on the ship that accommodated the Sharrixians. Victoria had seen it all sixteen years before, so the doors were nothing new for her. Ashten had also seen the ship when it was first docked in the shipyard at Celtarenia.

"The air quality in here has been reduced significantly," Ashten said.

"Once I'm on the bridge, I should be able to restore full power to the ship. That should fix this stale air that was created from the ship being in auxiliary power mode," Versill said.

"Is that the brig?" Victoria asked as they passed a security area.

Versill stopped and looked into the doorway.

"Yes. This confirms my assumption. We'll check it out later," Versill said.

They continued down the corridor to where it ended at a corridor intersection. Turning right, Versill led them a short distance and turned left into a stairwell. They followed her up the steps.

"This has an interesting layout," Tauren said.

"They actually based our newer battleships off from this large scout ship design, except for the rounded, outer hull. I would normally take the elevator, but not with the ship at reduced power," Versill said.

"Understood," Victoria said.

Exiting the stairwell, they followed Versill a short distance to a door on the right that led to the bridge of the *Credence.*

"Here we are," Versill said.

She walked over to the center chair of the bridge's console and looked at the controls in the dim lighting. The others stood behind her. There were three chairs at the console as well as one behind them and two additional chairs off to the far right of the bridge. After familiarizing herself with the controls, Versill flicked several switches to activate the ship's computer. She began typing several commands on the keyboard. Suddenly, the ship's lights brightened fully, the air circulation system accelerated to its normal mode, and full power was restored to all the electronics. Versill engaged the *Credence's* engines and nothing happened. She stared at the console for a long moment.

"Perhaps, try again," Ashten said.

"No. I need to go to the engine area and check the power termination modules. If you all want to stay here on the bridge, I'll be back in a few minutes," Versill said.

She left the bridge and took the fully restored elevator down to the lowest level. Making her way down a long service corridor, Versill proceeded to the engine area of the ship. The metal grating beneath her feet rattled as she walked along. Soon, the service corridor opened up into a large engine area. The large, cylinder engines could be seen below through the grating. She turned onto a catwalk that led to a set of power termination modules. Opening the panel, she looked inside. Sure enough, all of the modules had become disabled. Versill flicked several switches, closed the panel, and headed back toward the bridge.

Not having a crew sucks, she thought.

Versill returned to the bridge and found the three humans sitting in a few of the chairs.

"We made ourselves comfortable," Victoria said.

"No worries. Just as I thought, the power termination modules had become disabled once the ship's auxiliary power was activated. Now, the engines should fire up immediately," Versill said.

Victoria and Ashten sat in the chairs on either side of the center console and Tauren sat in the seat behind them, leaving the center console chair open for Versill. Versill sat down and engaged the *Credence's* engines once again. This time, they started in an instant, the distant roar making its way to the bridge. Victoria reached for her comm.

"You are clear to release the docking arm," she said.

They felt a shift in the artificial gravity for a brief moment before the *Credence* was free from the shipyard docking station. Versill rotated the ship to the starboard side and the docking station came into full view through the bridge's observation window. In the distance, various ships of different models, sizes, and shapes could be seen docked in the yard. The bright crescent of Celtarenia appeared beyond the shipyard docks, which orbited the planet. Versill made some adjustments and the *Credence* moved away from Celtarenia.

"Okay, since this ship is not equipped with a modern navigation system, we will need to navigate remotely from our shuttle's nav system," Tauren said.

Tauren removed a computer pad from his pocket and synced it to the navigation system of the shuttle that was parked down in the docking bay. He then sent a signal from the computer pad to the *Credence's* computer system.

"Doing this, I will be able to navigate the *Credence* back to Anneriss via the shuttle's nav system," Tauren said.

"That's pretty slick," Versill said as she turned toward Tauren.

"Thanks," he said.

"I've had our team prepare a modern navigation system module for you. So, when we return to Anneriss, I will have our technicians install it on the *Credence.* We don't need you getting lost out there," Victoria said.

"Thank you. With the Stormrider fighter ship's modern nav system, I wouldn't get lost, but I don't think I could sync the fighter ship to the *Credence,* like Tauren is doing with the shuttle's nav system. Although we have updated our own galactic maps in recent years, it's nice that both of our species have at least exchanged galactic navigation databases since you've first contacted us," Versill said.

"I understand the Sharrixians have adopted the Marrithious Galaxy name that we use," Victoria said.

"Yes, we have. We really didn't have a name for it previous to that," Versill said.

"Now, if we can just avoid war..." Commander Ashten said.

• • •

The *Credence* exited lightspeed-plus and drifted in orbit above Anneriss.

Versill turned to Tauren who sat behind her. "If I can get a lift to the base so I can get my fighter ship, it would be most appreciated," she said.

"Yes, I can do that. Then I'll come back with the technicians to have the nav system installed, as General Ediira had mentioned," Tauren said.

"Commander Ashten and I can man the *Credence* until you're back, if that works for you," Victoria said.

"I was going to ask if you would. Thank you," Versill said.

Versill and Tauren left the bridge and headed for the docking bay. It was much faster since they were able to use the elevator. Before long, they entered the docking bay and proceeded toward the shuttle.

"Would you like to sit up front with me?" he asked.

"Sure."

They entered the shuttle and Versill was careful to duck down as they made their way to the two front seats. The two of them fastened themselves in and Tauren engaged the engines. The military shuttle smoothly exited the docking bay of the *Credence* and flew toward the surface of Anneriss.

"Well, when I get back home to Lairdain Tannis, I'm either going to be a hero or I'll be killed," Versill said.

"Well, let's hope it's the hero. How long has your queen empress been in power?" Tauren asked.

"Queen Empress Aminarra has been in power for thirty-five years, I believe. Since just before I was born… She lives in the Lythinarr Palace. It is such a beautiful structure…at least from the outside. I've never actually been *in* the palace. Only very special guards and dignitaries get to enter the palace."

"What's it like on Lairdain Tannis? Is it similar to any of the planets that you've been to on this side of the Marrithious Galaxy?" he asked.

"Yeah, a little. A large portion of the planet is a desert. Although the Sharrixian Government has other planets in its territory, almost all of us live on our home planet," she said.

The two of them were quiet for the remainder of the trip to Anneriss. Soon, the shuttle settled into the docking bay of the military base. Tauren disabled the shuttle's engines and the two of them unfastened their seat belts. Exiting the shuttle, they walked over to the center of the docking bay as two technicians approached them. Each of the technicians held the handle of a metal case that contained the sophisticated navigation equipment.

"We are ready to install the nav system on the *Credence*," one of them said.

"Okay. Go ahead and board the shuttle. I will be there shortly," Tauren said.

The two of them continued onto the shuttle with the equipment.

"Well, Tauren, it was nice chatting with you," Versill said.

"Indeed, it was, Versill. I'm going to check on the prisoners and see if the other shuttle is ready. I may see you back up on the *Credence*," Tauren said.

"Okay. See you soon," Versill said.

She made her way across the docking bay toward the Stormrider fighter ship. Its dark gray, metallic look and sleek design put a smile on Versill's face. She climbed aboard, closed the canopy, and put on her helmet. Maneuvering the Stormrider toward the exit, she quickly jetted out of the docking bay and flew up toward the *Credence* at lightning speed. Versill felt good to be in a familiar craft.

After Versill landed the Stormrider in the docking bay, she headed for the bridge. When the bridge door slid open, Victoria and Ashten turned toward her.

"Hello. I have the Stormrider parked in the docking bay. Tauren should be here at any moment with the technicians who will install the modern nav system. The prisoner shuttle will also be here shortly. I need to familiarize myself with the brig on the second level. Would you two like to join me?" Versill asked.

Victoria and Ashten stood up.

"Yes. It's been a bit uneventful on the bridge," Victoria said.

"But we did see a comet in the distance of space," Ashten said.

"Awesome," Versill said.

Victoria and Ashten followed Versill into the corridor toward the elevator. Soon, they were in the long corridor on the second level.

"So, Victoria, once I'm back on Lairdain Tannis, I will contact you on a schedule for the trial of the prisoners so that you can be present,"

Versill said.

"Well, we hope to add a couple more criminals to that list. There is still work to be done. We have to find Bryson Wieler and their boss. You know, we've spent a lot of years digging deep into their organization. They've been very secretive about everything they do, so it has taken a lot longer than we originally anticipated," Victoria said.

"So, Wilcox Brown is also investigating this group?" Versill asked.

"Well…in a round-about way, yes. Wilcox and Nancy are investigating the missing deed to Staraliss for their client. It just happened to lead them to the same group that we've been investigating," Victoria said.

Versill stopped in front of the door that led to the security area. They stepped into the main room. Like most of the *Credence*, the walls were white. A desk sat to the left where prisoners could be processed, if need be. Across the room was the brig. Versill walked over to the large cell and activated a laser lock from the wall panel. Blue beams crossed the doorway, securing the cell.

"Nice!" Ashten said.

"Well, that should work until I can get them to the fleet at Rafith Astonn. From there, I will let High Commander Shirom take them to Lairdain Tannis," Versill said.

Versill disabled the laser lock.

"We should head to the docking bay and see if the shuttles have arrived," Victoria said.

"Yes. The docking bay is not far from here," Versill said.

She led them out of the security area, down the corridor, and through a door that led to the upper level of the docking bay. As they stood on the metal grating that overlooked the bay, they noticed that both shuttles had arrived. The technicians were waiting outside of the shuttle that Tauren piloted, the navigation equipment in hand. Tauren stepped out of the shuttle to join them.

"Sorry for the wait," Victoria said from the stairs.

Victoria, Ashten, and Versill made their way down the steps to the docking bay floor.

"No problem. Actually, we just arrived before the prisoner shuttle," Tauren said.

The sound of the second shuttle's engines winding down could be heard as it faded to silence. The airlock door opened and a security officer exited the shuttle.

"Hello, General Ediira… Commander Ashten… Where are we moving the prisoners to?" the security officer asked.

"The prisoners will be staying in the shuttle until these technicians get the new nav system installed on the bridge. If your team could wait here in the docking bay and guard them until we are finished on the bridge, that would be great," Victoria said. "I just want to be sure there are no issues with the install first."

"Roger that," the security officer said.

Versill stepped over to the technicians.

"If you two would follow us, we will take you to the bridge," Versill said.

Tauren retreated into the shuttle to wait. With equipment in hand, the two technicians followed Versill, Victoria, and Ashten to the bridge.

A heavily armed security guard stood outside the prisoner shuttle in the docking bay. He held a large laser rifle in his gloved hands. The guard wore a light gray military uniform. The security officer who had spoken with Victoria earlier exited the shuttle and stood next to the armed guard.

"I just heard from Victoria over the comm. They have successfully installed the nav system and are en route to the docking bay. Let's begin preparing for the prisoner transfer," the security officer told the guard.

"Roger that," the security guard said.

They both disappeared into the shuttle. Moments later, the prisoners were escorted out of the shuttle, each in handcuffs and ankle shackles. They stood in a line in the docking bay with heavily armed guards on either side of them, a guard behind them, and the main security officer in front of them.

Victoria, Ashten, Versill, and the two technicians arrived at the upper level of the docking bay. They looked down at the prisoners.

"I'll wait up here," Versill said.

"As soon as we clear the stairs, the prisoners can be transported up to the brig. Versill will lead the way," Victoria said.

Victoria, Ashten, and the two technicians went down the stairs, their boots making a distinct sound on the grated, metal steps. When they reached the bottom of the steps and went toward their shuttle, the main security officer went up the stairs ahead of the group and stood next to Versill, pointing his laser rifle over the yellow railing at the prisoners.

"All right. Walk up the stairs, slowly," the security officer said.

Quinlan Zale, Chaslin Anders, other Settlement Agency agents, and their security staff were escorted up the stairs toward the second level. From there, Versill led them to the security area. Once inside, they each had their handcuffs and ankle shackles removed before being put into the brig. After the last prisoner was placed into the security cell, Versill activated the laser locks. The intense blue beams suddenly crossed the doorway, preventing escape. Versill and the military group left the security area and returned to the docking bay where the others waited.

"I thank you and your security team for transferring the prisoners," Victoria said.

The main security officer turned around. "You're welcome, General Ediira," he said.

The security team entered the shuttle where their pilot was waiting for them. Moments later, the shuttle departed from the docking bay of the *Credence.*

Victoria looked at the remaining shuttle and then over to the Stormrider fighter ship. She turned toward Versill and held out her hand to the tall alien. Versill shook Victoria's hand and then she shook Ashten's.

"It was a pleasure working with you both. Now, I must hurry and get to Rafith Astonn as quickly as the *Credence* can fly. I will contact you with information regarding the trial," Versill said.

"It has been a pleasure working with you as well," Victoria said.

"Yes, it has. Thank you for your help with the investigation. As soon as we find the others, we will contact you to have them brought to Lairdain Tannis as well," Ashten said.

"Okay. Thank you," Versill said.

"Safe travels. Godspeed," Victoria said.

Victoria and Ashten entered the shuttle where Tauren and the two technicians waited. Versill waved at Tauren, who could be seen through the shuttle's observation window. After waving back, Tauren maneuvered the shuttle toward the docking bay exit and launched into space. Versill stood there alone in the docking bay watching the shuttle depart. As it slowly disappeared into the darkness of space,

Versill sighed. She turned toward the metal stairs and headed for the bridge.

Thanks to the technicians installing a modern navigation system, Versill would be able to safely get to her destination. When the *Credence* was initially launched for its outbound flight to the other side of the galaxy to investigate the portal incident, the crew did not expect their navigation system to malfunction. The death of the crew was an unfortunate event.

From the bridge, Versill sat at the console and looked out the observation window at the distant stars that filled the tapestry of space. She engaged the engines and the *Credence* disappeared from Anneriss at lightspeed-plus.

Chapter Eighteen

"There is a large ship approaching that just exited lightspeed-plus, sir," an officer said.

The officer swiveled around in his seat toward Admiral Novish Shirom. Novish looked past several officers at the console of the bridge. Through the observation window, a ship could be seen in the distance as it approached Rafith Astonn.

"Is it broadcasting its identity?" Novish asked the officer.

"One moment… Sir, it is registered as the *Credence*," the officer said in surprise.

"That would be Versill, returning from a special mission that she was assigned to. Prepare a shuttle for prisoner transfer. We now have the humans who murdered our Gatherers. Also, inform Commander Othan, Commander Prilston, and Commander Jafer that the approaching ship is a friendly," Novish said.

"Versill has prisoners? Ah, yes sir," the officer said.

The officer quickly made arrangements for the shuttle and then contacted the commanders. Novish knew this information would cause shock and confusion with the other commanders.

"Admiral Shirom, can you please explain the situation with the *Credence* that was just mentioned?" Commander Gedlo Othan asked.

"Is Queen Empress Aminarra aware of this?" Commander Covlan Prilston asked.

"This is great news, Admiral Shirom. Thank you for making us aware of the situation," Commander Jafer said.

"Versill was sent on a special mission and has returned with the human prisoners who were involved with the death of our Gatherers at the portal. She also has the remains of the original *Credence* crew, and information about the human military's investigation. All this was done to achieve the goals we wanted without going to war," Novish said.

The comm was silent as the commanders contemplated the new information. Minutes later, the *Credence* stopped near Rafith Astonn and drifted. Novish smiled at the sight of the rounded ship that he had not seen in twenty years.

"Admiral Shirom, this is Versill reporting in from the *Credence*," she said.

"Congratulations on a successful mission, Versill. Because of your heroism, we have avoided the Marrithious Galactic War. I will immediately send a shuttle over to the *Credence* to transfer the prisoners to the *Credence Revenge*," Novish said.

"Thank you, sir. I am honored to serve. Not only do I have the human prisoners who caused this, but I also have the skeletal remains of the original crew of the *Credence* who have been preserved in chambers by the human military," Versill said.

"Queen Empress Aminarra has already declared war on the humans. We are just waiting for her blessing to launch the assault. I'm sure she has returned to the Lythinarr Palace. Once the interference from the supernova in the Pixellis System subsides, we will be able to receive her order," Commander Gedlo said.

"The entire point was to get justice for our Gatherers. We have now achieved that goal," Novish said.

"Pardon me for interjecting, Commander Othan," Versill said. "General Victoria Ediira from the human military received special permission from the Marrithious Government leader, Essir Phensaa, to relinquish control of the prisoners and assign justice to the Sharrixian Government."

"I see. Well, it will be interesting to see what Queen Empress

Aminarra has to say about this updated situation," Gedlo Othan said.

"I'll be down in the docking bay when the shuttle returns so I can oversee the prisoner transfer," Novish said.

Novish stood up from his chair and left the bridge. After going through a maze of corridors, he made his way back to the ship's communications system. Moving along the narrow service aisle, Novish opened the panel and disconnected the small, gray box that he had installed earlier. He put the small module into his pocket and reconnected the wire harness into the terminal.

Open communications have been restored, Novish thought.

Novish proceeded to the docking bay.

Quinlan Zale, Chaslin Anders and the other prisoners from the Settlement Agency were very frightened to see a multitude of tall Sharrixian military guards and personnel. Novish slowly walked back and forth along the line of prisoners, looking at them with contempt.

"Take them to the battleship brig," Novish said.

He motioned for the guards to take them away. The guards immediately escorted them toward a corridor that was adjacent to the docking bay. As they walked along the corridor, Chaslin turned to Quinlan.

"I may not have met our boss, but she sure as hell isn't going to help us out of this after all we did for her. This is bullshit," Chaslin said.

"Bryson and I recently met with her and she threatened to kill us if we didn't fix a few things," Quinlan said.

"What things?" Chaslin asked.

"Her daughter—"

"Both of you, shut up!" one of the guards shouted.

The end of the guard's laser rifle came barreling down on Chaslin's cheek bone, sending him to the floor. Chaslin picked himself up from the floor of the corridor and wiped a trickle of blood from his face. The guard separated the two of them, putting Chaslin at the back of the line. When the group of prisoners reached the brig, they were separated into four groups and put into different cells. The guard who had struck Chaslin made sure he went into a different cell than Quinlan. Unlike the brig on the *Credence,* the brig on the *Credence Revenge* did not have laser lock doors. Instead, there were thick, solid doors that secured the cells.

• • •

On the bridge of the *Credence Revenge,* Novish settled back into his seat that overlooked the officers at the console. He knew the queen empress would hear his transmission since the open communications had been reactivated.

"Commander Othan, Commander Prilston, and Commander Jafer. We have secured the prisoners in the brig of the *Credence Revenge.* The fleet will now head home to Lairdain Tannis for the humans to stand trial," Novish said. "Versill, the *Credence* is only an exploration vessel, but do you think you can keep up with the fleet?"

"I will do my best, sir," Versill said.

"Finally, I can hear the fleet now. The galactic interference must have subsided." The voice of Queen Empress Aminarra came over the comm.

"Queen Empress Aminarra… It does appear that the interference from the supernova in the Pixellis System has diminished," Novish said.

"You have my authority to launch the assault on the humans," Queen Empress Aminarra said.

"Queen Empress Aminarra, there have been new developments since we have lost open communications with you," Novish said.

"What did I hear about prisoners, Versill, and the *Credence?*" Queen Empress Aminarra asked.

"Versill has returned with the humans who are responsible for the deaths of our Gatherers. She has also returned with the *Credence* and the remains of the crew," Novish said.

"What? Who sent Versill to do this?" Queen Empress Aminarra asked.

"I sent Versill on a special mission across the galaxy to help the human military with their investigation before our fleet even arrived here at Rafith Astonn. I figured Versill was the perfect officer for the job since she had already met with General Victoria Ediira previously," Novish said.

"This is unacceptable! I would have never allowed this! You are to have the *Credence* and Versill brought back to Lairdain Tannis at once! Working directly with the human military is treason! And you, Admiral Shirom, are hereby relieved of your duties as admiral. You are to return to Lairdain Tannis at once with the *Credence Revenge* and

Versill with the *Credence.*

"Commander Gedlo Othan, you are now admiral of the fleet. Admiral Othan, Commander, Prilston, and Commander Jafer, you are to launch the assault with the *Arcinaris,* the *Lhasariss,* and the *Shartannis* at once. I will send other battleships to attach to the fleet as necessary," Queen Empress Aminarra said.

Silence fell over the comm for a long moment.

"I accept my position as admiral and we will launch the assault in five minutes," Gedlo said.

"You're making a big mistake," Novish said.

Minutes later, the *Arcinaris* and the *Lhasariss* disappeared from Rafith Astonn. Novish was surprised to still see the *Shartannis* outside his observation window.

"Commander Jafer?" Novish inquired.

"I stand with you, sir," Jafer said.

"Commander Jafer, need I remind you that this is treason?" Queen Empress Aminarra asked.

I have never seen Queen Empress Aminarra act like this. I should have waited to activate the open communications, Novish thought.

"Versill, I'm sorry. Let's head back to Lairdain Tannis," Novish said.

"But…" Versill began, but trailed off.

I can't even warn General Ediira, Versill thought.

Silence filled the comm as the three ships turned toward Lairdain Tannis and engaged their engines.

Wilcox Brown sat in a seat behind Commander Stone, who was piloting a heavily armed military ship. In the navigator's seat was Commander Aolliam. Nancy Louray sat behind Aolliam. On the ship's long range scanners, another ship could be seen.

"Thank you, Wilcox and Nancy, for your continued work with the military. You've both been a vital part of bringing down this criminal organization," Stone said.

"We are glad to help. At some point, it would be nice to find the deed to Staraliss. That's why we started this case in the first place," Wilcox said.

"Since we began tracking Bryson Wieler a couple of weeks ago, he's been avoiding any significant moves. Do you think he knows we're tracking him?" Aolliam asked.

"If he knew, he would simply disconnect the homing beacon. For some reason, he is not going back to his boss. Perhaps he is afraid of the boss's wrath because of the group's failure," Stone said.

"Well, his supplies have to run out at some point," Nancy said.

"True," Stone said.

"According to the computer, the current flight that Bryson Wieler is on has been the longest since we've started tracking him. Up until now, he's just orbited random planets and has stayed in orbit for a couple of days at a time. This time, it appears that he has a destination in mind," Aolliam said.

"He must be getting desperate. I think you are right, Nancy. He's probably running out of food and supplies," Wilcox said.

"Well, I'm certainly grateful for the facilities and supplies we have on this military ship. A couple of weeks without food, a shower, and some place to sleep would be terrible," Nancy said.

"He just increased his speed," Aolliam said.

"Then, I will increase our speed," Stone said.

Stone increased the military vessel's speed to the higher end of the lightspeed-plus spectrum.

"He's increasing his speed even more. I think we may have been detected on his scanners," Stone said.

"That's a negative. We are in stealth mode. Unless he has some high-tech equipment that can read interstellar waves, there is no way he is picking us up. I just think he is finally desperate enough to go to his boss," Aolliam said.

"What is his trajectory at this point?" Stone asked.

Aolliam performed a couple of calculations. Unless he makes a correction in his course, it appears that his destination is Adanarr," Aolliam said.

Wilcox and Nancy looked at each other.

"Adanarr? That's where our client's mother lives," Nancy said.

"She was a bit suspicious during our interview. Do you think Mercedes Brantt is their boss?" Wilcox asked.

"I don't know. Why would she try to kill her own daughter?" Nancy asked.

Wilcox sighed.

"We'll arrive on Adanarr in a few minutes. Once we exit lightspeed-plus, keep your distance until we lock in on his destination," Aolliam said.

"Roger that," Stone said.

In the distance, the sphere of Adanarr could be seen. The ship exited lightspeed-plus and drifted toward the atmosphere of the planet. Following Bryson's ship through the large city of Torontarr, Stone kept a distance. Stone made some quick adjustments on the control panel and the ship just hovered in place. He waited for Bryson to land and exit the ship before continuing onward. Once Wilcox visually saw Bryson's ship on the landing pad, he knew where they were headed.

"That's Mercedes Brantt's house," Wilcox said.

Stone landed the military ship in the distance and the four of them unfastened their seat belts. Stone and Aolliam walked to a small area in the back of the ship and opened a cabinet. They each grabbed two laser rifles from a rack. Stone handed one of them to Wilcox and Aolliam handed one of them to Nancy. Nancy looked at the large rifle.

"I've only used a laser pistol before," Nancy said.

"You'll do just fine," Aolliam said.

With laser rifles in hand, the four of them exited the ship and walked through the trees toward Mercedes Brantt's luxurious home.

"If things get ugly, you two stay behind us," Stone said.

"Yes, sir," Wilcox said.

They quickly maneuvered across the beautiful yard, moved past several shrubs, and up the stone steps to the front door. The door was ajar. Peering into the large living room, they saw Mercedes Brant holding a laser pistol at Bryson Wieler.

The living room had white walls and a light brown, hardwood floor. A table and a light gray couch and chair rested on a lavender rug on the left of the room. Many beautiful decorations were displayed throughout the room. To the far right, an open staircase led to the second level. The intricate rail followed the stairs to the top and across a long mezzanine that overlooked the entire living room.

"I told you and Quinlan the last time you were here for the meeting that you needed to fix shit. Wilcox Brown and Nancy Louray came here for their investigation and told me my daughter had been abducted. *My* daughter! You and Quinlan sat there and lied to me, saying that you weren't involved. Well, Coradelle left me a message and told me otherwise. Now, you are telling me the military has taken our team and they were given to the Sharrixians? You are all idiots! *Idiots!*" Mercedes shouted.

"I'm sorry we screwed up. Maybe, if you give me the deed to Staraliss, I can fix this with Wilcox Brown," Bryson said, desperately.

"The deed to Staraliss is not going to save you. It might save me, however. You, Bryson Wieler, are already dead," Mercedes said.

She pulled the trigger on the laser pistol and a blue beam struck Bryson in the chest, burning a hole through his heart. The intense heat cauterized all blood flow and he fell backwards against a brown, wooden cabinet before falling to the hardwood floor with a thud. The sudden movement of the cabinet caused a tall, sparkling, white vase to wobble back and forth until it fell off the cabinet and smashed onto the floor, shattering into hundreds of pieces.

"Not my Sharrixian vase! Damn it!"

Mercedes walked over to the shattered pieces and kneeled down to have a closer look. The smell of burned flesh lingered in the air. She looked over at Bryson's body. Stone, Aolliam, Wilcox, and Nancy quickly stormed through the front door, pointing their laser rifles at Mercedes. She turned toward them, surprised at their presence.

"Don't move!" Stone shouted. "Drop your weapon!"

Mercedes tossed her laser pistol over the hardwood floor and onto the lavender rug. She frowned at Wilcox Brown in anger.

"Well, Wilcox Brown, it looks like you've managed to take down my entire organization," Mercedes said.

"Nancy and I may have helped, but the Marrithious Government military has been on to your organization for years. I simply want the deed to Staraliss. The planet belongs to Coradelle. Speaking of your daughter…if it wasn't for Nancy here saving her life, your own thugs would have killed her with the black crystals," Wilcox said.

"I know. Coradelle contacted me about it and verified what you two originally told me. So, you want the deed? I'll get you the deed to Staraliss. I keep it upstairs in my bedroom," Mercedes said.

Wilcox looked at Stone.

"That's fine. I'll go up the stairs ahead of you. Any sudden moves and you'll be joining Bryson," Stone said.

Commander Stone walked up the wooden steps to the mezzanine and pointed his laser rifle at Mercedes as she slowly walked up the steps. Aolliam was behind her with his rifle concentrated on her back. Wilcox and Nancy followed. Once they were all on the second level, Mercedes led them past several rooms, around a corner, and down an elegantly decorated hallway to another stairway that led to a third level.   Again, Stone went ahead of them and carefully watched Mercedes come up the stairs. The third level of the luxurious home had a long hallway that was decorated similar to the one on the second level. There were a few doors along the hall. Mercedes led them to the last door on the right.

"My bedroom…   I keep the deed over there in the dresser," Mercedes said, pointing to the left.

The bedroom was gorgeous with beautiful furnishings and wall decorations. Elegant carpeting covered the floor. A tall bed was centered against the far wall of the room with an intricately decorated blue and white comforter. On the left, a large, wooden dresser sat against the back wall. Several jewelry boxes sat on top of the dresser. To the left of the dresser, an odd-looking mirror sat in a large, metal frame against the wall. To the right, a painted portrait of a Sharrixian woman, dressed in red, hung on the wall. After seeing the painting, Wilcox and Nancy looked at each other.

How does Mercedes have a Sharrixian vase and a painting of a Sharrixian? Wilcox thought.

Mercedes walked over to the dresser. "I keep the deed in the top right drawer," she said.

"Stop. I'll open the drawer," Stone said.

He walked past Mercedes and opened the top right drawer. Inside, there were three binders. Aolliam walked over to have a look. As they all peered into the drawer, Mercedes ran and dove through the large mirror on the wall, disappearing from sight.

"What the fuck?" Stone said.

They all looked at the mirror as it rippled with a shimmering effect. Aolliam walked over to it and noticed a wire next to it that connected to a device on the wall. He unplugged the wire from the metal frame and suddenly a low humming frequency could be heard. The smooth mirror-like surface became a shimmering, bluish field of energy.

"That's the same sound we heard at the portal on Staraliss," Wilcox said. "That's no mirror. It's another portal!"

"Umm… I need to contact General Ediira," Stone said.

As Stone reached for his comm, Wilcox walked over to the dresser and set his laser rifle on top of it. He removed the binders from the dresser drawer and looked through each of them. The first binder was full of papers regarding the group's criminal organization. The next binder had the deed to Staraliss in it.

"Yes!" Wilcox exclaimed. "We now have the deed to Staraliss. Coradelle's case is finally complete."

"Is it? Her own mother is behind everything. At this point, the last thing Coradelle will care about is some backwater planet," Nancy said.

Wilcox sighed. "You're right, Nancy," he said.

"I know I'm right," Nancy said.

Wilcox continued to the last binder and opened it. There were pages that had been ripped out of some tablet that were numbered seven through eleven. Wilcox studied the pages for a long moment.

"Ah… You guys need to see this," Wilcox said.

Stone was on his comm, but Aolliam and Nancy stepped over to have a look.

"These are pages from the surviving Sharrixian Gatherer's testimony. His name was Tajenipp. He is the Gatherer who Versill told us about when we were preparing to raid the Settlement Agency. He is the Gatherer who made it back through the portal to tell his people what had happened on Staraliss. The story that all the Sharrixians know is probably from pages one through six of his testimony. These are pages seven through eleven and appear to have been ripped out of a tablet. Look at this. Versill didn't mention any of this. Apparently, Tajenipp witnessed Mercedes coming through the portal from Staraliss—you know, when Robert Hershall left her stranded there for a short time. Tajenipp saw Mercedes meet with Queen Empress Aminarra. He wrote that it was like a childhood story when Queen Empress Aminarra used a green crystal to have special powers over Mercedes. Tajenipp ends this testimony with great fear for his life because the Queen Empress Aminarra noticed that he witnessed her controlling Mercedes with the green crystal. And it is signed by Tajenipp," Wilcox said.

"I wonder what Mercedes is doing with these pages," Nancy said.

Stone ended his communication on the comm and they immediately filled him in on their findings.

"Well, this just keeps getting more interesting," Stone said, looking at the pages. "I was just told by General Ediira that we are preparing for war against two incoming Sharrixian battleships."

Nancy immediately remembered her vision about a war.

"Not four battleships?" Aolliam asked. "Versill said there were four. I wonder what happened to the other two. Their queen empress must not care that we caught the prisoners who are responsible for the

Gatherers deaths."

"Oh, and General Ediira has given us permission to pursue Mercedes through this portal," Stone said.

"Let's not leave the deed nor these papers behind," Nancy said. "Since you two officers have a slim backpack, we can slip them in one of yours."

"Yeah, that works. Put them in mine," Aolliam said.

Nancy closed the binder and put all three inside Aolliam's backpack, zipping it closed. She closed the dresser drawer and looked at the three of them.

"Are we ready for this?" Wilcox asked, grabbing his laser rifle from the top of the dresser.

One by one, they stepped through the portal and disappeared.

Chapter Nineteen

Wilcox, Nancy, Stone, and Aolliam found themselves in a very extravagant master bedroom. Each of them turned around and looked at the portal they had just stepped through, its pseudo-mirror surface rippling. They saw the same sized portal in an identical metal frame. A similar noise-cancelation device sat next to it, eliminating the portal's low-frequency sound. The master bedroom had a red theme. The large bed had an eloquently embroidered, red comforter. Across the room, there were soft red chairs on either side of a large, wooden dresser. To their right was a large walk-in closet full of beautiful, tall dresses of many varieties. To their left was a tall, closed door with black crystal embellishments embedded into the wood. Large paintings were fixed on the walls, each with a gold frame. Three of the four paintings were of beautiful Lairdain Tannis landscapes. The painting that hung on the wall above the bed, however, shocked them. It was a painted portrait of Mercedes Brantt with a black, metal collar that connected to a heavy-duty chain.

"That is very strange. Where the hell are we?" Wilcox asked.

"I have a feeling we are not on Adanarr anymore," Nancy said.

"Let's continue our pursuit, shall we?" Stone asked.

Being careful not to touch any of the black crystals that decorated the tall door, Aolliam opened it, pointing his laser rifle to the other side. Beyond the door was a stairway that led downward and opened up into a lower level of the master bedroom. Decorated with the same red theme, the room had two more chairs, a closet full of shoes, and a long, red bench. There were two doors in the lower section of the bedroom. The door on the right led to a large, luxurious bathroom. In one corner, a long tub was elevated two steps above the marble floor. A long mirror ran the length of a golden, marble countertop with a sink in the center of it. Upon discovering it was a bathroom, they turned back to the other door in the lower bedroom. They opened it and exited into a long hallway with many windows on the opposite side, along its entire length. A thin rug with intricate patterns ran the full length of the hall. Candles were located at even intervals along the wall opposite of the windows. Wilcox and the others stepped over and peered out the windows. A courtyard full of flowers sat three stories below.

"Lily of the valley...my favorite flower," Nancy said as she peered down into the courtyard.

"It appears we are in the tower of some castle or palace," Wilcox said.

"Shall we go left or right?" Aolliam asked.

"Let's split up. Aolliam and I will take the left. Wilcox, you and Nancy can take the right," Stone said.

"Okay," Wilcox said.

Wilcox and Nancy walked down the long hallway and opened several of the tall doors along its length to discover guest rooms. At the end of the hallway, they discovered it turned perpendicular and continued. The new hallway ended at two stairways. One was a spiral staircase that led upward to an opening in the tall ceiling. The other was a traditional stairway that led downward.

"Which way?" Nancy asked.

"Mercedes could have gone anywhere. Let's go up the spiral stairwell. This place reminds me of Everett Quarton's North Harbor Mansion on Velassine," Wilcox said.

"Oh, this is much more elegant," Nancy said.

They made their way up the spiral stairs. It led to a small, open hall with a window, but the stairs continued upward to the next level.

Nancy looked out the window.

"We're in a tall tower," she said.

Wilcox continued up the stairs to the next level. The spiral staircase ended at a small reading room with a tan chaise lounge chair, a small bookshelf that contained several books, and a tall lamp.

"Well, she's not up here. Let's head back down to the other stairway," Wilcox said.

Nancy turned around and walked back down the spiral staircase. When they reached the large hallway, they walked down the traditional stairway. Before them was a large library, full of books. It was carpeted with a solid, light gray fabric. Bookshelves surrounded the parameter of the room. There was another tan chaise lounge chair in the center of the library. They noticed a set of double doors at the far end of the library. One of the two doors was ajar. Wilcox opened the door and they caught a glimpse of Mercedes Brantt running along a mezzanine. They quickly chased after her.

Stone and Aolliam went down a stairway that led to a small office. A large, wooden desk sat along the back wall. There were several book cases and filing cabinets in the room. The walls were decorated with pictures of former Sharrixian monarchs. A comm sat on the desk that had several cables connected to it. The cables ran down the desk and disappeared under a metal plate on the wooden floor.

"Listen," Stone said.

They heard chatter between Admiral Othan and Commander Prilston. Admiral Othan called for Queen Empress Aminarra on the comm. Stone and Aolliam looked at each other. They realized it was an open communications set-up.

"Not gonna answer it..." Aolliam said. "This must be the queen empress's palace."

"Do you think these cables are connected to a signal booster?" Stone asked.

"Absolutely. Whether it is necessary or not, Queen Empress Aminarra has this comm boosted. Perhaps she was having issues communicating," Aolliam said.

Stone disconnected the comm from the cables and found that they could still hear the conversation between Gedlo and Covlan clearly. He turned down the volume and put the comm into his pocket.

Aolliam opened a set of double doors and they both saw Mercedes running along a mezzanine from a set of identical, tall doors on the far side. Wilcox and Nancy ran after her along the mezzanine from the opposite direction. The mezzanine ran along the upper level of a grand foyer. The white railing along the edge was decorated with fancy embellishments and purple crystals. Mercedes ran toward a wide, carpeted stairway that led down to the main floor. Toward the bottom of the steps, the stairs became wider and more curved. Flowing fountains of water were located on either side of the stairway, along the marble floor of the grand foyer. Before Mercedes reached the bottom of the curved steps, she tripped and fell down several stairs to the hard floor below. She tried to pick herself up, but it was too late. Stone grabbed her by the back of the shirt and slammed her against the railing of the stairway.

"You're not going anywhere," Stone said.

Aolliam grabbed her arms and positioned her hands behind her back. He put a pair of handcuffs on her.

"Let go of me! Queen Empress Aminarra will *kill* you," Mercedes shouted.

Her voice echoed into the heights of the grand foyer. Two tall Sharrixians came running into the grand foyer when they heard the commotion. Wilcox, Nancy, Stone, and Aolliam pointed their laser rifles at the aliens. Seeing four large weapons pointed at them, they immediately stopped and put their hands in the air.

"Humans? Don't shoot! Why are you here in the Lythinarr Palace? Queen Empress Aminarra will not be pleased. She had every right to declare war on you," one of them said.

"Who are you two? Where is Queen Empress Aminarra?" Aolliam asked.

"We are dignitaries for the queen empress. She is currently at the Sharrixian Government Building taking care of treasonists in our military. You are on Lairdain Tannis," the second dignitary said.

"How did you get here in the Lythinarr Palace?" the first dignitary asked.

"Guards!" the second dignitary shouted.

Two Sharrixian Palace Guards came running into the grand foyer. Their special, blue uniforms stood out against the gold and white, marble floor. The guards opened fire on the group at the bottom of the steps. Commander Aolliam took a direct shot in the leg. He fell to the marble floor in agony, the laser beam separating his leg at the knee. The bottom portion of the leg fell against the steps. Stone, Wilcox, and Nancy opened fire on the two palace guards. The dignitary who called for the guards was caught in the crossfire. He was shot and killed, falling to the marble floor. The remaining dignitary dove for cover along the base of the flowing fountain of water. Intense blue laser beams flew across the grand foyer. The two guards took hits in their chests. They both fell dead to the floor, smoke rising from the laser wounds.

"My leg!" Aolliam shouted.

Intense pain filled his cries, echoing throughout the grand foyer.

Two more Sharrixian Palace Guards came from the opposite direction and opened fire. Aolliam was hit twice in the head and immediately died, his body falling against the stairs, next to his leg. Smoke rose from the open wounds in his skull. Wilcox sent a barrage of quick laser bursts toward the palace guards, waving his laser rifle back and forth. They both fell dead to the marble floor.

"No! Aolliam, no!" Stone shouted, his voice echoing in the high arches of the grand foyer.

Stone grabbed Mercedes by the handcuffs, pulling her arms and walked her over to the remaining dignitary who was crouched down behind the base of the round fountain. Stone handed Wilcox another pair of handcuffs. Wilcox put the cuffs on the Sharrixian dignitary. Nancy looked back at Aolliam's body that was slumped against the stairs. She walked over to him, set her laser rifle against the stairway railing, and prayed over him.

"Dear Father in Heaven, please receive Aolliam with open arms. Help us get through this ordeal safely. In Jesus's name, I pray. Amen."

Nancy removed Aolliam's backpack containing the three binders and put it on herself. Grabbing both Aolliam's laser rifle and her own, she walked back over to the fountain, a rifle in each hand.

Stone looked at Mercedes. "You have some explaining to do, Mercedes," he said.

"Queen Empress Aminarra controls me when she wants to. I can't say that it's been all bad," Mercedes said.

"No. You have made a shit-ton of credits from selling crystals on the black market. You are Queen Empress Aminarra's sycophant," Stone said.

"Why would Queen Empress Aminarra want you to harvest the

crystals that caused the Gatherers to die? What is her motive? She obviously has declared war on the humans. This makes no sense," Wilcox said.

"She wouldn't start a war with us," Mercedes said.

"She already has," the dignitary said.

Mercedes looked up at the tall Sharrixian as if she had been betrayed. "How could she do this to me?" she asked.

Stone looked over at the dignitary. "Are there more palace guards?" he asked.

"Just the four," the dignitary said.

"What is your name?" Stone asked.

"My name is Nilliss," the dignitary said.

"Nilliss, you need to take us to Queen Empress Aminarra right now. We have turned over to your military the people responsible for the death of your Gatherers," Stone said.

"That is not what the queen empress has said. She is currently at the Sharrixian Government Building, which is some distance from here. We will need to take a ship," the dignitary said.

"Well, the queen empress is lying. Take us to a ship. I'll fly. You just follow instructions," Stone said.

With Mercedes and Nilliss in handcuffs, they made their way out the front door of the Lythinarr Palace. Nilliss led them to a ship that rested on a landing pad on the palace grounds. They climbed aboard and Stone engaged the engine. Commander Stone found the coordinates to the Sharrixian Government Building pre-programmed into the navigation system. He quickly lifted from the landing pad and flew in that direction.

"So, Mercedes, how is it that there is a portal in your bedroom?" Nancy asked.

"Queen Empress Aminarra made it for me using a special green crystal. Somehow, she has harnessed the power of the green crystal and programmed the exact galactic coordinates to my bedroom wall. She had a metal frame built around it and added noise cancelation. She said it is the only crystal of its kind that exists. I believe only humans can be controlled with it, just like the blue, purple, and black crystals only affect humans," Mercedes said.

"I presume you met the queen empress after going through the other portal from Staraliss when Robert Hershall left you stranded there for a short time?" Nancy asked.

"Yes. The queen empress was visiting the Gatherers at the time when I came through. I was shocked that the portal led to another planet. I saw the Crystal Field and the Gatherers and was mesmerized by the sparkling crystals and the tall aliens. I picked up a purple one and felt very strange. That's when Queen Empress Aminarra grabbed me and held up a green crystal to my eyes. I dropped the purple crystal and fell into a trance. She spoke words to me and I obeyed her every word…but I enjoyed it. She brought me back to the Lythinarr Palace and later created a special portal for me, using the green crystal. It is a very, very powerful crystal. Do you suppose there is a large, green crystal beneath the rock at the Crystal Field where the portal connects Staraliss to Lairdain Tannis?" Mercedes asked.

"You must not trust Queen Empress Aminarra fully, or you would not have torn out the pages from the Gatherer's testimony," Wilcox said.

"You've seen the pages?" Mercedes asked.

"We did see the pages. Tajenipp was afraid for his life after he saw Queen Empress Aminarra controlling you. Did she kill Tajenipp?" Wilcox asked.

There was a long pause. "Yes. It was later, after I had set up my organization and we went back to Staraliss for the initial gathering of the crystals. After seeing what she had previously done to me and then later seeing his fellow Gatherers killed, Tajenipp must have been scared for his life. Queen Empress Aminarra killed him right in front of me. I later found Tajenipp's testimony and tore the pages out as an insurance policy of sorts, just in case Queen Empress Aminarra went against me. She doesn't know where the pages disappeared to," Mercedes said.

"So, she controls you and you enjoy it, but you don't fully trust her?" Nancy asked.

"It's complicated. It has everything to do with that green crystal. Queen Empress Aminarra has made me rich by allowing my group to harvest crystals, so I just keep obeying her. But sometimes, when she has the crystal, I can't help it. The fact that she has declared war over this confuses me. Why would she do this to me twenty years later?"

"Well, it appears that your insurance policy of keeping those pages has paid off," Wilcox Brown said.

"If Queen Empress Aminarra killed Tajenipp and has some special control over you, then High Commander Shirom was correct. There are prisoners who were brought back to Lairdain Tannis?" Nilliss asked.

"Yes, there are. We had investigated this group for years, and sent the prisoners off with Versill in the *Credence* to be tried on Lairdain Tannis" Stone said.

"We need to hurry. Queen Empress Aminarra is about to have High Commander Novish Shirom, Commander Jafer, and a special officer named Versill all executed. But you won't make it far into the Sharrixian Government Building without my help. Our military is everywhere and I know a back way in," Nilliss said.

The *Arcinaris* and the *Lhasariss* both exited lightspeed-plus in a remote part of the Marrithious Government's territory.

"Commander Prilston, let's scan this sector of the Marrithious Galaxy to get an assessment of the Marrithious Government's military capabilities. It would be good to compare it to our target list. Things could have changed since we've gathered this data," Admiral Gedlo Othan said.

"Okay. I'll run the scans now. I will report when it's complete," Covlan Prilston said.

"It looks like the humans have picked us up on their long-range scanners," Admiral Othan said.

"I have the report. They have seven battleships at various locations. Some of those locations match our target list. The planet Sharmyra is a high-priority target. Apparently, it is their military headquarters," Covlan said.

"Let that be our first target, then. Once we are there, we'll see if we need to have Queen Empress Aminarra send more of our battleships," Gedlo said.

"Hopefully, she will answer the comm next time," Covlan said.

Together, the two Sharrixian battleships left for the Sharmyra Star System.

Marshall ran to the open door of a transport ship that was parked in the docking bay of the military base on Anneriss. He looked up at General Victoria Ediira as she carried a crate.

"General Ediira, we've picked up two Sharrixian battleships on our long range scanners. They appear to be on a course to Sharmyra. I have already warned Commander Ashten," Marshall said.

Victoria set down the crate that she was carrying inside the transport ship and looked at Marshall.

"This is not good. Apparently, things did not go well for Versill when she returned. Thanks for letting me know," Victoria said.

She sprinted from the transport ship's open ramp and ran across the docking bay toward the communications room. Victoria opened up all military frequencies.

"This is General Ediira. We have a high alert situation. We expect an attack by two confirmed Sharrixian battleships. They are currently en route to Sharmyra. We currently have one battleship stationed there. Commander Ashten, be sure the *Kalaress* is ready for battle. I want all personnel at full readiness. Have your pilots get to their Angel Wing fighter ships in the docking bays immediately.

"Commander Stone and Commander Aolliam were responsible for setting up a military post at the portal on Staraliss. I believe it is under the command of Striker. Is that correct?" Victoria asked.

"This is Commander Striker. Affirmative, General Ediira. Commander Stone and Commander Aolliam assigned this task to me. I'm pleased to report that we have a small outpost set up here now. We've removed the four Sharrixian skeletons from the sand and have put them in preservation chambers to be returned to the Sharrixians. There has been no activity at the portal," Striker said.

"That is about to change. I want you to measure the portal to see if an Angel Wing fighter ship can safely fit through the opening," Victoria said.

"That is one of the first things we did. Yes, an Angel Wing will comfortably fit through the portal," Striker said.

"Where is the nearest battleship to Staraliss located at this moment?" Victoria asked.

"This is Commander Wells aboard the *Tansonn*. We just left the planet Noderell after securing the warehouse there and cleaning up the dead. We are not far from Staraliss," a new voice said.

Commander Wells was one of several Axynnian Commanders in the Marrithious Government military.

"Commander Wells, proceed to the planet Staraliss. As long as your navigation system is in sync with the galactic database, you will be looking for Staraliss. If it is not updated, then you will be looking for Shext. Get there as quickly as possible. I need you to send a squadron of Angel Wing fighter ships down to Staraliss. They will be operating under Commander Striker while on this mission. Commander Striker, send them through the portal to Lairdain Tannis and assess all military targets. Communications from the other side of the portal will be questionable. One of them is to fly back through to Staraliss and report. And for whatever it's worth, don't touch any crystals on the other side, specifically the black ones," Victoria said.

"Understood. We will change course now and fly to Staraliss," Commander Wells said.

"We will have things ready here as well. My team has created a short conduit that we can wedge into the portal to completely open it up and see through to the other side. The last thing we need is a mid-air collision at the portal," Commander Striker said.

"Roger that. This is the situation that Commander Morphus helped us prepare for after Versill mentioned what might be coming. Although we were expecting four battleships and there are only two, let's be vigilant. There could be more coming. Commander Morphus, I want you to send a second battleship to Sharmyra," Victoria said.

"This is Commander Morphus. I'm already en route to Sharmyra with the *MX710 Blackstar* to join with the *Kalaress*. We will be arriving at any moment."

"Nice. The *MX710 Blackstar* alone could wipe out the two Sharrixian battleships that I'm seeing on the scanners. Keep me informed of events as they unfold. I am currently on Anneriss, breaking down the base here. I will reach out to Essir Phensaa to keep our leader aware of the situation," Victoria said.

The *Arcinaris* and the *Lhasariss* exited lightspeed-plus at Sharmyra.

"Oh, this is not good," Admiral Othan said.

Gedlo looked out the observation window from the bridge of the *Lhasariss*. Positioned in space before them were two Marrithious Government battleships, one of which was three times the size of the others. The *Kalaress* and the *MX710 Blackstar* faced them at a short distance. Covlan had the same feeling as Gedlo as he stared out the observation window from the *Arcinaris*.

"Launch all Stormrider fighter ships," Gedlo commanded.

"Launching," Covlan said.

"Queen Empress Aminarra, we need more battleships sent

immediately," Gedlo said.

There was no response from the queen empress. Moments later, forty Stormriders exited the docking bays of each battleship. They headed toward the Marrithious Government ships.

"Launch the Angel Wing fighters," Commander Ashten said over the comm.

A swarm of one hundred and fifty Angel Wing fighter ships launched from both the *Kalaress* and the *MX710 Blackstar*. They quickly intercepted the Stormrider fighters. Blue laser fire brightened the darkness of space as the two groups engaged in space battle. A pair of Angel Wings quickly overtook a Stormrider, their lasers slicing through the craft. It erupted with a silent explosion. Before one of the two Angel Wings could circle back around, it became a target for a Stormrider and was struck in the aft section, destroying the ship. The other Angel Wing pilot saw his partner get destroyed and went after the Stormrider. Quickly trailing behind it, the pilot fired. The Stormrider exploded into cosmic dust. In another dog fight, four Angel Wings engaged with two Stormriders. The laser fire was intense. The beams struck fighters from each side, causing great damage to the hulls. One of the four Angel Wings lost its controls as the engines became disabled. It drifted toward the *Arcinaris,* unable to maneuver nor fire. The *Arcinaris,* opened fire on the Angel Wing fighter ship and destroyed it. The other three Angel Wings of that group did not waste any time taking out the two Stormriders. After they destroyed them, they split up and pursued other Stormriders.

"Maneuver the *MX710 Blackstar* above these dog fights. Concentrate forward laser cannons on the Sharrixian battleship on the starboard side," Commander Morphus said.

The team at the control console in front of Morphus went to work, quickly flicking switches and adjusting controls. The *MX710 Blackstar* rose above the dog fights and began to fire on the *Arcinaris*. The large diameter of the ship's laser cannons was impressive. The massive bolts of blue energy sped toward the *Arcinaris*. With the first hit, the defense shields of the *Arcinaris* were immediately disabled. A second hit ripped a hole through the hull, just underneath the bridge section. Fire burst from the ship and the bridge sagged downward slightly. The stabilizers on the *Arcinaris* began to fail as the ship drifted at an awkward angle. Both Sharrixian battleships began to exchange laser fire with the *MX710 Blackstar.* The *Kalaress* also rose above the dog fights, joining the *MX710 Blackstar.*

The fighter ships continued to strike at each other. A few of the Stormriders that had been damaged just drifted helplessly in space among the action. An Angel Wing pilot was being chased and did not see one of the drifting ships in front of him until it was too late. He collided with the Stormrider and they both exploded in a blinding light. The other two drifting Stormriders from that group were easily picked off by a pair of Angel Wings.

"Concentrate all laser fire on the damaged battleship," Commander Ashten said.

Both Marrithious Government battleships began a barrage of laser fire against the *Arcinaris.* With its defense shields down and multiple laser beams piercing through its unprotected hull, several of which hit the bridge, the battleship exploded with a blinding light. Several large chunks of metal shrapnel struck the *Lhasariss* and disintegrated against its defense shields.

"Commander Prilston!" Gedlo shouted. "Queen Empress Aminarra, do you copy?"

There was no immediate response from Queen Empress Aminarra. Gedlo had to make a quick decision. He was outnumbered and outgunned.

"All Stormrider fighter ships, retreat to the *Lhasariss.* You're going to have to squeeze into the docking bays on this ship because the *Arcinaris* was destroyed. If you cannot fit, make your way back to Lairdain Tannis alone," Gedlo said.

The Stormriders immediately disengaged and retreated to the *Lhasariss.* The Angel Wings ceased fire when the Stormriders retreated. After the *Lhasariss* docking bays were full, several of the Stormriders passed the docking bays when the pilots saw that there was no room left. The *Lhasariss* turned away from the Marrithious Government ships and entered lightspeed-plus. The four Stormriders that were left behind drifted for a moment before also disappearing at lightspeed-plus.

"All Angel Wings, return to your assigned battleship," Ashten said.

"Give me a damage report," Morphus said.

"We have minor damage on the port side of the *Kalaress*," Ashten said.

Morphus waited for his team to report.

"We have no damage. We did lose a few Angel Wings, however. I'll send a report to General Ediira," Morphus said.

Moments later, they received a reply from Victoria.

"Have the damage to the *Kalaress* repaired immediately. Give me a list of the Angel Wing pilots that we have lost so I can contact their families. We have the remaining battleship on long-range scanners. It appears to be returning across the galaxy to Lairdain Tannis. Stay at full alert, just in case," Victoria said.

Wave after wave of Angel Wing fighter ships passed through the portal on Staraliss. The conduit that Commander Striker's team had put into place made the flight through the portal much easier for the pilots. After assessing the potential military targets, one of the fighters returned to Staraliss through the portal with a report for Commander Striker. The pilot landed at the new outpost and exited his ship.

"There is a government building in a canyon that seems to be the only large military target. There appears to be a couple smaller bases in some distant cities. There is also a palace that we believe is their queen empress's residence," the pilot said.

"Overtake the main military building in the canyon. Next, the other two smaller bases in the other cities, and last the palace. Keep in mind that they may have other forces on Lairdain Tannis as well as in space and on other planets. The squadron must be vigilant at all times. That is an alien world," Commander Striker said.

"Yes, sir. Oh, and we are getting some ground fire just on the other side of the portal," the pilot said.

"Okay. Thank you," Striker said.

The pilot returned to his Angel Wing, engaged the engine, and flew back through the portal to Lairdain Tannis. Another officer exited the outpost building and joined Commander Striker at the portal. The two of them watched through the portal as the Angel Wing disappeared into the Lairdain Tannis sky.

"Hey, Owen. It was reported that the fighter pilots are getting some ground fire on the other side of the portal. Also, it looks like our squadron has located a main target," Striker said.

"Good. I was just coming out here to ask—"

Suddenly, a blue laser beam flew past Striker's head. Both officers dove to the ground.

"Those shots came through the portal," Striker said.

"I can see two Sharrixian military officers through the conduit. I only see two of them," Owen said.

"Okay. You take cover on the right side of the rock wall. I'll take the left," Striker said.

"Roger that," Owen said.

They both split up and ran toward either side of the tan rock wall. More lasers were fired through the conduit. Striker turned and peered around the rock wall through the portal. He spotted one of the officers behind a small rock outcrop. He quickly shot a burst of laser fire at the Sharrixian and struck him in the chest. He fell dead to the sand. The other Sharrixian officer opened fire in a continuous barrage. Several of the shots hit the trees in the forest behind them, next to the outpost building. Owen peered around the rock wall and returned fire at the remaining Sharrixian. Owen was immediately struck with a laser beam and fell dead to the sand.

"Owen! No! Ahhh, damn!" Striker exclaimed.

Striker turned and fired through the portal. His beam sliced through the Sharrixian and the alien went down. After some time with no return fire, Striker went over and kneeled down next to Owen. He picked up the body and walked toward the outpost.

Novish Shirom, Jafer, and Versill stood before a military tribunal in the Sharrixian Government Building. Three judges sat along a bench in front of them. One female and two males. The male who sat in the middle was Chief Justice Xalarrton. Queen Empress Aminarra Vistona sat in a throne next to the bench. It was just one of several thrones she used as queen empress. Other than the sitting monarch, the chief justice had the second highest authority in the Sharrixian Government. A small number of other Sharrixians were seated behind Novish, Jafer, and Versill. The three judges finished reading a long list of charges against Versill, then Jafer. Novish knew he was next. He wanted to explain that he was willing to take full responsibility for the charges against Versill and Jafer.

"Novish Shirom, you are charged with conspiring with the enemy, disobeying Queen Empress Aminarra's orders, sending an officer through the portal, tampering with commun—"

The judge was cut short by the courtroom doors bursting open. Everyone's attention turned toward a government official.

"How dare you interrupt this trial!" Queen Empress Aminarra said.

"Queen Empress Aminarra, I know you gave strict instructions not to be interrupted, but people are trying to contact you," the man said.

Queen Empress Aminarra stood up from the throne, her elegant red dress coming into full view. She pointed toward the door.

"Out!" Queen Empress Aminarra shouted.

"We're under attack!" the man shouted back.

A dumbfounded look came over the queen empress.

"Speak," she finally said.

"The fleet tried to contact you to attach more battleships to the fleet. Commander Prilston and his crew perished. They were defeated and the *Arcinaris* was destroyed, along with a number of Stormrider fighter ships. Admiral Gedlo is returning to Lairdain Tannis with the *Lhasariss*. Also, it was reported by the portal guards at the Crystal Field that a squadron of Angel Wing fighter ships have entered through the portal and will arrive here at any moment," the man said.

"Put the building into full lockdown. Mobilize our defense team," Queen Empress Aminarra said.

"Right away," the officer said.

He quickly left the room. The two guards who stood on either side of the entrance closed the doors behind him.

Suddenly, laser fire could be heard in the distance, followed by explosions. Thunderous sounds rolled through the building as waves of Angel Wing fighters swarmed the Sharrixian Government Building.

"Take cover!" Queen Empress Aminarra said.

Queen Empress Aminarra crouched down behind her throne as the three judges ducked under their long bench. The Sharrixians behind Novish, Jafer, and Versill stood up from their seats and ran out of the room, closing the doors behind them. Novish, Jafer, and Versill looked at each other and turned toward the exit. The two guards who stood on either side of the doors readied their rifles in case the three of them tried to escape.

• • •

Being Queen Empress Aminarra's special dignitary at the Lythinarr Palace gave Nilliss special access to many areas of the Sharrixian Government Building that were otherwise restricted. After landing in a private docking bay, Nilliss led the humans along a concrete path that overlooked Deslorr Canyon. Wilcox peered over the edge at the raging waters below. The path led to a tall, gray, metal door. After struggling to enter his code into the keypad with the handcuffs behind his back, Nilliss finally completed the sequence and the door slid aside. They found themselves in a service elevator.

"If you could press the button for the third floor, that would be great," Nilliss said.

Wilcox pressed the button and the door closed.

"So, you are certain Queen Empress Aminarra will be in the courtroom?" Stone asked.

"Yes. She seemed extremely determined to have the three officers tried and killed as quickly as possible. I still cannot believe that she is behind everything. I'm embarrassed for my people. And I understand you need to keep the handcuffs on me until this is sorted out," Nilliss said.

Silence filled the elevator as it rose. Soon, it stopped and the door opened. They stepped out and into a narrow service corridor.

Abruptly, the building shook and they heard a loud snap behind them. They turned to see the elevator free fall down the shaft just before the door closed shut.

"What the hell was—"

The building shook again and several explosions could be heard in the distance. The overhead illuminator fell from the ceiling and crashed onto the floor. The corridor immediately went dark. Instinctively, Stone grabbed a flashlight from his gear. He turned it on and the intense light brightened the entire length of the corridor.

"It sounds like we are under attack. If the building goes into lockdown, my codes will not work," Nilliss said.

Nilliss hurried along the service corridor. Stone was behind him, followed by Mercedes, Wilcox, and Nancy. Stone held the flashlight in one hand and his laser rifle in the other. Wilcox had his laser rifle at the ready in case Mercedes made any sudden moves. Nancy still held a laser rifle in each hand. After passing a couple of doors, Nilliss stopped in front of one.

"This is it. We are at the back of the courtroom," Nilliss said.

Stone held his light up to the keypad and Nilliss reached around with his cuffed hands and pressed the code. Nothing happened. He tried it again. The door would not open.

"They've gone into lockdown. It looks like we are stuck here," Nilliss said.

"Stand back," Stone said.

"You're going to fire that thing in this little corridor?" Nilliss asked.

"Yes. Back up," Stone said.

He fired his laser rifle at the control panel, completely destroying it. The door still did not open. He began a firestorm of concentrated laser power on the door latch. The intense blue beams brightened the dark corridor. The others crouched back and shielded their eyes as sparks flew. The metal along the door melted, dripping down the door frame. It opened.

"Okay, we're in," Stone said.

Once again, Nilliss took the lead. They followed him through back offices. Any office personnel who had been there had already cleared out before the lockdown. Nilliss stopped at a wooden door.

"This leads to the courtroom. There will be two armed courtroom guards, so be careful," Nilliss said.

Stone slowly opened the door and peeked through the crack. He spotted the guards on the right side of the room.

"If we stay down, we can get behind a bench that runs the length of this wall. That will keep us out of sight. The problem is that there are what appear to be three judges behind the bench at the moment," Stone said.

Once again the building shook as more Angel Wings concentrated their firepower onto the building.

"That didn't sound good," Nilliss said.

"I'm going in," Stone said.

"We're right behind you," Wilcox said.

Stone opened the door and they each crouched down behind the bench. The surprised look on the faces of the judges was priceless. Stone quickly maneuvered around the end of the bench and pointed his laser rifle at the two guards.

"Put down your weapons!" he shouted.

Wilcox and Nancy immediately revealed themselves from behind the bench with their laser rifles drawn. The two guards looked as if they were going to raise their weapons.

"Okay, for *you!*" Nancy said.

Nancy stepped around in front of the queen empress's throne and raised the two laser rifles she held in either hand. She fired both lasers above their heads, sending debris down over them.

"Drop the weapons!" Nancy shouted.

The guards both lowered their laser rifles to the floor. Queen Empress Aminarra peeked from around the back of her throne and Nancy turned toward her.

"Queen Empress Aminarra, I presume," Nancy said.

"Who are you people?" Queen Empress Aminarra asked.

Wilcox walked over and obtained the two guards' weapons. Each of the rifles had straps. He slung them both over his shoulder.

The three judges stood up from behind the long bench. Novish, Jafer, and Versill each looked as surprised as the rest. Mercedes stood close to Wilcox, her hands still cuffed behind her back. Queen Empress Aminarra turned toward Nilliss and noticed that he too was in handcuffs. She looked at Mercedes with compassion. But the look that Mercedes gave the queen empress was anything but mutual.

"I gave up *everything* for you! You lied to me!" Mercedes shouted, staring at the queen empress.

"Queen Empress Aminarra, we have evidence against you. We have evidence that you are behind everything. The death of the Gatherer Tajenipp, controlling Mercedes with the green crystal, causing the other Gatherers to be killed by the humans so you would have the excuse you needed for war, lying to your people about the prisoners who Versill returned, attempting to kill these three military officers for trying to stop your Marrithious Galactic War, but most of all...for shaming our people," Nilliss said.

"Show me proof!" Queen Empress Aminarra said.

"We'll show the judges proof," Nancy said.

She walked over to the bench and set down both laser rifles. Removing the backpack, Nancy removed the binder with the torn pages of Tajenipp's testimony. She handed the pages to one of the judges. The tall Sharrixian judge read the pages aloud and looked at Queen Empress Aminarra.

"If I may speak... The prisoners are still aboard the *Credence Revenge.* They are the ones the humans have arrested and released to Versill for Sharrixian justice. The prisoners are responsible for killing, apparently, four of the Gatherers...but not Tajenipp, as we previously thought," Novish said.

"And is there other evidence against Queen Empress Aminarra?" the female judge asked.

"I am living evidence of what Queen Empress Aminarra has done. She's been controlling me for twenty years. It's difficult to explain what the green crystal does to me. I…I become a minion under her control. But it's like an addiction. I'm free, but I come back for more instructions, as if I'm in a trance sometimes," Mercedes said as tears pooled in her eyes.

"You have betrayed me, Mercedes. You had the missing pages from Tajenipp's testimony this entire time, didn't you? I should have ended you a long time ago," Queen Empress Aminarra said.

"You have betrayed *me!* You made me believe we could continue to harvest crystals. For twenty years, you've been planning this. Yes, I took the pages. Something deep inside of me knew not to trust you. But, ohhh…the green crystal. You made me do things… You made me do things that I regret," Mercedes said, tears flowing down her cheeks. "I've killed for you. I've put my own daughter in danger for you! *Why?* Why did you start this war?" Mercedes asked.

Queen Empress Aminarra knew at that point that her master plan had failed. She was not going to get out of the mess that was exposed before the court.

"Oh, Mercedes… You've always just been my pet slave. You were always so happy to do my bidding. You became rich, did you not? I started this war because I wanted to conquer all of you humans. I wanted to control the entire Marrithious Galaxy…even the Axynnians. If Admiral Othan is running back home, then I have misjudged your military power. The death of the Gatherers was the excuse I needed to make it happen. And you and your group helped me to achieve that, Mercedes. I just needed the Sharrixian Council to want it badly enough that any Sharrixian losses would be on them, not me. I waited years to convince them."

"I always thought you were against war, while the council was all for it. Did you control the council with the green crystal too?" Novish asked.

"Don't be a fool! Our crystals don't affect Sharrixians. Only the humans are affected by our crystals. I'm not actually sure about the Axynnians. I never had the chance to experiment with them," Queen Empress Aminarra said.

"Where is the green crystal now?" Mercedes asked.

Queen Empress Aminarra laughed for a long moment. "You will never find it," she said.

"The portal in your master bedroom is still working, so the crystal must be close," Mercedes said.

Queen Empress Aminarra Vistona remained silent.

"The presentation of evidence and testimony, including your own statements, Queen Empress Aminarra, has given us judges the overwhelming proof that it is *you* who is the treasonist. I never thought I would have to arrest my own queen empress. Guards, I need you to place Queen Empress Aminarra Vistona under arrest for treason and murder, among many other crimes. If we survive this attack on the Sharrixian Government Building, then we will set up a trial date for her. Aminarra Vistona, you are hereby removed as the sovereign head of state for the Sharrixian people," Chief Justice Xalarrton said.

The two guards were reluctant, but knew the authority of the chief justice. They walked over to where Aminarra stood next to her throne and handcuffed her.

"Speaking of the attack, I'll see if I can stop the attack on this building," Commander Stone said.

He reached into his pocket for his comm. From the two comms in his pocket, the one he removed was from the office in the Lythinarr Palace. He immediately handed it to Versill.

"Since I know who you are, Versill, I'll hand this comm to you. This comm is from the Lythinarr Palace. Perhaps, you can contact your military and deescalate things. I'll do the same," Stone said.

Versill took the comm from Stone and handed it to Novish. Stone reached back into his pocket for the correct comm.

"This is Commander Stone. Can anyone hear my signal?" he asked.

"Commander Stone? How are we picking up your signal on Lairdain Tannis? Our Angel Wing comms cannot reach all the way across the galaxy without a booster," a pilot said.

"Cease fire on the Sharrixian Government Building. I am inside," Stone said.

"Umm… All fighters in the squadron, cease fire now! Commander Stone, there are Stormriders from the Sharrixian Government Building defenses still shooting at us. We will stand by for further instructions," the pilot said.

"Roger that," Stone said.

Novish turned the volume up on the comm and walked over to Chief Justice Xalarrton.

"This is High Commander Novish Shirom. We are still on open communications, so Admiral Gedlo Othan, you should be able to hear me."

"This is Admiral Othan. It was my understanding that you were arrested for treason," Gedlo said.

"New evidence has created a change in events. It is Aminarra Vistona who is under arrest for treason. I have Chief Justice Xalarrton here to confirm my statements," Novish said.

The chief justice received the comm from Novish.

"Admiral Gedlo. This is Chief Justice Xalarrton. I declare that High Commander Novish Shirom has been fully restored to his position of power over the Sharrixian military and has full authority over you and the other commanders. Commander Jafer and officer Versill have also been restored to their positions. Aminarra Vistona has, indeed, been arrested for treason and removed as a monarch," Xalarrton said.

"I see," Gedlo said.

Xalarrton handed the comm back to Novish.

"All Sharrixian Government Building defenses, stand down. Cease fire! Commander Othan, if you are on your way back to Lairdain Tannis, you are to stand down and not engage in any fight on or off the planet,"

"Yes, sir," Gedlo said. "We lost the *Arcinaris* with Commander Covlan Prilston and his crew. Most of the remaining Stormrider fighter ships squeezed into the docking bays of the *Arcinaris,* but there are several that could not fit and are not far behind us."

"It is unfortunate about Commander Prilston. That battle should have *never* taken place. Have the extra Stormriders land in the docking bay of the *Shartannis* when they arrive. It is currently in orbit above Lairdain Tannis, along with the *Credence* and the *Credence Revenge.* Each ship is currently being manned by a small military crew," Novish said.

"Understood," Gedlo said.

"If there are any other Sharrixian battleships en route from the planets Rassioth, Ryth Oparrian, or Narross Selontious, you need to return to your bases and follow your normal schedule," Novish said.

The three judges huddled together and spoke in a low manner for several minutes.

"High Commander Novish Shirom, by my authority as chief justice of the Sharrixian court, I hereby declare you to be our new Sharrixian emperor," Xalarrton said.

Novish Shirom put a hand over his bumpy head in surprise, his jaw dropping. He knew Chief Justice Xalarrton had the second highest authority in the government, just below the monarch, but he did not expect this.

"It is with great honor that I accept," Novish said.

Chapter Twenty

A DIPLOMATIC SHIP from the Marrithious Government arrived at the Sharrixian Government Building on Lairdain Tannis. Several crews could be seen in the distance making repairs to the damaged sections of the building that took place the week before during the Battle of Deslorr Canyon. The ship hovered above Deslorr Canyon, awaiting clearance to land in the docking bay. The sun brightened the canyon and the desert beyond. Below, the rapid flowing water could be seen making its way along the jagged rocks. Soon, the ship proceeded onto the docking platform that extended slightly outward beyond the edge of the building.

On board the ship was the leader of the Marrithious Government, Essir Phensaa, along with General Victoria Ediira, Commander Stone, Wilcox Brown, and Nancy Louray. Since the two investigators had previously been commissioned by the military to collaborate on the investigation, their request to join the leader and military personnel on the trip was granted.

Essir Phensaa was a man in his forties with light brown hair. He sat next to General Victoria Ediira. Each of the passengers on the ship were dressed appropriately for the trial of the prisoners from Mercedes Brantt's criminal group.

"It will be nice to get this peace treaty signed," Essir said.

"Yes, it will," Victoria said.

"Also, it will be nice to finally get justice for the Gatherers and others who Mercedes Brantt's group of criminals have killed. It is my understanding that Sharrixian justice is swift and harsh," Essir said.

"According to Versill, it won't end well for any of them," Victoria said.

"I was surprised when Chief Justice Xalarrton wanted Mercedes Brantt to stand trial in a Marrithious Government court," Wilcox said.

"Yes, I was as well, when I found out. They had the leader of the group in their hands, but because of Aminarra's involvement with Mercedes, Chief Justice Xalarrton felt that Mercedes should be tried by her own species. He did reiterate that he was grateful for us turning over the group who actually killed the four Gatherers, however," Victoria said.

"I assume the trial for Mercedes Brantt will happen soon," Nancy said.

"Yes, it will. In fact, the arraignment is finished and the trial is set for next week. I know you two plan to be there as well," Victoria said.

"Yes. We need to present the deed to Staraliss as one of the court's exhibits. Coradelle Hershall will be there as well," Wilcox said.

Victoria looked over at Commander Stone, who had been fairly quiet the entire trip across the Marrithious Galaxy. She knew he was depressed.

"Hey… Are you okay?" Victoria asked.

Stone looked up at her with no facial expression and then sighed.

"Aolliam and I have worked together for many years. We always had each other's back. In the Lythinarr Palace that day, I didn't have his back," Stone said.

"We had a surprise attack from the Sharrixian Palace Guards. There's not much you could have done to have his back. The open staircase was a vulnerable location. I'm sure the fact that we are back on Lairdain Tannis doesn't help. Commander Aolliam will be remembered as a great warrior," Wilcox said.

"There is a military memorial service planned for Commander Aolliam, the Angel Wing pilots who lost their lives in the Battle of Sharmyra, and an officer who was shot near the portal at the Staraliss outpost. They will be honored," Essir Phensaa said.

"You should not blame yourself for that, Commander Stone. Commander Aolliam is in good hands right now in Heaven. You can be certain of that," Nancy said.

"The kind words from all of you are appreciated," Stone said.

After the ship came to a rest in the docking bay, the airlock door was opened by the pilot. Each of them exited the ship and they were greeted by two tall Sharrixians.

"General Ediira!" Versill said.

"Versill, it's nice to see you again. I would like you to meet the leader of the Marrithious Government, Essir Phensaa. And you already know Commander Stone, Wilcox Brown, and Nancy Louray," Victoria said, gesturing toward each of them.

"Leader Essir Phensaa, it is an honor to meet you. I would like to introduce all of you to Emperor Novish Shirom," Versill said, stepping aside.

Novish stepped forward and reached out his patterned hand toward Essir Phensaa. Essir looked up at the tall Sharrixian and shook his hand.

"It is, indeed, an honor to meet you, Essir," Novish said.

"It is an honor to meet you as well. Congratulations on your new position as monarch," Essir said.

"We finally get to meet in person," Victoria said.

Novish looked over at Victoria and also shook her hand.

"Yes. We have been communicating across the Marrithious Galaxy for some time. It is certainly nice to meet you in person, General Ediira. It is nice to meet *all* of you," Novish said, looking at the others. "I appreciate you all being here for today's important events. I would also like to attend the trial for Mercedes Brantt when it occurs. As we head to the conference room, Versill will explain today's agenda."

Novish started walking across the docking bay, the rest of them following. Versill turned toward the others.

"We are proceeding to the new conference room—which was formerly the Sharrixian Council room—so Essir Phensaa and Emperor Novish can both sign the Lairdain Tannis Treaty. Then, with the peace treaty signed, the end of the Marrithious Galactic War will be official. One of the first things Emperor Novish did when he became monarch was to dissolve the Sharrixian Council. Aminarra was manipulating them to advocate for war and they didn't even realize it. From the conference room, we will proceed to the courtroom for the trial of the human prisoners who are responsible for the death of our four Gatherers, one of whom was Emperor Novish's uncle, Riilan. This will also be justice for others they have killed. The blood of the fifth Gatherer, Tajenipp, is on Aminarra Vistona's hands. Just so you know, the humans in this trial *will* be put to death. Our court has zero tolerance for these types of crimes," Versill said.

"Riilan was the skeleton I pulled from the sand on Staraliss. His name patch was still intact. I actually have a picture of it on my comm. I'm sorry for your loss," Wilcox said.

As they walked, Novish turned toward Wilcox.

"Thank you, Wilcox. I'd like you to send me that picture when you get a chance. I appreciate the military putting his remains, as well as the others, in preservation chambers. We will be honoring them later today," Novish said.

"Yes. Immediately after the trial for the humans, we will attend the high-profile trial for Aminarra Vistona, former queen empress. She has a long list of offenses. Aminarra will also be put to death. After both trials, we will be heading over to the large hall to attend the memorial service that Emperor Novish had mentioned. It is for the Gatherers found on Staraliss, Tajenipp, and the original crew of the *Credence,* who died in space. After the service, in the same hall, there will be an honor ceremony for yours truly in my role to bring peace. Emperor Novish insisted…" Versill said.

After a set of doors swiftly slid aside, they entered into a long corridor.

"An honor ceremony? So, you *are* a hero to your people, after all," Victoria said.

"I am. But we were almost killed by Aminarra. It's strange and surreal how things like that can change in an instant," Versill said.

"God works in mysterious ways," Nancy said.

Emperor Novish turned toward Nancy and leaned downward slightly.

"That, He does, Nancy. That, He does," Novish said.

Nancy Louray was hard at work in the kitchen, making her renowned mashed potatoes. Other food items cooked on her stove as well. She whipped the potatoes until her arm became tired. Suddenly, there was a knock at the door of her apartment. Nancy looked in that direction.

"Just a minute," she said.

She walked through the living room to answer the door.

"Hi, Nancy!"

"Avalaur! It's nice to see you and the whole family. Come on in," Nancy said.

Avalaur, her husband, and two children stepped into Nancy's living room.

"Whatever you're cooking, it smells incredibly delicious," Avalaur said.

"Thank you. How are you, Alex?" Nancy asked.

"I'm doing well. Thanks for asking. We appreciate you inviting us over for the celebration," Alex said.

Nancy closed the door behind them.

"Do you kids like games?" Nancy asked.

"Yes," they replied simultaneously.

"Okay. Let me show you the games closet. You two can pick out whatever games you want to play. Just be sure not to lose any of the pieces," Nancy said.

She brought the two children to her games closet and opened the door. The children's eyes became wide in surprise at the massive assortment of board games.

"Pick what ever you want. You can play them in the family room down the hall. Okay?"

"Thanks, Miss Nancy," the boy said.

"Thank you," the girl said.

Nancy went back into the living room, where Avalaur and Alex made themselves comfortable on the couch.

"Dinner is almost ready. We're just waiting on Wilcox," Nancy said.

"And how is the whole thing going with revealing your feelings to him?" Avalaur asked.

"Umm… It's… Let me put it this way, he knows how I feel now," Nancy said.

"Well, that's a step in the right direction," Avalaur said.

There was another knock at the door.

"That must be Wilcox now. Shhh!" Nancy said.

She turned toward Avalaur and put her index finger vertically up to her lips to indicate for Avalaur not to mention anything about the conversation to Wilcox. Nancy opened the door. Before her, Wilcox

Brown stood with his usual fedora hat on, his black hair poking out from the sides. In his hand was a bouquet of colorful flowers.

"Hi, Nancy. These are for you," Wilcox said.

A look of surprise came across Nancy's face as she accepted the bouquet.

"Well, thank you, Wilcox. This arrangement is absolutely beautiful. Come on in," Nancy said.

She closed the door behind Wilcox.

"This is an old friend of mine, Avalaur, and her husband, Alex. Their kids are playing in the other room. Avalaur, Alex, this is Wilcox Brown," she said.

"It's nice to meet you," Alex said.

He stood up and shook Wilcox's hand.

"Yes, it's nice to meet you. Nancy always has so many nice things to say about you," Avalaur said.

"It's nice to meet you both as well," Wilcox said.

Nancy smiled at Wilcox as she smelled the flowers.

"These are so beautiful, Wilcox. I'm going to go put these in a vase," Nancy said.

She disappeared into the kitchen.

"It was nice for Nancy to have this little event to celebrate our agency solving the most complex case we've had to date," Wilcox said.

"Yes. This is perfect. Over dinner, I'd like to hear more about your adventures on this case," Avalaur said.

Wilcox sat down in the living room chair and removed his hat. He set it on the back of the chair.

"We have the Mercedes Brantt trial in a couple of days as well," Wilcox said.

"Yeah, Nancy mentioned that. She also said the trials you two saw on Lairdain Tannis were very sobering," Avalaur said.

"Yes, there was some serious charges against Mercedes Brantt's group and also against the former queen empress herself. Their executions were carried out immediately after the trials. Although we could have, we chose not to attend those. Besides, we had a couple of ceremonies to attend. One of them was for the Sharrixian officer named Versill. She is the one who came through the portal to help our Marrithious military with their investigation. Versill was honored as a hero," Wilcox said.

Nancy walked back into the living room.

"Speaking of heroes…" Avalaur said.

"What?" Nancy asked.

"Nancy, you are a hero as well. Among many other things that you helped with during this investigation, you rescued Coradelle Hershall on Noderell…even though I wrongly said it would be chasing a dead end," Wilcox said.

"They would have killed her too, so it would have been a literal dead end, all right. I'm glad I didn't listen to you. Anyway, dinner is ready. I've already made all of your plates. If you want to get the kids, then we can start eating. I have some bubbly to drink, if any of you want some. Otherwise, I have cola, coffee, water, and juice," Nancy said.

Avalaur gathered her children and brought them into the kitchen. They each sat down at the table. The aroma that rose from each plate was tantalizing. The bouquet of flowers that Wilcox had given Nancy sat in a vase at the center of the table.

"This looks so good. Thank you for all of your efforts, Nancy," Avalaur said.

Nancy smiled. "You're welcome. I really enjoy the company. I'd like to pray. Shall we?"

"Yes," Wilcox said.

"Dear Heavenly Father, we come to You today in prayer and thanksgiving. Thank You for this food. Please nourish it to our bodies. Thank You for this time together with friends. Please keep us all safe in our travels. Please provide Your hand of protection over us. Thank You for getting us through our recent case and helping us to solve the mystery of the missing deed. Thank You for getting us safely past that ordeal and specifically for helping me rescue Coradelle. There has been a lot who have died over this crystal greed. Please be with the loved ones of those left behind. I pray for Commander Stone as well with the loss of his friend Commander Aolliam. Please comfort him with Your Holy Spirit. Thank You that we were able to give Remywl Yortix closure on what happened to his uncle, Everett Quarton. Thank You that the Marrithious Galaxy is a lot safer now than when we began this investigation. I pray this all in Jesus's name. Amen," Nancy said.

The military trial for Mercedes Brantt was in progress on the planet Sharmyra at the Marrithious Government military headquarters. In attendance was the Marrithious Government leader, Essir Phensaa, along with General Victoria Ediira, Commander Stone, Commander Ashten, Wilcox Brown, Nancy Louray, Coradelle Hershall, Emperor Novish Shirom, and Versill. The trial was well under way. Mercedes Brantt sat in a separate section with armed military officers on either side of her. She looked up at Judge Thaosium, who was looking over some papers. The courtroom was fairly quiet.

"Wilcox Brown, do you have the Staraliss deed exhibit?" Thaosium asked.

"Yes, Your Honor."

"Can you please bring that to me?" Thaosium asked.

Wilcox brought the document up to the bench, handed it to the judge, and returned to his seat. Judge Thaosium looked over the deed and set it on one of the piles of evidence.

"I've heard testimony from Mercedes Brantt. I've seen all the evidence, some of which was presented during her arraignment, including others who witnessed her murdering Bryson Wieler," Thaosium said, rummaging through a few papers to find a note. "I do have a note here from Coradelle Hershall, requesting to address her mother, Mercedes Brantt. Coradelle Hershall, permission is granted. You may step forward and speak."

Coradelle stood up and made her way toward the front of the courtroom.

"Thank you, Your Honor," Coradelle said. She turned toward her mother. "Mom, first and foremost, I want to say that I've always tried to be close to you, but you have always pushed me away. Now, I know it was because you were preoccupied with your criminal organization. Even if it wasn't by your own hands, you had your group kill my father with a black crystal…and others as well. I don't understand why you hated him so much. Robert Hershall was a good man. You can blame all of this on the former queen empress of the Sharrixians all you want, but you are responsible for making many of those decisions. You've made countless credits with your crystal avarice. Even if the blue crystals are helpful for healing, the purple ones make humans fall in love when they would not normally do so, forcing a one-way relationship. And the black ones…" Coradelle shook her head. "The black ones were used to kill my father. And they were going to kill *me* with them." She began to cry. "I'm devastated to learn of your involvement with this. I'm ashamed of you, mother. I wish we could have had a close relationship. I wish you would have loved me."

Wiping the tears from her eyes, Coradelle returned to her seat. Mercedes began weeping when she saw the pain in her daughter's eyes.

"Wilcox Brown, you may retrieve the deed to Staraliss and present it to its rightful owner, the heir to Robert Hershall's estate, Coradelle Hershall. Mercedes Brantt, with your statements from earlier and all the evidence presented against you, I hereby sentence you to death. Execution will be set for this afternoon," Thaosium said.

The courtroom became quiet. The only sound was Mercedes Brantt sobbing heavily.

Immediately after Mercedes Brantt's trial, a meeting took place in a conference room in the Marrithious Government military headquarters on Sharmyra. Essir Phensaa sat next to General Victoria Ediira. Emperor Novish Shirom and Versill sat across from them. Also present was Commander Stone, Commander Ashten, Wilcox Brown, Nancy Louray, and Coradelle Hershall.

"Thank you all for attending this meeting," Essir Phensaa said. "As leader of the Marrithious Government, I want to thank Emperor Novish Shirom for traveling across the galaxy to attend Mercedes Brantt's trial. Justice for the Gatherers is now complete, including your uncle Riilan. But that does not make the pain any less significant for those who were affected by this entire ordeal. The sad thing about greed is that it can come in many forms and it can hurt many innocent people."

"Thank you for having me and Versill here," Novish said.

"Wilcox Brown, I present this certificate to you for your agency's outstanding work in the Coradelle Hershall case to find the missing deed to Staraliss," Essir said. He handed Wilcox a framed certificate. "I would also like to personally thank both you and Nancy Louray for helping General Victoria Ediira with the military investigation into Mercedes Brantt's criminal organization. You both played a vital role in solving this lengthy investigation, which crossed over into your own investigation. And Nancy, your bravery and heroism in rescuing Coradelle Hershall from Noderell is very honorable. I present these medals of honor to both of you." He handed medals to Wilcox and Nancy.

"Thank you," Wilcox said.

"Thank you," Nancy said.

"Versill, you also played a vital role in helping General Victoria Ediira with her investigation. I have a medal for you as well," Essir said. He handed a medal to Versill.

"Thank you, Leader Phensaa," Versill said.

She reached across the conference room table and accepted the medal.

"General Ediira, Commander Stone, and Commander Ashten, there will be a military ceremony this evening where all of you will be honored for your work. Other commanders and officers will also be honored," Essir said.

"We look forward to it, sir," Victoria said.

"Wilcox, as you mentioned to me earlier, I believe you have a few words to say," Essir said.

"Yes. Coradelle Hershall, I would like to present to you the missing deed to Staraliss. You are the rightful owner of the planet," Wilcox said.

He removed the deed from a binder and handed it over to Coradelle, who sat next to Nancy. She took the document and looked at it for a long moment and saw her father's signature.

"Thank you, Wilcox and Nancy, for all of your hard work in solving my case. I probably didn't pay you as much as you deserve for my case. I know it became a crazy rabbit hole for you. I will recommend the Wilcox Brown Agency as private investigators any time. And Nancy, thank you for rescuing me and saving my life. Thank you for your prayers," Coradelle said.

"You're welcome," Nancy said.

"And now, Emperor Novish Shirom has some things he would like to discuss," Essir said.

"Yes. I wanted my trip across the Marrithious Galaxy to be as efficient as possible, so I figured I would discuss some things after attending the trial. First, I would like to thank you for returning the load of crystals that you found in the warehouse on Noderell as well as the black crystals that were found inside the container in the town of Timber Wolf on Ryamesh. The Sharrixian Government will be putting safeguards in place regarding the crystals. The crystals do not affect Sharrixians, so these safeguards would be in place for the protection of the humans and Axynnians. We have recently found out that the blue crystals heal Axynnians, so it is assumed the purple and black crystals would affect them as well. Since it is now permitted for citizens of the

Marrithious Government and citizens of the Sharrixian Government to enter into each other's territory, we have removed any black and purple crystals from public areas in which humans and Axynnians might come into contact with them. As you may know, we have used them in the architecture of our buildings for years. Since the blue crystals are actually beneficial to you for healing, we will permit contact with, and purchase of the blue crystals. Theft of crystals is punishable, however," Novish said.

"That is understandable. I know there were crystals sold on the black market through Mercedes Brantt's organization. We have put laws into place for possessing the black and purple crystals, with harsh penalties for those who do. We will continue to search for those. For the blue crystals, it is acceptable for anyone to possess them," Essir said.

"All the crystals that were returned to us had originally come from the Crystal Field out in the Lairdain Tannis desert by the portal. And that is where they were returned…the blue ones, the purple ones, and the black ones. The second thing I want to discuss is the portal itself. It is forbidden for non-Sharrixians to enter the Crystal Field via the portal or physically going out to the Crystal Field in the Lairdain Tannis desert, due to the dangers of the black crystals. Although two of our portal guards died in the Marrithious Galactic War, our Crystal Field is constantly guarded for everyone's safety.

"It is now presumed that a large, green crystal lies deep within the rock below the portal that creates the natural phenomenon. We do not plan to start cutting through the rock to find it. As far as the smaller green crystal that Aminarra Vistona possessed, it was found in the Lythinarr Palace, within her master bedroom. When the metal frame was removed from the wall, the portal connecting to Mercedes Brantt's house disappeared. When it was returned to the wall, the portal would reappear within the metal frame. As soon as the metal frame was disassembled, the portal no longer worked. In addition to finding the green crystal inside a compartment within the metal frame, a module was discovered within the metal framework that was an integral part of the *Credence's* original nav system. Apparently, Aminarra channeled the power of the crystal to the high-tech galactic mapping technology in the module to create the exact galactic coordinates in Mercedes Brantt's house. So basically, Aminarra sent the crew of the *Credence* on their outbound flight without a proper nav system. The nav system was not outdated, but malfunctioned because part of it was missing. That's why they became lost and starved to death. This was just discovered after Aminarra Vistona had already been executed. She is also responsible for the deaths of the four Sharrixian crew members of the *Credence.*

"I am now living in the Lythinarr Palace, which was made for the sitting monarch. The green crystal that she possessed has been transferred to a military storage facility under armed guard. Whoever will end up with Mercedes Brantt's house will need to remove the metal frame from the wall on that side. It is nonfunctional at this point," Novish said.

"Interesting…" Commander Ashten said.

"We can take care of the metal frame on this side. We were already there to remove the body of Bryson Wieler," Victoria said. "Oh, and we arrested the remaining stragglers who sold crystals on the black market for Mercedes."

"If I may…" Coradelle Hershall said. "I would like to sell the planet Staraliss to the Sharrixians. It will prevent any further criminals from going through to get crystals."

Coradelle looked at the deed that she held and then at the tall alien emperor who sat across the conference room table from her. Novish turned from Coradelle to Essir.

"That would certainly solve the problem of non-Sharrixians coming through the portal, but it would also create a new potential issue. The Sharrixian Government would then have territory inside Marrithious Government territory," Novish said.

"Yes, it certainly would. We already have a military outpost on Staraliss to guard against portal entry. So, I don't think that would be a good idea, Coradelle," Victoria said.

"I'm just trying to help. Since the military is occupying my planet anyway, I don't have much need for it. Would the Marrithious Government like to purchase it, then?" Coradelle asked.

"Consider it sold. We will give you more than a fair price for the planet," Essir said.

"Well, good. I will have some credits to fix the back door to my house that was broken into," Coradelle said.

"I'm sure you'll have plenty left over," Commander Stone said.

"You may even end up with your mother's house on Adanarr. It will have to go through the Settlement Agency, however. Now that the criminals are out of that agency, it should run like it's supposed to," Victoria said.

"Inheriting the house would be nice, but I'll probably sell it because of everything that has happened there. I will let my friend Alivia Bexley and also Maxboro Lawson know the outcome of the case as well," Coradelle said.

"Well, I am very pleased that a new relationship has been formed between our two governments," Novish said.

"Yes. I am grateful that we have worked together on the Lairdain Tannis Treaty and also that safeguards for the crystals have been implemented," Essir said.

"Peace…it's a beautiful thing," Wilcox said.

The sun was shining in the city of Kethan. Wilcox Brown and Nancy Louray had just landed on Kesron. After exiting the *Enigma*, they made their way around to the front sidewalk toward the office. Pausing in front of the old building, Nancy unlocked the door. Wilcox looked up at his old sign.

Wilcox Brown Agency, Private Investigators… He silently read the sign.

In his hand, he held the framed certificate that Essir Phensaa had given to his agency. Nancy opened the door, the familiar bells jingling. After entering the office, Wilcox set the certificate on his desk and removed his fedora hat, placing it on top of the coatrack.

"I'm glad you finally made an appointment to get the *Enigma's* door hinge fixed. Hey would you like a cup of coffee?" Nancy asked.

"That would be great. I want to mount this framed certificate on the wall," Wilcox said.

Nancy walked toward the back of the office to make some fresh coffee. Wilcox followed her to the back and opened a closet door.

"Do you know where the ladder is?" he asked.

"Yes. You left the ladder down the hall by the back window when you repaired the window lock," Nancy said.

"Ah. Thank you."

Wilcox walked down the narrow hall, beyond the bathroom, and spotted the ladder next to the back window. He took it and walked back toward his desk. Wilcox opened a drawer in a cabinet next to the wall and removed a hammer and some nails.

"Where should I put the certificate?" he asked.

Nancy walked back toward his desk with a cup of coffee in each hand and looked up at the wall.

"Right there in that open spot. Center it right below the clock," she said.

"Yeah, I think that would look great."

Wilcox opened the ladder and began to hang the certificate.

"The coffee is ready," Nancy said.

She set his black coffee on his desk and sipped hers while she watched him hang the certificate.

"Be careful on the ladder. Oh, I see that I missed a cobweb on the ceiling when I was cleaning yesterday," Nancy said.

"Well, you must be slacking. I'm joking. You always do a phenomenal job around here, Nancy," Wilcox said.

He stepped down from the ladder and bumped his head on a file cabinet.

"Did you knock some sense in?" she asked.

Wilcox looked at her. "I probably did."

"Kidding…"

They both looked up at the framed certificate that hung on the wall.

"It looks nice," Wilcox said.

"It's perfect. And it's a great recognition that Essir Phensaa has awarded the agency," Nancy said.

Wilcox turned around and smiled at Nancy.

"Thank you, Nancy, for being by my side in all of our investigative work. You are much appreciated."

Nancy smiled back at Wilcox and set her coffee cup on top of the filing cabinet next to her desk.

"You're welcome," she said.

Suddenly, Wilcox picked Nancy up and set her on her own desk. He stood against the desk, her legs on either side of him and he stared into her green eyes. A surprised look came over her.

"What—" she began.

Wilcox interrupted her with a long, passionate kiss, his tongue dancing around hers. When he finally broke away, she breathed in deeply and smiled.

"There are no purple crystals around this time. I'm in love with you, Nancy. I'm sorry that I've suppressed my feelings for so long. But no more…" Wilcox said.

"I've been waiting a long time to hear those words, Wilcox Brown. I've been in love with you for a very long time," Nancy said.

Wilcox leaned in and wrapped his arms around Nancy, kissing her once more.

APPENDIX

TERMINOLOGY GLOSSARY

Chapter references are where the term first appears in the novel.
(Some terms may contain slight spoilers.)

A

Adamorr - (Chapter 1) He was an Axynnian who lived on the planet Xeralosa. Adamorr had amber eyes. He was a friend of Wilcox Brown.

Adanarr - (Chapter 12) A planet within the Marrithious Government's territory.

Alex - (Chapter 20) He lived on the planet Symphainia. Alex was the husband of Avalaur and the father of their two children, a boy and a girl.

Anders, Chaslin - (Chapter 2) He was a settlement agent at the Settlement Agency on the planet Anneriss. Chaslin had brown hair.

Angel Wing - (Chapter 9) A Marrithious Government military fighter ship.

Anneriss - (Chapter 2) A planet within the Marrithious Government's territory. Anneriss was the location of a secret Marrithious Government military base.

Aolliam, Commander - (Chapter 7) He was a commander in the Marrithious Government military. Aolliam had brown hair.

Arcinaris - (Chapter 11) A Sharrixian Government battleship under the leadership of Commander Covlan Prilston. The *Arcinaris* was destroyed in the Battle of Sharmyra during the Marrithious Galactic War.

Ashten, Commander - (Chapter 9) He was a commander in the Marrithious Government military. Ashten commanded the battleship *Kalaress* in the Battle of Sharmyra during the Marrithious Galactic War. Ashten had whitish-gray hair.

Avalaur - (Chapter 1) She lived on the planet Symphainia. Avalaur had blond hair. She was the wife of Alex and the mother of their two children, a boy and a girl. Avalaur was a friend of Nancy Louray.

Axynnian - (Chapter 1) One of the three intelligent species in the Marrithious Galaxy, second most common to humans. Axynnians had amber eyes and short, light brown fur.

B

Battle of Deslorr Canyon - (Chapter 20) One of the battles during the brief Marrithious Galactic War. The Battle of Deslorr Canyon took place at Deslorr Canyon on the planet Lairdain Tannis where the Sharrixian Government Building was located.

Battle of Sharmyra - (Chapter 20) One of the battles during the brief Marrithious Galactic War. The Battle of Sharmyra took place in space, near the planet Sharmyra.

Bexley, Alivia - (Chapter 1) She lived in the city of Emysh on the planet Ryamesh. Alivia had blond hair. Alivia was a friend of Coradelle Hershall.

Brantt, Mercedes - (Chapter 2) She lived outside the city of Torontarr on the planet Adanarr. Mercedes had blond hair and blue eyes. She was the mother of Coradelle Hershall.

Brown, Wilcox - (Chapter 1) He lived in the city of Kethan on the planet Kesron. Wilcox was a private investigator who owned the Wilcox Brown Agency in the city of Kethan. He was in the business of solving mysteries for over thirty years. Wilcox had black hair and green eyes. He often wore a fedora hat. Wilcox owned a spaceship named *Enigma,* but he did not like space travel.

C

Celtarenia - (Chapter 17) A planet located in the Celtarenia Star System, within the Marrithious Government's territory. Celtarenia was the location of a Marrithious Government military shipyard.

Celtarenia Star System - (Chapter 14) A star system in the Marrithious Galaxy, within the Marrithious Government's territory.

comm - (Chapter 1) A communicator device that had multiple functions.

Corbinn, Commander Mawtesh - (Chapter 13) He was a commander in the Marrithious Government military. Mawtesh was part of the alien ship military investigation and worked undercover at the Settlement Agency.

Country Barn - (Chapter 1) A restaurant on the outskirts of the city of Kethan on the planet Kesron. The Country Barn had been renovated from an old barn.

Credence - (Chapter 3) A Sharrixian scout spaceship that had been sent outbound on a flight across the Marrithious Galaxy to investigate the deaths of the Gatherers. The *Credence* had a crew of four Sharrixians, all who died from starvation when their ship malfunctioned and became lost in space.

Credence Revenge - (Chapter 11) A Sharrixian Government battleship under the leadership of Admiral Novish Shirom.

Crystal Field - (Chapter 3) It was a desert area on the planet Lairdain Tannis near the portal. The Crystal Field contained countless blue, purple, and black crystals, which protruded from the sand. Sharrixian Gatherers harvested crystals in the field to be used for architectural and design purposes in buildings.

D

Deslorr Canyon - (Chapter 3) A rocky canyon with high walls and a flowing river at the bottom, located on the planet Lairdain Tannis.

docking bay P27A - (Chapter 9) The main docking bay for the public relations headquarters for the Marrithious Government military on the planet Sharmyra.

E

Ediira, General Victoria - (Chapter 1) She was the highest ranking military officer in the Marrithious Government military. Victoria had short, blond hair and brown eyes.

Emperor Novish Shirom - (*See* Shirom, Emperor Novish)

Emysh - (Chapter 8) A city on the planet Ryamesh.

Enigma - (Chapter 1) A spaceship owned by Wilcox Brown.

F

Falpherr's Place - (Chapter 11) An intoxication joint on the planet Sarloh's World, known for its criminal activity.

G

Gatherers - (Chapter 3) A group of Sharrixians who gathered crystals from the Crystal Field on the planet Lairdain Tannis to be used for architectural and design purposes in buildings.

Grand Meadows - (Chapter 3) A city on the planet Lairdain Tannis.

H

Hershall, Coradelle - (Chapter 1) She lived in the city of Emysh on the planet Ryamesh. Coradelle had long, blonde hair and blue eyes. She was the daughter of Mercedes Brantt and Robert Hershall. Coradelle was a friend of Alivia Bexley.

Hershall, Robert - (Chapter 2) He lived in the city of Emysh on the planet Ryamesh. Robert was the father of Coradelle Hershall.

I

Industrial Drive - (Chapter 8) A street in the town of Timber Wolf on the planet Ryamesh.

intoxication joint - (Chapter 11) A drinking establishment.

J

Jafer, Commander - (Chapter 11) He was a Sharrixian commander in the Sharrixian Government military. Jafer commanded the battleship *Shartannis.*

Jim - (Chapter 11) He lived on the planet Sarloh's World. Jim worked on the technical aspects of spaceship design. He was an old friend of Nancy Louray.

K

Kalaress - (Chapter 19) A Marrithious Government military battleship under the leadership of Commander Ashten. The *Kalaress* was involved in the Battle of Sharmyra during the Marrithious Galactic War.

Kawthas - (Chapter 5) A town on the planet Velassine.

Kesron - (Chapter 1) A planet within the Marrithious Government's territory.

Kethan - (Chapter 1) A city on the planet Kesron.

Knablean's Cafe - (Chapter 11) One of the oldest restaurants on the planet Sarloh's World.

L

Lairdain Tannis - (Chapter 3) A planet that was the seat of the Sharrixian Government.

Lairdain Tannis Treaty - (Chapter 20) A treaty between the Sharrixian Government and the Marrithious Government that officially ended the Marrithious Galactic War.

Lake Methora - (Chapter 5) A lake with dark blue water located on the planet Velassine.

Lawson, Maxboro - (Chapter 2) He lived in the town of Timber Wolf on the planet Ryamesh. Maxboro had gray hair. He was an old friend of Robert Hershall.

Legend of the Green Crystal, The - (Chapter 12) A Sharrixian children's book.

Leti - (Chapter 12) A city on the planet Lairdain Tannis.

Lhasariss - (Chapter 11) A Sharrixian Government battleship under the leadership of Admiral Gedlo Othan. The *Lhasariss* was involved in the Battle of Sharmyra during the Marrithious Galactic War.

lightspeed-plus - (Chapter 1) A general term used to reference spaceship speeds beyond that of light.

Louray, Nancy - (Chapter 1) She lived in the city of Kethan on the planet Kesron. Nancy was an investigative assistant for the Wilcox Brown Agency in the city of Kethan. She had dark brown hair and green eyes. Nancy owned a spaceship named *Nellie*.

Lythinarr Palace - (Chapter 3) The home of the sitting monarch of the Sharrixian Government, located on the planet Lairdain Tannis. The palace was decorated with crystals from the Crystal Field.

M

Marauve - (Chapter 5) A planet within the Marrithious Government's territory.

Marrithious Galactic War - (Chapter 12) A brief war between the Sharrixian Government and the Marrithious Government. The Marrithious Galactic War included the Battle of Sharmyra, the Battle of Deslorr Canyon, and a skirmish at the portal.

Marrithious Galaxy - (Chapter 1) A galaxy controlled by two governments, located across the galaxy from each other. The Marrithious Government was home to both humans and Axynnians. The Sharrixian Government was home to Sharrixians.

Marrithious Government - (Chapter 1) A government within the Marrithious Galaxy that had both human and Axynnian citizens. The seat of the government was on the planet Ovlarr.

Marshall - (Chapter 12) He was an officer in the Marrithious Government military.

Merritt - (Chapter 12) He was a criminal who sold crystals on the black market.

Morphus, Commander - (Chapter 14) He was a commander in the Marrithious Government military. Morphus commanded the battleship *MX710 Blackstar* in the Battle of Sharmyra during the Marrithious Galactic War.

MX710 Blackstar - (Chapter 19) A Marrithious Government military battleship under the leadership of Commander Morphus. The *MX710 Blackstar* was involved in the Battle of Sharmyra during the Marrithious Galactic War.

N

Narross Selontious - (Chapter 12) A planet within the Sharrixian Government's territory.

Nellie - (Chapter 8) A spaceship owned by Nancy Louray.

Nilliss - (Chapter 19) He was a Sharrixian dignitary in the Sharrixian Government monarch who worked at the Lythinarr Palace.

Noderell - (Chapter 8) A planet within the Marrithious Government's territory. Noderell was the location of many warehouses used for logistics.

North Harbor - (Chapter 6) A harbor of Lake Methora on the planet Velassine.

North Harbor Mansion - (Chapter 5) A mansion at the North Harbor of Lake Methora on the planet Velassine that was owned by the private investigator Everett Quarton.

O

Othan, Admiral Gedlo - (Chapter 3) He was a Sharrixian admiral in the Sharrixian Government military. Gedlo commanded the battleship *Lhasariss* in the Battle of Sharmyra during the Marrithious Galactic War.

Ovlarr - (Chapter 14) A planet that was the seat of the Marrithious Government.

Owen - (Chapter 19) He was an officer in the Marrithious Government military.

P

Phensaa, Essir - (Chapter 14) He was the leader of the Marrithious Government. Essir had light brown hair.

PI Index Database - (Chapter 5) An obscure private investigator database that was still accessible.

Pixellis Star System - (Chapter 3) A star system in the center of the Marrithious Galaxy that contained a star that had gone supernova, causing intermittent communication issues across the galaxy.

portal - (Chapter 3) A natural phenomenon within a rock wall that created a galactic portal, connecting the planet Lairdain Tannis to the planet Staraliss, which were physically across the galaxy from each other.

Prilston, Commander Covlan - (Chapter 3) He was a Sharrixian commander in the Sharrixian Government military. Covlan commanded the battleship *Arcinaris* in the Battle of Sharmyra during the Marrithious Galactic War.

Q

Quarton, Everett - (Chapter 5) He lived in the North Harbor Mansion on the planet Velassine. Everett was a private investigator with his agency located on the planet Marauve. He was the widower to an Axynnian woman named Shandarr Quarton. Everett had a nephew named Remywl Yortix.

Quarton, Shandarr - (Chapter 5) She was an Axynnian who had lived on the planet Velassine. Shandarr was the late wife of Everett Quarton. She had amber eyes.

Queen Empress Aminarra Vistona   (*See* Vistona, Queen Empress Aminarra)

R

Rafith Astonn - (Chapter 3) A planet located half way across the Marrithious Galaxy that was neither in the Marrithious Government's territory nor the Sharrixian Government's territory.

Rassioth - (Chapter 12) A planet within the Sharrixian Government's territory.

Riilan - (Chapter 3) He was one of the Sharrixian Gatherers who was attacked by the humans who were harvesting crystals. Riilan was the uncle of Emperor Novish Shirom.

Robin Avenue - (Chapter 8) A street in the town of Timber Wolf on the planet Ryamesh.

Ryamesh - (Chapter 1) A planet within the Marrithious Government's territory.

Ryth Oparrian - (Chapter 12) A planet within the Sharrixian Government's territory.

S

Sarloh's World - (Chapter 11) A planet within the Marrithious Government's territory.

Settlement Agency - (Chapter 1) An agency that settled estates and inheritances by distributing property to the rightful beneficiaries. It was located on the planet Anneriss.

Sharmyra - (Chapter 9) A planet located in the Sharmyra Star System, within the Marrithious Government's territory. Sharmyra was the location of the public relations headquarters and administrative offices for the Marrithious Government military.

Sharmyra Star System - (Chapter 9) A star system in the Marrithious Galaxy, within the Marrithious Government's territory.

Sharrixian - (Chapter 3) One of the three intelligent species in the Marrithious Galaxy. Sharrixians had light orange, beige, green, and black patterned skin, bumpy heads with little to no hair, and they were approximately three meters tall.

Sharrixian Council - (Chapter 3) A Sharrixian Government council that made important political decisions.

Sharrixian Government - (Chapter 3) A government within the Marrithious Galaxy that had Sharrixian citizens. The seat of the government was on the planet Lairdain Tannis.

Sharrixian Government Building - (Chapter 3) The headquarters for the Sharrixian Government. The Sharrixian Government Building was constructed into the Deslorr Canyon wall on the planet Lairdain Tannis. The building was decorated with crystals from the Crystal Field.

Sharrixian Palace Guard - (Chapter 19) Special Lythinarr Palace guards for the monarch of the Sharrixian Government.

Shartannis - (Chapter 11) A Sharrixian Government battleship under the leadership of Commander Jafer.

Shext - (Chapter 6) A planet name illegally given to Staraliss and changed in the galactic navigation database.

Shirom, Emperor Novish - (Chapter 3) He was a Sharrixian who lived on the planet Lairdain Tannis. Novish was the high commander in the Sharrixian Government military. He served as admiral in the initial battleship fleet that gathered at the planet Rafith Astonn just before the Marrithious Galactic War. Novish was later named emperor by Chief Justice Xalarrton. Emperor Novish had greenish-gray eyes.

Space Agency - (Chapter 1) A defunct organization that operated in the Marrithious Government's territory to manage all things space related.

Staraliss - (Chapter 2) A planet located in the Tenebrous Region of the Marrithious Galaxy, within the Marrithious Government's territory. Staraliss was purchased by Robert Hershall, but he never received the deed to the planet.

Stone, Commander - (Chapter 7) He was a commander in the Marrithious Government military. Stone had black hair.

Stormrider - (Chapter 3) A Sharrixian Government military fighter ship.

Striker, Commander - (Chapter 19) He was a commander in the Marrithious Government military who was responsible for setting up an outpost on the planet Staraliss.

Symphainia - (Chapter 1) A planet within the Marrithious Government's territory.

T

Tajenipp - (Chapter 18) He was one of the Sharrixian Gatherers who was attacked by the humans who were harvesting crystals. Tajenipp was the only one who made it back through the portal alive.

Tansonn - (Chapter 19) A Marrithious Government military battleship under the leadership of Commander Wells. The *Tansonn* was involved in the Marrithious Galactic War by providing Angel Wing fighter ships to Commander Striker for the Battle of Deslorr Canyon.

Tauren - (Chapter 17) He was a shuttle pilot in the Marrithious Government military.

Tenebrous Region - (Chapter 7) A remote region of the Marrithious Galaxy that was located within the Marrithious Government's territory. The planet Staraliss was located in the Tenebrous Region.

Thaosium, Judge - (Chapter 20) He was the high judge of the Marrithious Government court.

The Lush Vine - (Chapter 1) A restaurant located on the planet Xeralosa.

Timber Wolf - (Chapter 8) An industrial town on the planet Ryamesh. Timber Wolf was home to the Timber Wolf Railway.

Timber Wolf Railway (TWR) - (Chapter 8) It was a freight railway company with its yard office located in the town of Timber Wolf on the planet Ryamesh.

Torontarr - (Chapter 13) One of the largest cities on the planet Adanarr.

V

Velassine - (Chapter 5) A planet within the Marrithious Government's territory.

Versill - (Chapter 3) She was a Sharrixian special operations military officer for the Sharrixian Government. Versill had greenish-gray eyes.

Vistona, Queen Empress Aminarra - (Chapter 3) She was a Sharrixian who lived in the Lythinarr Palace on the planet Lairdain Tannis. Queen Empress Aminarra was leader of the Sharrixian Government for thirty-five years. She had greenish-gray eyes.

W

Wells, Commander - (Chapter 19) He was an Axynnian commander in the Marrithious Government military. Wells commanded the battleship *Tansonn* during the Marrithious Galactic War. He had amber eyes.

Wieler, Bryson - (Chapter 2) He was a real estate agent who worked closely with the Settlement Agency. Bryson had brown hair.

Wilcox Brown Agency - (Chapter 1) A private investigator agency in the city of Kethan on the planet Kesron. The Wilcox Brown Agency was owned by Wilcox Brown and had been in business for over thirty years.

X

Xalarrton, Chief Justice - (Chapter 19) He was a Sharrixian who lived on the planet Lairdain Tannis. Chief Justice Xalarrton was head of the Sharrixian Government court and second highest in command of the Sharrixian Government.

Xeralosa - (Chapter 1) A planet within the Marrithious Government's territory.

Y

Yortix, Remywl - (Chapter 5) He lived in the town of Kawthas on the planet Velassine. Remywl had long, brown hair. He was Everett Quarton's nephew.

Z

Zale, Quinlan - (Chapter 4) He was the director of the Settlement Agency on the planet Anneriss. Quinlan had brown hair.

Troy D. Wymer is a science fiction space opera novelist from Michigan, US. He started writing in 1984, but it wasn't until 2016 that he formed the WymerNovels imprint and began to publish novels. Troy enjoys reading, writing, and listening to various subgenres of metal music.